M000113796

RESCUING WENDY

Delta Force Heroes, Book 8

SUSAN STOKER

CHAPTER ONE

Aspen "Blade" Carlisle stared at his phone impatiently. It was ridiculous how much he was looking forward to Wendy calling him. Yeah, he could always call *her*, but he didn't know what her plans were and didn't want to interrupt anything.

He'd met her a couple of months ago when she'd cold-called him, trying to sell him a life insurance policy. He hadn't needed one, but he'd been surprised by how much he'd enjoyed their brief banter. He'd invited her to call him back, and she had.

They'd progressed from Wendy calling him a couple times a week to exchanging cell phone numbers. She still sometimes called him when she was working, but they also texted each other, and now spoke when she wasn't working at her telemarketing job.

Blade liked just about everything about Wendy that he'd learned so far.

When she'd asked about *his* job, and he'd been honest and said he couldn't really talk much about it, she hadn't pried.

He admired the way she'd stepped in to raise her brother when her parents had died in a nasty car wreck. Jack had been only six when their mom and dad had been killed. Blade didn't know exactly how old the boy was now, just that he was a teenager, but Wendy couldn't have been much over legal age herself when she'd suddenly become responsible for her little brother.

Blade liked how Wendy always asked about his day and how he was doing. He'd dated a couple of women who were only interested in talking about themselves, or what was happening in their own lives. They'd been self-absorbed and it had turned him off in a big way. Wendy went out of her way to ask about his friends, how he was feeling, if he'd had a good day, and she didn't ever seem bored with whatever he wanted to talk about.

He respected how passionate she was about her job as an aide at the assisted-living complex where she worked. At times, she was a bit self-recriminating that she wasn't doing more, that she wasn't a nurse, but most of the time she seemed to truly like her work, and she talked about the older men and women who lived at the facility as if they were pseudo grandparents.

The one thing that bothered Blade was that he could tell Wendy wasn't all that confident in herself. She was constantly deflecting any compliments and went out of her way to turn conversation away from herself and her brother onto him.

They hadn't exchanged photos of each other. It hadn't come up, and Blade was enjoying getting to know Wendy without the pressure of dating. But the more he got to know her, the more curious he got, and the more he wanted to see if they clicked in person as well as they clicked on the phone. One night, they *had* briefly talked about what they looked like, and after he'd given her the basics on himself, all she'd said about herself was that she was "average height, average weight, and had average brown hair." He'd complained that he wanted to know more, but she'd changed the subject.

His cell phone rang then, the shrill sound echoing throughout the living area of his condo. Blade's sister, Casey, had helped him pick the three-level condo months ago, and he still hadn't fully furnished it yet. It was too big, but he couldn't resist purchasing and renovating it. There were no rugs covering the beautiful dark hardwood floors, and a couch and a TV was all he had in the large open living space. He didn't need anything more and hadn't bothered trying to make it look homey.

Casey complained that it looked like a bachelor pad, and Blade had retorted that's because it *was* a bachelor pad. His sister had rolled her eyes at him, but hadn't brought it up again.

"Hey, Wen," Blade said after making sure it was Wendy calling and not some other random telemarketer.

"Hi, Aspen. This an okay time to call?"

He smiled. He loved how she called him by his given name instead of his nickname. The first time they'd talked, he'd told her his name and she'd said that she loved how unique it was. He also really appreciated that she made sure she wasn't interrupting or bothering him whenever she called. Blade reassured her. "Of course. Anytime you want to call is fine with me. Besides, I've told you before, if I can't talk, I won't answer the phone."

"I know, I just wanted to make sure. How was your day?"

Blade smiled. There she went again, asking about him. "It was good. Me and my friends had PT this morning, some paperwork we had to do, two briefings to attend, then I went to the gun range. I finished dinner a bit ago, and now I'm sitting on my couch talking to you."

"Sounds like a busy day," Wendy observed.

"Yup. What about you? How was *your* day? How's Mister Clark doing?"

She sighed and Blade tensed. She'd talked about the ninety-one-year-old resident of the assisted-living

4

facility the other day. She'd been concerned about him, as his health had been going downhill recently. She'd been appalled that his two children had been notified but hadn't bothered to come see him, even though they lived not too far away up in Fort Worth.

"He passed away today," Wendy said quietly, her normally perky voice subdued and sad.

"Oh, sweetheart, I'm so sorry," Blade told her. He wished he could take her in his arms and comfort her.

"It's okay," Wendy told him. "It was time. He didn't know who anyone was anymore, and he even told me a couple days ago that he was ready to go. He was amazing, Aspen. I wish you could've met him. He fought in World War II, and the stories he told about some of the things he did over there were amazing."

"I wish I could've met him too." And he did. Blade used to take the time to volunteer at some of the veterans' homes, but he hadn't done it in a while. He made a mental note to start doing that again soon.

"I went to work early this morning because I had a bad feeling about him. The night nurse told me that she didn't think he had very much time left. His stupid kids still hadn't bothered to come down, even though I made a point to call them both yesterday and let them know that it was only a matter of time before their father died. I sat by his bed holding his hand, and didn't think he knew I was there, but about an hour later he opened his eyes. He thought I was his wife—she died ten years ago—and he started recounting the most beautiful memories of her.

"He talked about their honeymoon and how lucky he thought he was that she'd married him. He reminisced about the times their children were born and how happy he'd been. He even brought up a memory of the two of them on the rooftop of an apartment in Paris, and how they watched the lights of the Eiffel Tower twinkle as they made love."

Blade could feel the pain in her voice, as well as the sadness.

"I just let him talk. Didn't tell him that I wasn't his love. After a while, he stopped talking and we just sat there in silence. Eventually, his breathing slowed and he died. It was beautiful and sad at the same time, Aspen. I never wanted to let go of his hand. I wanted him to wake up and tell me more stories. Talk to me about how proud he was to serve his country. But eventually I had to get on with my work."

"Did his kids ever show up?" Blade asked.

"Yeah," Wendy said bitterly. "About five hours later. When they were told that he'd passed, I heard his son bitching that he'd driven all the way down from Fort Worth for *nothing*. His daughter merely looked at her watch, then told her brother she was emailing her lawyer to see about getting his will executed. It was awful. I was going to tell them the beautiful stories Mister Clark had told me about his wife, but after hearing how uncaring they were, I decided to keep those memories to myself."

"I'm glad you were there for him," Blade told her.

"Me too."

"Are you all right?" he asked.

"Not really," Wendy said. "I mean, I see people die all the time. It's kind of part of the job of working at an assisted-living facility. But for some reason, Mister Clark really got to me."

"It's because you're a good person," Blade said. "And you could no more ignore an old man who just wanted some peace before he passed than you could a starving dog on the street."

She was silent for a while after he'd spoken, and Blade had the momentary thought that maybe he'd gone too far. Yeah, they'd been talking for a couple of months, and yeah, they'd gotten past the bullshit answers to the "how was your day" questions, but he hadn't been quite so blatant about his admiration of her before.

"You're right," Wendy told him. "But it still hurts."

"You wouldn't be the person you are if it didn't. You're compassionate, hardworking, honest, and a little too easygoing sometimes. I would've told his kids off if I was there."

She chuckled. "I could totally see you doing that. But it wouldn't have brought Mister Clark back, and it wouldn't change the fact that his kids didn't appreciate him. All it would've done is make things awkward. I'd give anything to have my dad back," Wendy said softly. "He wasn't always the best father, he worked too hard and wasn't home a lot, but he loved me and Jack."

"Can you talk about what happened to your folks?" Blade hadn't asked before. He knew her parents had been killed when she was a teenager, but that was about it. He hadn't really felt they were in a place in their friendship where it was appropriate. But it seemed like she needed to talk about them tonight.

She sighed, and once again Blade wished he was sitting next to her and could comfort her in person.

"My dad worked in IT and was gone a lot. He traveled most weeks from Monday through Thursday. He'd go to companies and help them set up and customize different software packages. It was a Saturday, and Mom was feeling down. Dad took her out on a date. I was babysitting Jack, and they were hit by a drunk driver."

"Jesus, Wen. That's awful."

"I read the police report and apparently when the cops got there, they found my parents holding hands in the wreckage of their car. They were both dead, but the coroner's report said my dad survived the initial impact. My mom died right away. He passed away not too much later after the paramedics arrived. He'd latched onto my mom's hand and refused to let go."

Blade didn't know what to say. Literally, he opened

his mouth and nothing came out. He couldn't imagine anything worse.

But Wendy, being Wendy, moved past the awkward moment for him as if what she'd just said hadn't rocked him.

"I've tried to live my life in a way that would make my parents proud of me. I've mis-stepped along the way, but I've done my best to make sure Jack never forgets how wonderful our parents were."

"Where's your brother now?" Blade asked, wanting to make sure Wendy wasn't alone after her horrible day.

"He's in his room. I tried to help him with his homework earlier, which was a joke because he's way smarter than I'll ever be. Then we watched TV for a while, and now he's on the phone with one of his friends."

"Did you tell him that you had a bad day?" Blade asked.

"No."

"Why not? I'm sure he would've tried to cheer you up."

"Because I don't want to bring him down. He had a tough few years in middle school. He was bullied, but thank God, he didn't turn to drugs or give up or anything. Now he's loving high school. Being a sophomore is so much better for him than being a freshman was."

"Wen, you shouldn't keep things to yourself," Blade

lectured. "He's your brother, I'm sure he'd want to know when you're having a tough time."

"I didn't keep my crappy day to myself," she said quietly. "I told *you*."

Blade blinked and stared at the muted TV for a beat. There was a commercial on with a half-dressed woman hawking some lotion, but Blade didn't give a crap about anything other than Wendy's words at that moment.

"So you did," he said after a while. "Thank you."

"For what?"

"For trusting me with your real feelings. You have no idea how much I appreciate that."

"So, enough about me," Wendy said, her embarrassment easy to hear in her tone. "What do you usually do for PT?"

Blade allowed the change in conversation. It went back to being light and somewhat superficial, but he knew that something had changed, at least for him. She'd opened up. Told him some extremely emotional and personal things about herself. Of course, he had a million questions about what she *didn't* say.

Why was Jack bullied? What happened to her and her brother after their parents died? Why did she always put herself down...like the comment about her not being as smart as her brother?

Blade had been frustrated before when he could tell she was holding back...as if she had some deep dark secret. And he believed there was something that made her as cautious as she was. However, telling him about her parents, and about Mister Clark, was a good first step forward.

But what was it a first step *toward*?

And with a clarity that hit him like a bullet piercing the target he'd shot at earlier in the day, he realized that her trusting him, opening up to him, was the first step toward making their friendship more than a "phone" one. More than just casual friends.

He wanted to meet her.

Wanted to see her face-to-face as she asked about his day.

Wanted to know if her voice was as soothing to him in person as it was over the phone.

"I want to meet you," Blade blurted, interrupting whatever it was that she was saying.

There was silence on the phone for a beat before she asked, "Why?"

"Why?" Blade echoed. "Because I like you. Because you make me laugh. Because I'm interested in you."

"You're interested in me?"

Blade smiled. She was cute when she was flustered. "Yeah, Wen. I am. We've been talking for two months. I think you like me, at least a little, otherwise you wouldn't keep talking to me. Let's meet."

"I'm not sure that's the best idea," Wendy finally said.

"Why?" It was his turn to question her now.

"Because I'm really busy, and you are too. And we don't really know each other. I mean, I could be a serial killer or something. Haven't you watched any of those killer shows on TV? Like *Snapped* or *Deadly Women*? I could be luring you into my web to hurt you."

"Are you?"

"That's beside the point," she huffed.

Blade's smile grew. "Actually, I think that's exactly the point."

"I'm just not sure it's a good idea," she semi-repeated. "I...I'm not all that pretty."

"Wendy," Blade reprimanded. "I like you for who you are, not because of what you look like. But I have a feeling that you're way underestimating yourself. You do that a lot. If it makes you feel better, we can text each other pictures of ourselves first. Then if you think I'm a troll, you can make up some excuse not to meet me."

"I don't want to exchange pictures. And you're not a troll," she huffed.

"How do you know? I could have a hunchback and my eyes could be uneven and squinty, and maybe I have resting bitch face all the time," he teased.

Wendy giggled. "Whatever."

"Meet with me," Blade said. "As a friend. With no pressure for anything more for now. I can't imagine I'd like you any less than I do right now. And I have a feeling seeing you face-to-face will only make our friendship grow."

"I'm not sure..." Wendy hedged.

"This weekend," Blade went on quickly. "Friday night, after your shift at the assisted-living facility. You already said earlier this week that you're not working that night for the telemarketing company. You can come straight from work and we'll have an informal dinner somewhere. What about that new trendy sports bar in downtown Temple?"

He held his breath as Wendy thought about his question.

"I like you, Aspen. A lot. And I'm afraid if we meet, it'll change our relationship."

"It won't."

"You can't guarantee that," she argued.

"Wendy, the only way our relationship will change is if we let it. We're still gonna talk all the time. You're still going to call me and pretend to try to sell me something so you can hear a friendly voice when you're at your telemarketing job. I'm still gonna wait with bated breath for you to call when you say you're gonna call and laugh when you send me a funny joke via text. The way I see it, things can only get better from here on out. Yeah, our relationship might change, and honestly, right now I'm hoping it *does* change. I feel closer to you than I've felt to any woman in a hell of a long time. I see that as a good thing. You know what I was thinking tonight before you called?"

"What?" Wendy asked.

"That I wished I was waiting for you to show up at my door instead of waiting for you to call. I'd love to hang out with you. Watch a movie. Talk. Eat. I'm comfortable with you, and there aren't a lot of women I can say that about. There's something about you that makes me put down my guard."

"I feel the same way," Wendy said quietly. "But I'm nervous."

"About what? Not about me?" Blade asked.

"Yes and no."

"I'd never hurt you, Wen. Never."

"It's not that," she said immediately.

"Then what?"

"It's just..."

Blade heard her take a deep breath before continuing.

"There are things you don't know about me. About what I've done in the past. Things I've never told anyone."

Blade clenched his teeth and felt his free hand fisting. "Did someone hurt you?"

"What? No."

"Stalk you? Do you have an ex that won't leave you alone?"

"Aspen, no, it's nothing like that."

Blade breathed a sigh of relief. "Whatever it is, it'll be okay."

She chuckled softly. "That's so like you."

When she didn't elaborate, Blade asked, "What is?"

"You're always so positive. So worried about others. It's not normal...but I like it."

"If more people looked on the bright side of things, maybe there'd be less anxiety, depression, and general grouchiness in the world."

"True," she responded.

"So?" Blade asked. "Are we on for Friday?"

"Are you sure?"

"I'm sure."

"Okay then."

She didn't sound very excited about the prospect, and suddenly Blade was disappointed. "You know what? If you really don't want to, it's okay. I don't want to push you into anything you don't want to do. I know *I'm* excited about the prospect of meeting you, but if this is something you're going to dread, or something that you really, really don't want to do, then let's not do it."

"I want to," Wendy immediately contradicted. "As I said, I'm just nervous about it. You're the first person in a very long time I've felt as if I have a true connection with, and I don't want to screw it up. The last thing I want to do is let you down. It'll kill me if we meet and you decide I'm not who you thought I'd be, or if you don't want me calling you anymore."

"Your calls are the highlight of my day, sweetheart," Blade told her honestly. "Unless you get totally shit-faced and start dancing on the tables, you aren't going to let me down, and I'm definitely going to want to keep talking to you afterward. Okay?"

"Okay. How will I know who you are? Maybe we should exchange pictures after all," Wendy said in a perkier tone.

"I kinda like the idea of seeing you for the first time Friday night," Blade said.

"So like a true blind date," Wendy said with a little giggle. Then she sobered and quickly added, "Not that this is a date or anything, I just meant—"

"Oh, it's a date, all right," Blade interrupted. "And, yes, it's truly a blind date. But so you'll know it's me, I'll be wearing a pair of jeans, a black T-shirt, and I'll bring you a bag of chocolate Kisses because I know how much you enjoy them."

"Oh...you don't have to do that," she protested.

"I know, but I'm going to anyway," Blade told her. "What will you be wearing, so I'll know it's you?"

"Um...I usually wear scrubs at the facility, but I'll wear jeans on Friday instead. Um...jeez...you can't ask me on Tuesday what I'm going to wear Friday," she teased. "I'm a woman. I'll have to take everything out of my closet, scrutinize it, and I'll change my mind about half a dozen times."

Blade chuckled. "Point taken. How about you just

text me sometime before Friday night and let me know then."

"I can do that."

"Great. It's a date then."

"Aspen?"

"Yeah, darlin'?"

"Thanks."

"For what?"

"For being so amazing. For being easy to talk to. For not hanging up on me during that first call I made when I tried to sell you life insurance. Just...thanks."

"You don't have to thank me, Wendy. I'm just as thankful that you called me back that second time. And the third. And the fourth. That you trusted me enough to give me your cell number. And that you want to meet in person after all this time. I'm the one who should be thanking *you*. Oh, and I want to meet your brother sometime too. That is...if you think it's okay."

"He wants to meet you too."

"You've told him about me?"

"Yeah, Aspen. He knows about you," she said.

Blade swallowed hard. Wendy might be nervous to meet him, but he was glad she felt comfortable enough that she'd talked to her brother about him. "I'd like to know more about him...if you're willing to share."

"Of course. Friday?"

"Absolutely. I'll be waiting for you in the bar area," Blade told her. "Around five?"

"Five is perfect."

"I'm going to let you go, Wen, but you should know something."

"What's that?" she asked.

"I haven't dated anyone in years. This isn't something I usually do. There's something about you that I can't resist and don't want to resist. Friday is going to be the start of something between us. Unless we find that we can't stand each other, which I can't see happening, I want to be exclusive. I don't want you dating anyone else."

"I don't want to see anyone else," Wendy said quietly. "And between working two jobs and raising Jack, I haven't dated much either."

Blade couldn't help but feel a sense of pleasure wash over him at her words. "Okay, sweetheart. I'm going to let you go. I'm looking forward to meeting you. To seeing you in person."

"Me too."

"Sleep well. Bye."

"Bye."

Blade hung up the phone and knew he had a goofy grin on his face, but he couldn't help it. He wanted to call Casey and tell her that he was finally going to meet the woman he couldn't stop thinking about. He'd told his sister all about Wendy, and she'd been thrilled for him.

It could be because Casey was disgustingly happy

with his teammate and friend, Beatle, but Blade knew it was more because she wanted *him* to be happy. He was close to his sister, and he knew if something, God forbid, had happened to their parents, both he and Casey would've done whatever was necessary to be there for each other.

Blade sat on the couch and stared at the TV for a long while before finally pushing to his feet and heading upstairs to his bedroom. He wanted to meet Wendy tonight. Or tomorrow, but knew she had to work. He also knew without a doubt the rest of the week was going to crawl by. He couldn't wait until Friday.

CHAPTER TWO

Wendy Tucker opened the door of the new sports bar and slowly walked inside. She was exactly on time for her date with Aspen, but he'd texted her a couple minutes ago to tell her he was running late. He said he'd explain when he got there, but it had to do with his work.

She wasn't thrilled to have to hang out by herself in the bar and wait for him—being social really wasn't her thing. Jackson always made fun of her for spilling her life story to complete strangers when she was nervous, and in social situations she was usually nervous. She was always afraid she'd say the wrong thing to the wrong person and have law enforcement beating down her door as a result.

She'd tried to change—to be more cautious about what she blurted out—but she always seemed to run off at the mouth when she was unsure. She was surprised she hadn't been found already because of what she'd blabbed to people in the past.

Wendy was beginning to think, after all these years, that she just might be in the clear.

She had planned on arriving at the bar at least ten minutes early, but she'd been running late as well because she'd had to change clothes after a resident at the assisted-living facility had gotten sick all over her. Wendy had been assisting a nurse in getting him from his bed to a chair so they could change his sheets when he'd literally puked up his entire lunch all over her shirt, and it had dripped down her body, soaking her jeans. By the time she'd gotten him into the chair, she could even feel the sticky, disgusting mess on her skin under her clothes.

After a shower, she'd had no other clothes to change into other than a pair of scrubs. She'd been hoping to wear something a bit more feminine to meet Aspen for the first time, but she didn't have time to go home between the end of her shift and the time she was supposed to meet him at the bar.

She'd texted him that morning to let him know she'd be wearing a pair of jeans and a cute black blouse, which she thought slimmed her curves and showed off a bit of skin without being slutty, but that outfit was currently soaking in a sink at the assisted-living facility in the hopes it could be salvaged. Wendy was going to text

Aspen and let him know about her new outfit, but figured she'd just tell him when he got there. Explaining why she'd changed her mind and what had happened was a long story, and she was actually looking forward to telling it to him face-to-face for once. She knew he'd be appropriately appalled and amused at the same time. And she'd know who *he* was because of the chocolate he said he'd bring for her, so she'd just have to approach him when he got there instead of waiting for him to find her.

She wandered over to the main bar area and hiked herself up onto a barstool at the end of the long bar. She still had a direct line of sight to the front door, so she'd be able to see Aspen when he entered.

"Good afternoon," the pretty woman behind the bar said as Wendy got herself settled. "What can I get for you?"

"I'm thinking a soda, please," Wendy said.

"You got it." The bartender nodded and turned to make the drink.

"A soda?" a dark-haired woman asked. "It's Friday night, surely you need and want something a bit stronger than that."

Wendy turned to face the woman sitting on the barstool next to hers. She appeared to be alone, but she was smiling brightly and seemed friendly enough. She was tall and slender, wearing a short skirt and a black shirt with an extremely low neckline. The push-up bra the woman wore made it more than clear she'd enhanced what God had given her. She had long brown hair that lay in curls over her boobs, successfully bringing attention to them. Her makeup was heavy but done in a tasteful way. Her legs were crossed, and she swung one back and forth, bringing Wendy's gaze down to the bright red, four-inch heels on her feet.

She looked like she was ready for one hell of a night out, and Wendy felt extremely frumpy next to her in her basic cotton scrubs.

Remembering the woman's comment about her choice of drink, Wendy was a bit defensive, but she tried not to take the other woman's words personally.

"I could probably use something stronger, but I'm meeting a man for the first time tonight, and I want to make sure I'm not tipsy or anything when he shows up."

"I'm Christine," the other woman said, holding out her hand.

Wendy shook it. "Wendy."

"So...blind date, huh?" Christine asked.

"Sort of, yes. We've talked on the phone a lot, but haven't seen each other in person. We decided to go for it tonight. Of course, if the evening goes the way my day did, it might not be a good thing."

"I figured something must have happened because I wouldn't be caught dead wearing those scrub things in public...nonetheless to meet a man, especially for the first time."

Wendy wrinkled her nose. She wanted to tell Christine to fuck off, that not everyone was born with the genes she obviously had. But it was easier to let things roll off her back than get into an argument.

"Yeah, well, I got thrown up on at work and didn't have a choice."

"Ewwww!" Christine said. "You poor thing. Where do you work?"

"Cottonwood Estates. It's a senior living community. We offer independent living for those who can still be on their own but want either a place with others their age they can hang out with or who need a bit of assistance with house cleaning and maybe one meal a day. We also have memory care, nursing home care, assisted living, and even rehabilitation."

"So, you work with old people," Christine said with a straight face.

Wendy struggled to keep her face clear of emotion. She really didn't like the woman sitting next to her all that much, but never liked to cause a scene. She'd learned a long time ago that it was better to be nice and blend in than to cause a stink and bring attention to herself.

"The elderly, yes."

The bartender came over with her soda and placed it on a napkin in front of Wendy with a smile. Wendy picked up her drink and took a big swallow as Christine asked, "So you got puked on today and had to change.

Did you tell the guy you're meeting? What's his name again?"

"Aspen, and no, I figured I'd tell him the whole story when he got here," Wendy told Christine.

"Aspen? What kind of name is that?" the other woman asked.

Wendy gritted her teeth. She'd loved Aspen's name from the first time she'd heard it.

"It's English."

"Isn't it that ski resort town out in Colorado?" Christine asked.

"Yeah. It's also the name of a tree."

"Hmmm. What's he do?"

"Who, Aspen?"

"Yeah."

Wendy sucked down another swallow of the soda and wished that Aspen would walk through the door and save her from Christine's nosey questions. She'd get up and move but that would be super rude, and she didn't want to cause a scene. She hated confrontation, and the last thing she wanted was for Christine to get huffy with her. "He's in the Army."

"Ah, a military man. I bet he's muscular, huh?"

Wendy shrugged. "I guess. He works out a lot. He's always talking about how he does PT with his friends."

"What time's he supposed to get here?"

Wendy looked at her watch and thought to herself, *Not soon enough*. But instead, she said, "We were supposed to meet at five, but he texted and said he was running late. He should be here any minute."

"How are you going to know who he is? I mean, you said that you hadn't met each other in person before. Let me guess, he'll be carrying a red rose, right? That's so romantic!"

"Nope, a bag of chocolate Kisses. I told him how much I loved them during one of our phone calls."

Christine rolled her eyes then looked Wendy up and down. "Yeah, that's obvious."

Wendy gaped at her. She knew she wasn't exactly model thin, but this bitch pointing it out was so out of line it wasn't even funny. So what if she wasn't stick thin? But of course, now that Christine had pointed it out, Wendy began to feel self-conscious. She'd told Aspen that she wasn't skinny...hadn't she? Suddenly she couldn't remember. What if he was expecting a tall, slender woman? She'd told him she had brown hair, but that was about it. Shit.

"Hey, you've got something between your teeth," Christine said.

Wendy's hand shot to her mouth and she covered it. "Really?"

"Yeah, it's something black. Maybe you should run to the restroom and take care of it before Aspen gets here, huh?"

Wendy put down her drink and nodded. "Yeah, I think I will. Thank you so much for pointing it out."

She suddenly felt guilty for thinking mean things about Christine. She couldn't be all bad if she was trying to save her from embarrassment around her blind date.

"No problem." The other woman waved off her thanks. "Us women have to stick together."

Wendy hopped off the barstool and headed for the back of the bar. When she got there, she had to stand in line behind three other women waiting to use the facilities. Of course. It was one room, and only one woman could enter and use the bathroom at a time. Even during the short time she'd been talking to Christine, the bar had begun to fill up. Apparently, it was very popular with the working crowd.

After several minutes, it was finally Wendy's turn. She closed and locked the door behind her and leaned over the small sink. She curled her lips back and bared her teeth, looking for whatever was in them. She turned her head one way then another and couldn't see anything.

She turned on the water anyway and scooped some into her mouth and swished. After spitting the water out, she bared her teeth again. Still nothing. Running her tongue over her teeth, Wendy couldn't feel anything, either. Thank God whatever had been in her teeth must have worked itself free.

She took a step back and eyed herself. She'd put on some mascara after work and had brushed a bit of blush over her cheeks. She was wearing shiny lip gloss and had pulled her hair back. It had been in a ponytail all day, and she couldn't leave it down because there was a weird kink in it, so she'd just pulled it up into a messy, hopefully, artsy bun instead.

Sighing, Wendy studied her reflection. She wasn't a beauty, but she wasn't ugly either. She had high cheekbones and really long lashes. She remembered her mom complimenting her on how pretty her dark brown eyes were. Her hair was thick and generally didn't do anything she wanted it to, but Wendy still loved it. She refused to cut it short and had always worn it below her shoulders.

Yeah, the scrubs weren't exactly the height of fashion, but Aspen knew where she worked. Knew she worked with the elderly. She had a feeling he'd think her story was hilarious. At least she hoped he would. The man she'd gotten to know over the phone wouldn't care that she was wearing scrubs instead of fashionable jeans and a nice blouse.

Taking one last look at her reflection, Wendy took a deep breath and headed out of the restroom and back to the bar.

Her first thought, upon seeing Christine was no longer in the seat next to where Wendy had been sitting, was what a relief. She glanced around as she walked back to her stool and saw the other woman was now sitting on the other end of the bar.

But she wasn't alone.

A man was with her.

He had his back to Wendy, so she couldn't see his face—but he wore a black T-shirt and a pair of jeans. She saw a pair of cowboy boots on his feet as well.

Christine had her legs crossed and had spun the barstool around so her legs were almost touching the man's. She was smiling and laughing, and occasionally she'd reach out a hand and touch the man's knee. They were sitting close together, their heads bent toward each other.

In the ten minutes Wendy had been gone, the bar had gotten even busier. There was a football game on the television at the end of the room. The chatter was loud, and everywhere she seemed to look there were couples laughing and smiling at each other.

Wendy's stomach tightened. Feeling extremely out of place, she stood next to her barstool and pulled out her phone to check to see if Aspen had sent her a text. He had.

Eleven minutes ago.

She'd missed the vibration notifying her of the message before she'd headed to the restroom.

Aspen: Be there in a minute or so. Can't wait to see you!

The churning in Wendy's belly intensified. Aspen was

here...somewhere. She didn't want him to think she'd ditched him. She'd been stood up once before and it was the worst feeling ever.

The more Wendy thought about Christine, and how she'd said Wendy had something in her teeth right around the time Aspen had texted, the leerier she got.

But the other woman couldn't have known, could she?

Jackson was constantly telling Wendy that she needed to stand up for herself more. That she needed to stop letting people walk all over her. She never complained in restaurants when the food was bad. She didn't return stuff she bought online when it didn't fit. And she never, *ever* caused a scene in public.

But this seemed to be as good a time as any to practice asserting herself more.

She slid a ten-dollar bill under her half-drunk glass of soda, enough for the cost of the drink and a good tip —Wendy had been a waitress once and knew how hard the work was and how important tips were—and took a deep breath.

She began to work her way toward Christine and the man, hoping against hope it wasn't Aspen sitting in front of the other woman. She had to push her way through the throngs of people now gathered around the bar, and as she got closer to the couple, she saw a clear bag sitting on the bar between them. It was tied off with a pink bow, and Wendy could clearly see the silver foil of the chocolates in the bag.

That *bitch*.

Christine knew Wendy was waiting for Aspen

Of course she did—Wendy had blabbed everything about their meeting to the other woman. How they'd never met. How she didn't know what he looked like, and how he didn't know what she looked like. Christine must've been laughing the whole time she'd been pumping her for information.

Christine didn't give a shit where Wendy worked. She wanted to get as much information as possible so she could pass herself off as Wendy to Aspen.

Taking a moment to give herself a pep talk—and to calm down, knowing she'd have to confront the lying bitch—Wendy heard low, masculine laughter coming from the man in front of Christine. Looking up, she caught him smiling at the other woman.

Her heart sank.

He looked like he was having the time of his life.

Christine had been touching his knee suggestively, and Aspen moved his hand right then to cover her own on his leg.

Wendy decided she needed to move to get a better look at him...because if she confronted Christine and the man in front of her wasn't Aspen, she'd feel like an ass.

Of course, it would be the coincidence of the

century if the guy Christine was meeting also happened to bring *her* a bag of chocolate, but Wendy supposed it could happen.

She edged her way around a large group of people standing near the bar, having a good time, until she could see the face of the man sitting in front of Christine.

Wendy almost gasped.

He was beautiful.

He had dark hair that was in a typical military cut. Short on the sides and a bit longer on top. His T-shirt wasn't tight, except around his biceps. His arms were cut and larger than those on most of the military men she'd seen. But it was his forearms that made Wendy's knees go weak. She could see the veins in his arms clearly. There was just something about those veins, covered by a fine mist of dark hair, that did it for her.

He had large hands and a five o'clock shadow. He'd told her once that he hated how quickly his facial hair grew...how he'd had to shave twice a day when he was in basic training because his drill sergeants gave him shit about being unshaven when he didn't.

To Wendy, the scruff on his face was irresistible and handsome...not something he should ever be worried about. His front teeth were slightly crooked; she could see them clearly because of the wide smile on his face.

The longer she stared at him, the more her anger

drained away—as did her will to correct him as to the identity of the woman sitting in front of him.

He looked happy. He was staring at Christine as if she was the most beautiful woman in the room...and she was.

Wendy looked down at her own light green scrubs, then back up to Christine's low-cut blouse. At her long legs showcased in the short skirt. Wendy couldn't compete with that. Didn't *want* to compete.

Looking her fill of Aspen once more, Wendy wished for the thousandth time that her life was different. That her parents hadn't died. That she hadn't become a surrogate mother to her brother. That she could've gone to college like most other women her age. That she didn't have to live life always looking over her shoulder.

Perhaps if her life had been different, she could be the kind of woman who had the confidence to boldly go up to Christine and confront her. To tell Aspen that he'd been duped. That *she* was the woman he'd come to meet.

But she wasn't that woman, and she didn't have the confidence to do any of that.

Allowing herself a rare moment of self-pity, Wendy stared at Aspen.

She'd obviously been staring at him for too long because suddenly his gaze broke away from the woman in front of him and met hers.

His brows furrowed for a moment as his beautiful

brown eyes raked her from head to toe and back up again. He opened his mouth as if he was going to say something, but just then, Christine's artfully manicured fingers rested on his cheek, and he looked away from Wendy to see what she wanted.

Using the distraction, Wendy sidestepped behind a group of people and headed for the door. Why would he look twice at *her* when he had Christine? She should be glad that he was happy. But just once she wanted a man to look at her the way Aspen was looking at Christine.

She almost snorted. As if.

It was time to get back to her real life. Aspen had been a nice distraction, but Jackson had two more years of high school. Maybe after he graduated she could try the dating thing again...when she had less to lose.

CHAPTER THREE

B lade tugged on his shirt and took a deep breath
before opening the door to the pub. He'd meant
to get there early and get a good seat. He knew the bar
was popular and would get crowded as people got off
work, and he wanted to find a corner booth and have a
bit of privacy as he got to know Wendy better.

But there had been an incident on the Army post
and his commander had asked him and the other Deltas
to be on standby, just in case. It had turned out to be
nothing and the team wasn't needed, but it had made
him late. He'd had to go home to change and grab the
plastic bag full of chocolate for Wendy before he could
leave for his date.

He'd sent her a text letting her know he was running
late, and she'd responded briefly that it was fine because
she'd just arrived.

Blade walked into the bar and looked around. He held the bag of chocolate so it could easily be seen and tried to figure out which of the women milling around the bar was Wendy.

"Hi. Aspen?"

He turned to see a beautiful woman standing in front of him. She bit her lip nervously as she looked up at him.

For a moment, all Blade could do was stare. She didn't look anything like he'd pictured in his head. She had brown hair like she'd told him, but otherwise, nothing else fit. She had on high heels, bringing her almost eye level to his six-three height. He couldn't remember if Wendy had ever told him how tall she was, but was distracted when the woman held out her hand to him.

Her nails were painted red and looked manicured. She had on a short skirt that showcased long, slender legs, and the black blouse she was wearing dipped low on her chest. It was more than obvious she was wearing some sort of push-up bra because her generous-sized breasts were pushed upward, giving him an amazing view of her cleavage.

"Wendy?" he asked, confused.

"That's me," the woman said, beaming. "It's so nice to meet you!" And with that, she stepped into his space and gave him a hug.

Blade's arms went around her automatically. She

smelled good, like some sort of flower. She held on to him for a beat longer than might have been appropriate if they hadn't been talking on the phone and getting to know each other for the last couple of months.

"It's good to finally meet you too," Blade told her when she pulled back. "I brought these for you," he said, holding out the bag of chocolate.

"Thanks! Want to go and sit at the bar for a while?"

Blade looked around and saw that all the booths were occupied. He sighed. Yeah, being late was definitely cramping his style. "Sure, that sounds good," he said.

Wendy grabbed his hand and started pulling him toward the far end of the bar. Blade tried not to be annoyed, but couldn't help the stab of disappointment that shot through him at her assertiveness. He didn't mind holding her hand and it wasn't that he had a problem walking behind her. Hell, her ass in that skirt, and the way her heels accentuated her shapely calves as she strutted to the bar should've had him as hard as a pike. But he'd pegged her as more...submissive.

That wasn't exactly the word he was looking for. Unsure, maybe? He figured that he'd need to take the lead to make her comfortable, then as she got to know him, she'd open up more.

But this assertive, confident Wendy was throwing him for a loop.

They arrived at the bar, and Blade put a hand on her

elbow and helped her onto the stool. She beamed at him as he got settled on the stool next to hers. Wendy rested her elbow on the bar and leaned into him as she asked, "Do I look okay?"

Blade blinked and tried not to blatantly stare at the way her position made her tits look like they were about to pop out of her shirt. The bar was loud and he could barely hear her. He raised his voice and said, "You look beautiful."

She smiled at him and straightened on her seat. "Thanks."

"What happened to the jeans and blouse?" he asked.

Wendy rolled her eyes. "I decided since I was meeting you for the first time, I should dress up. Look my best." She smoothed her hand down the front of her skirt, effectively drawing his eyes to her legs once more.

"How was work?" Blade asked, not liking how awkward things seemed. Even the first time he'd talked to Wendy on the phone, he hadn't felt this weird vibe from her. Maybe she was right, and meeting in person hadn't been the best idea. He'd told her nothing would change with their relationship, but he had a feeling he'd spoken too soon.

"You won't believe what happened," Wendy said.

"Tell me," Blade urged. The more he looked at her, the more he realized just how pretty she was. Whatever she'd done with her makeup made her eyes look huge on her face. Her smile was nice and he liked the way her hair fell in curls around her shoulders, brushing against the globes of her breasts as she moved.

He smiled back, encouraging her to talk about her day. It was the first time in a long while that she hadn't immediately asked how his day had been before he could ask about hers.

"I was helping this old guy from his bed to a chair and he barfed!" Wendy exclaimed with a grimace. Her slight nose crinkled up as she recounted the story. "I managed to leap out of the way before it got on me. Can you imagine? Ugh, puke is the worst. Anyway, he threw up all over the floor and there I was, trying to dodge flying chunks and not let go of him at the same time. I managed to get him in the chair without stepping in it, and the old geezer looked up at me and said, 'Darn, girl, you moved too fast. I was hoping for a wet T-shirt contest. You know it doesn't take much to get me worked up.'"

Blade laughed. Then he felt Wendy's hand on his knee and looked down. His hand moved without thought and covered hers as it tried to move up his thigh. He'd expected to feel something when she touched him. Tingles, lust, *something*. But all he felt was the weight of their combined hands on his leg.

Wendy was beaming at him, and if Blade wasn't mistaken, she'd somehow moved her stool closer. "Sounds like it was quite the day."

"Oh, it was. But the best part hopefully is still to come."

Uncomfortable with the way Wendy was staring at him, as if he were a lollipop and she wanted to lick him from head to toe, Blade looked away. His eyes roamed the now full bar. There were folks dressed in everything from suits, ties, and other obvious work attire, to jeans and T-shirts.

A yell went up on the other side of the bar from a group who was watching the football game on the television, and Blade started to turn his head to see what was going on. But at the last second, his gaze was caught by a woman standing not too far from him and Wendy.

She was wearing light green scrubs, the kind of thing that was more appropriate for a hospital or a doctor's office than a busy bar after work. She had on a pair of white tennis shoes and was clutching a purse in front of her.

Her dark hair was piled on top of her head in a messy bun that Blade had a sudden urge to take down. She wasn't short, but she wasn't exactly tall either. Her body was curvy, and the way the material of her clothes left the details of her body to his imagination left him wanting to press a hand at the small of her back and pull her into him, so he could see for himself how she was made.

Time seemed to stand still as they stared at each

other. His eyes went down to her toes, back up her body, and to her face once more. Blade felt as if he knew the woman, though he'd never seen her before.

His lips parted to call out to her, to invite her over to where he was sitting, when Wendy's fingers on his face broke whatever weird spell he'd been in.

"What are you looking at?" she asked.

Blade felt her fingers on his leg shift until she was using her long red nails to scratch the inside of his thigh. The hand she'd had on his cheek brushed against his shoulder, then she lightly ran her nails down his arm.

With a clarity that he should've had ten minutes ago, Blade knew without a doubt that the woman sitting in front of him wasn't Wendy.

He had no idea who she was, but the Wendy he knew wouldn't call any of the men she worked with at the home "old geezers." She also wouldn't be as aggressive as this woman. Not only that, but she still hadn't asked how his day had gone. In every single conversation they'd had, Wendy had immediately asked about his day before he could get a word in edgewise.

This woman may be pretending to be Wendy, but there was no comparison between the woman he'd gotten to know and this imposter.

Blade was disgusted with himself for being duped so easily. Some Special Forces soldier *he* was.

The only questions left...who was *this* woman, and where was Wendy?

Blade was normally extremely blunt. He didn't have time for games, but he had the urge to see this fake Wendy squirm a bit. "How's Josh?" he asked.

"Josh?" the woman asked in a high-pitched tone. "He's good."

"Is he enjoying fifth grade?"

"As much as anyone can, I suppose. Hey, what do you say we get out of here and go someplace where we can get to know each other better?"

Blade's eyes narrowed. With every word she spoke, she confirmed his suspicions. "Where do you want to go?" he asked, leaning close as if he was encouraging her.

The hand on his thigh moved again, and her fingers brushed against his cock. The thick jeans he was wearing kept him from actually feeling the gentle caress, but even if he could've felt her touch, he wouldn't have reacted. He was so angry with whoever this was, he couldn't have gotten hard if his life depended on it.

"There's a hotel near here. We could go there."

Blade's hand squeezed the one at his cock. Hard. "How much?" he bit out, not bothering to pretend he didn't know she wasn't his date anymore.

"What?" The woman's eyes widened in surprise.

"How much do you charge?" Blade asked again.

"But...this is a blind date," she stammered, trying to pull her hand out of his grasp, but Blade didn't let go.

"Cut the bullshit. You aren't Wendy, obviously. His name is Jack, not Josh, and he's definitely not in the fifth grade. You're dressed like a whore and you're coming on to me so hard, almost desperately, you can't be anything *but* a prostitute. I figure you thought you'd get me into the hotel, tease the shit out of me, maybe suck my cock a bit, show me your tits—which are about to fall out of your shirt as it is—then you'd spring your rates on me. So, I'm just wondering how much a lying, conniving bitch charges these days."

At his words, the mask she'd been wearing disappeared in a flash. She might've been pretty before, but now her ugliness came through loud and clear. Her lip curled. "That little mouse wouldn't have satisfied you for a second," she hissed. "Why would anyone want someone as clueless and naïve as her? Stupid bitch made it too easy to intercept you. Besides, who wears fucking *pajamas* to meet a blind date?"

At her words, Blade had confirmation the woman he'd locked eyes with was the real Wendy. *His* Wendy.

Knowing he needed to ditch the whore so he could find his date, he flung her hand away from his body and stood. Then he leaned in and brushed a finger over the top of her tits, which were heaving up and down in her agitation, and said quietly, "I would fuck Wendy in those pajamas every day and twice on Sunday before I'd even *think* about sticking my dick in your nasty-ass cunt."

"Asshole!" the woman spat.

"You're going to want to take your business elsewhere, because I'm going to make sure the bartender and owner know who you are and that you're trying to pick up unsuspecting men in their establishment," Blade threatened. "This is a friendly neighborhood bar, not a pickup joint."

"Fuck you," the woman said, but she put the strap of her purse over her shoulder and stalked away from him toward the door.

Blade forgot about the prostitute as soon as she turned her back on him and frantically looked around the bar for the woman in the green scrubs. After two circles of the crowded bar, he realized she was gone.

Running a hand over his face, Blade swore under his breath. She'd seen him with the whore and had obviously gotten the wrong idea. Not that he could blame her, really. Pulling out his phone, Blade checked for any messages. Nothing.

Not even a "fuck you," which he wouldn't've been surprised by. Pressing his lips together, he shot off a quick text.

Call me, Wen.

He waited for five minutes, and when Wendy didn't

respond, he sighed in frustration. He texted again. Then again. And again.

I thought she was you.
 Please talk to me.
 Are you okay?
 Where are you?
 At least let me know you got home all right.

She didn't respond to any of his texts, and as far as he could tell, she hadn't even *read* them. Since she was ignoring his texts, he tried calling her.

But she didn't pick up. He left a message.

Then he called back and left another.

All in all, Blade left five messages for Wendy, getting more and more concerned with each one. He was also slightly irritated.

He was the one who'd been duped. Why should she be mad at him? They hadn't exchanged pictures, so he didn't know what she looked like. He'd been carrying the chocolates; she should've come up to him. And why did she just stand there, staring at him with the whore? Why didn't she come up and tell him *she* was the woman he was there to meet?

All she had to do was approach and he would've

known. But she didn't. She'd stood back and watched him, then left. Just fucking left.

Blade slammed his fist on the steering wheel of his Jeep. This was stupid. She was the one in the wrong. Why was he spending so much time being pissed about what had happened?

Because he'd been looking forward to this date for a long time. Because he hadn't felt a connection with another woman like he felt with her.

Wendy closed the door to her apartment as softly as she could. If Jackson was in his room, she didn't want to make him aware of the fact she was home already. It was way too early. She should've driven around longer, but gas was expensive and the only thing she wanted to do was crawl into bed and cry.

Of course, she wasn't lucky enough for her brother to be in his room. Nope. He was sitting at the dining room table.

"You're back early," he observed unnecessarily.

"Yeah."

"Things didn't work out?" he asked.

"Not really."

"Not really? Either they did or they didn't," Jackson said in exasperation.

Wendy dropped her purse on the table and headed

into the small galley kitchen. She poured herself a glass of water and chugged it down as she leaned against the counter. She refused to look at Jackson and just stood in the kitchen, trying to put off the inevitable.

"What'd he do?" her brother asked. He'd stood and was leaning against the wall leading into the kitchen. His arms were crossed over his chest and he was glaring at her.

Wendy stared up at her brother in surprise. Sometimes just looking at him took her breath away. He looked so much like their dad, it was eerie. He had dark hair and eyes like she did, but his facial features were more like their dad than hers were. Full lips, square jaw, and even now she could see the scruff of his beard from where it had grown during the day. Their dad had told her once that he got so tired of shaving, he'd grown out his beard just to give him a break from it.

Wendy had loved his beard, and she could totally see her brother wearing one just like their dad had.

But she didn't have time to appreciate the similarities between her brother and their dad for long because Jackson was obviously impatient. He shifted on his feet and continued to glare at her. Jackson was normally very easygoing. Like her, it took a lot to rile him up. But unlike her, once he was riled, he acted on it. It had been a while since Wendy had been called down to school to deal with the aftermath of him getting into a physical altercation, but it had happened enough that she knew her brother wasn't afraid to jump in and fight if he needed to.

And right now, he looked like he wanted to fight Aspen for whatever he might've done to her.

"He didn't do anything," Wendy said with a sigh. "I did."

"Come on," Jackson said, grabbing hold of his sister's elbow and steering her to the table. He pulled out a chair and helped her sit. Then he grabbed the chair he'd been sitting in when she'd arrived home and turned it around. He straddled it and leaned his elbows on the back. "Talk, sis," he ordered.

Wendy looked down at her hands in her lap. She saw the green scrubs and felt humiliated all over again. Without prevarication, she told her brother about how she'd been puked on at work and didn't have anything to change into except the scrubs. She told him about being early to the bar. About meeting Christine, and how stupid she'd been, and how she'd told her all sorts of stuff about Aspen.

"She told me I had something in my teeth, and like the good little naïve girl I am, I trotted off to the bathroom to check it out. I guess she saw Aspen outside or something, because by the time I came out of the restroom, she was sitting with him at the bar."

"What? Are you serious?" Jackson asked, his hands clenching into fists. "What did Aspen say when you confronted them about it?"

Wendy looked away from her brother and studied the old, faded wallpaper as if it held the answers to life's toughest questions.

"You didn't confront them," Jackson concluded. "Oh, sis...seriously?"

Wendy turned to look at her brother. "You don't understand."

"Then explain it to me," he begged. "You were so excited about this. You've been talking to Aspen for months. I can hear it in your voice when you tell me something he said. You like this guy. I mean, *like* him. You even told him about our parents, and I don't think you've told anyone about them since we moved. I can't believe you let that bitch steal him right from under your nose, and you didn't do anything about it!"

"I couldn't," Wendy told him.

"Bullshit," Jackson retorted. "I've been telling you for years that you need to stand up for yourself more, but you just don't do it. And look what happened."

"He looked happy," Wendy blurted. She couldn't stand the sad look on her brother's face anymore and turned away. "I was going to go up to them. I swear. I stood there, working up the courage, and as I was watching them, he laughed at something she said. He was smiling so big, it almost blinded me. Jackson, he was obviously satisfied with her. They were practically holding hands. Yeah, she was a bitch, and she intercepted him when I was in the bathroom, but the bottom line was that Aspen looked absolutely content to be there with *her*."

"But she was pretending to be *you*."

"I know. But, Jackson, what if I went up to them and told him that *I* was Wendy, not her...and he was disappointed? I couldn't bear that. And you didn't see this other woman. She was beautiful. Short skirt, boobs out to here." Wendy waved her hands in front of her, demonstrating how big Christine's chest was. "The last thing I wanted was to see his happy countenance turn into disappointment that the woman he was talking to wasn't the one he was supposed to meet. I didn't want to be second best...and I'm *always* second best."

"But what if he *wasn't* disappointed?" Jackson argued. "It's *you* he got to know, not her."

"I know you're my brother, and you're kinda required to defend me no matter the situation, but seriously, Jackson, let it drop."

The teenager shook his head. "I can't believe you, sis. Seriously. I love you more than anything, but you were in the wrong tonight."

Wendy stared at her brother. She didn't like to see the look of irritation on his face, especially not directed at her. For most of his life, it had just been the two of them. They'd been through some pretty serious shit, and to see the disappointment on his face almost killed her.

"If I was Aspen, I'd be pissed," he said.

50

"But he thinks he's with me," Wendy said, her brows furrowed in confusion.

"I would bet a million dollars that he figured out that bitch wasn't you pretty quickly," Jackson said without a trace of doubt.

"Why?"

"You said that you had like a five-minute conversation with her before you went to the bathroom. You've talked to Aspen for hours and hours over the last couple months. You think he's really that stupid and won't figure out that she isn't you?"

"He's not stupid," Wendy defended quickly. "And, yeah, I figured eventually he'd realize it, but I also assumed by then, he wouldn't care."

"No, Wen. I bet if you had hung around for a bit longer, you would've seen him ditch her. And since you left, he didn't find you. He was probably worried. Then mad that you stood him up."

"I didn't stand him up," Wendy protested weakly. "In fact, he looked right at me and then turned back to *her*." Wendy didn't know when her brother had gotten so mature. He was only a sophomore. However, he was actually seventeen, even though the school thought he was a year younger. The deception had been necessary after their parents had died and they'd left town. But most of the time she still saw him as a little boy.

At the moment, she realized with a jolt that he was

almost a man. That he was actually older than she'd been when her entire life had changed on a dime.

"He saw you?" Jackson asked.

Wendy nodded.

"Jesus, Wen. Then I bet he's *really* pissed you didn't come up to him. Didn't stick around. That was a shitty thing to do."

Wendy should've been mad, but she was too exhausted and heartsick. She realized Jackson was right, but didn't know what she could do about the situation now. "I'm going to bed," she informed her brother. "Make sure everything is locked up and maybe get a start on your homework."

"Wendy—" Jackson began, but she held her hand up to stop him.

"I can't right now," she told him. "Please."

"What are you going to tell him when you call him next?"

"I'm not."

"Wen—" he started again, but she cut him off once more.

"I can't. You're right. I stood him up. I left and didn't tell him about the mistaken identity. He's probably pissed. Hell, for all I know, he's in bed with that bitch right now. I can't bear to talk to him again. To hear him yell at me. I'm embarrassed and disgusted with myself and if the roles were reversed, I wouldn't want to talk to *him* again. I'm sure he feels the same."

"He deserves an explanation," Jackson insisted.

Wendy shrugged. She knew her brother was right, but she couldn't think about it at the moment. "I'll see you in the morning." And with that, she turned and walked down the short hallway to the bedrooms. There were only three doors...two bedrooms and one bathroom. The apartment was small, but it was cheap. And cheap was all Wendy could afford, even with two jobs.

She wanted to slam the door in frustration, but refrained. It wasn't Jackson's fault she was too trusting. That she was naïve. And it wasn't his fault she was so devastated that Aspen looked happy with a woman who wasn't her.

Without bothering to change—what did it matter if she slept in the damn scrubs?—Wendy crawled into bed and hugged her extra pillow to her chest. She brought her knees up to curl into a ball and cried.

Jackson Tucker glared at his sister's back as she headed down the hall toward her room. He loved her but she was so clueless sometimes. He knew why she didn't like conflict, why she felt the need to fly under the radar, but it still frustrated him. All she had to do was walk up to Aspen and tell him that she was Wendy, and everything would've been okay.

He'd heard enough about the kind of man Aspen

Carlisle was to be ninety-nine percent sure of that. His sister gushed every time she hung up with him. He knew Aspen was in the Army, had a sister who had recently gone through something horrible, although Wendy wouldn't tell him what...he wasn't sure *she* knew. Jackson had even talked to Aspen one night. Wendy had forgotten her phone, and he'd answered when Aspen had called so he wouldn't be worried about his sister.

They'd talked for about ten minutes. Not about anything in particular, but the fact that Wendy didn't freak out when he'd told her about their conversation said a lot. Usually, Wendy was super protective of him. Not that she dated much, but in the past, she hadn't told a man that she was raising her little brother until at least the fifth date.

And just from that short conversation he'd had with Aspen, Jackson had a feeling the man would be pretty upset when he found out the woman he'd been talking to wasn't Wendy.

Just then, the phone in Wendy's purse began to vibrate.

Jackson looked down the hall and saw that his sister's door was still closed.

She'd be mad at him for butting in, but he couldn't let this rest. Not after he'd seen the sadness in his sister's eyes. If Aspen *did* figure out that the woman he was talking to wasn't Wendy, and he didn't care, Jackson needed to find out now. Aspen wouldn't be the man for his sister if he'd done that.

Reaching over, Jackson pulled Wendy's old, beaten-up black purse closer. He unzipped it and reached in to grab her phone. It wasn't top of the line, and his looked just like hers, but he knew it was all she could afford, and he'd never complained.

As he was pulling it out, it vibrated in his hand, scaring the shit out of him. He tapped in the password —Wendy insisted they both have access to each other's phones, just in case—and he clicked on the text icon.

She had several missed texts, as he'd expected, all from Aspen. All six messages seemed fairly calm. He was worried about her.

Jackson scowled. The least his sister could've done was let him know she'd made it home all right.

Then he saw that she also had at least one voicemail message.

Reading her texts was one thing, listening to her voicemail was something altogether different...

Just when he'd decided that it was in her best interest that he listen, the phone vibrated once again with an incoming call.

Jackson saw it was Aspen, and made a split-second decision. He stood and went into the small foyer of the apartment. Wendy might still hear him, but there was less of a chance here than sitting at the table.

"Hello?" he said quietly after he'd swiped to answer the call.

There was a pause on the other end of the phone before a male voice asked, "May I speak to Wendy?"

"This is Aspen, right?" Jackson asked. He'd seen his name on the phone before he answered, but wanted to be sure.

"Yes. Jack? Is your sister all right? She got home, didn't she?"

And with that question, Jackson relaxed. He could tell Aspen was upset, but the fact that he asked about Wendy first, and wanted to make sure she was home safe and sound, went a long way toward making Jackson think he was doing the right thing. "She's home. I can't say she's all right, but she's here."

"Did she talk to you?"

"Yeah. She told me what happened."

"I swear to God I didn't know that bitch wasn't Wendy. She introduced herself to me as your sister."

"I figured."

"I really need to talk to Wendy," Aspen said, the evenness of his voice breaking.

"Not happening tonight," Jackson told him.

"This is between her and me," Aspen said.

"That's where you're wrong. Anything that happens to me, I talk to her about, and anything that happens to *her*, she tells *me* about. We don't keep secrets, and I have to make sure you're not going to go off on her before I'll let you talk to her."

Jackson heard Aspen breathing on the other end of the line, but he didn't say anything for a long moment. Finally, he said, "I don't understand why she didn't call that bitch out."

"Wendy doesn't like conflict," Jackson said.

"I know."

"No, I don't think you do. She *really* doesn't like conflict. Will go out of her way to avoid it at all costs. Even if it means she gets screwed in the process. She doesn't even like to argue with *me*, and we're as close as siblings can be. So when she saw that woman with you, the woman she'd nervously babbled to before you got there, who she'd told *all* about her blind date and how nervous she was, she literally couldn't interrupt you two. That bitch told her she had something in her teeth, and Wendy went off to the bathroom to take care of it. That's when you came in and she made her move."

"I saw her," Aspen said quietly. "Our eyes met and I had a feeling that was her. She didn't even need to say anything. If she'd have come up to where we were sitting, I would've known."

"She said you looked happy," Jackson said.

"What?"

"My sister. She told me she was working up the nerve to go up to you, that she was trying to overcome her aversion to making a scene, but you were laughing and had your hands on that other woman and you looked happy. Wendy was willing to give up her chance with you because she didn't want to take the happiness from your eyes or make you lose your smile."

"Fucking hell!" Aspen swore. "That bitch told me a story about something that had supposedly happened at the long-term care facility tonight. It was funny. That's all that was."

"I bet Wendy told her the story when she was waiting for you," Jackson said.

"No doubt. Although I have a feeling Wendy's story was more sympathetic toward the resident than when the fake Wendy told it."

"Look, here's the thing. My sister is upset. She's embarrassed and has no intention of contacting you ever again."

"No," Aspen said immediately. "Not happening."

Jackson smiled. If Aspen was weak, or a different kind of man, he would've let that be that. But Jackson was a pretty good judge of character, and he'd had a feeling Aspen wouldn't let his sister blow him off that easily. "So you're saying you still want to meet Wendy?"

"No."

Jackson's stomach knotted. That wasn't what he was expecting to hear.

"I don't just want to meet her," Aspen went on. "I want to date her. Get to know her. Stand by her side when people give her shit. If she won't stick up for herself, I'll do it for her. I don't know what happened to make her not like conflict, but I want to do my best to show her that it's okay to speak her mind."

Jackson liked that. He didn't think it was possible, but he liked the thought of someone standing by his sister. Lord knew he wouldn't always be around to try to run interference for her and to make sure she wasn't taken advantage of. "I'm not going to give you our address," he warned.

"I wouldn't ask you to. That shit's not safe."

"Right. But I'm not opposed to telling you that she'll be at the assisted-living facility Monday morning. She's working the morning shift and will be at her phone job later that night."

"Go on," Aspen encouraged.

"I'll give you the name of the home on one condition," Jackson said.

"Name it."

"Don't fuck with her."

"Done," Aspen said immediately.

"I mean it," Jackson warned. "We talk about everything. I'll know all about your dates. Where you go, what you do, if you kissed her. What you ate at dinner and what you said to her. If you do anything to make her sad or cry, I'll kick your ass. At least I'll try. My sister has been through hell and has put her life on hold for me. She put my well-being and safety before her own, and I'll never stand by and let someone take advantage of her or hurt her. Got it?"

Jackson wasn't sure Aspen was going to comment, as there was silence on the line for a long, uncomfortable moment. When Aspen finally spoke, it wasn't what Jackson had thought he'd say.

"She put your safety before her own?"

"Yes. Still does."

"You don't know me, Jack, but I'm going to tell you something that your sister should really hear from me first. I liked Wendy from the first time she called me. Something about her made me want to get to know her better. But when I saw her tonight, standing in the middle of a crowded bar, in her scrubs, all I wanted to do was pull her against me and shield her from the world. I have no doubt she's strong as fuck and would kick my ass if I tried to do something she didn't like, but that need to protect her is still there. Never again, if I can help it, will she have to put herself in danger, for you or for anyone else. I'll bend over backward to make sure she has whatever she needs to feel safe, to be safe, and to make *you* safe."

"And if she doesn't need or want that?" Jackson pressed. "She might not like conflict, but she doesn't stand for *me* protecting her. I can't imagine she'd let someone else come in and treat her like she's weak."

"She's not weak. I have a feeling I only know a fraction of her story, of your story. But what I do know is that she's one hell of a woman, and I can't wait to get to know her better. I'm really close with a group of men, and their wives and girlfriends are some of the strongest women I've met...but that doesn't mean their men won't do everything in their power so they don't *have* to be strong. Does that make sense?"

Strangely enough, it did. "Yeah. She works at Cottonwood Estates. It's that huge retirement home on the south end of town. Do you know it?"

"Yes."

"She works until two, then she'll come home to see me and make sure I've got dinner before she heads off to her other job at six-thirty. She wouldn't appreciate you being there right when she starts her shift, because she'll feel like she needs to get inside and start helping with the morning routines of the residents, but if you went by around one-thirty, you could catch her right as she's leaving."

"Thank you," Aspen said.

"Don't hurt her."

"Never. Jack?"

"Yeah?"

"She really said she didn't come over because she thought I looked happy?"

"That's what she said."

"She was wrong. I was uncomfortable as hell and was upset because the Wendy who I thought was sitting in front of me was nothing like the woman I'd gotten to know over the phone. I might've been laughing, but I wasn't fucking happy."

"You don't have to convince *me*," Jackson told him. "You have to convince my sister."

"I will. I owe you for this."

"No, you don't," Jackson countered. "I didn't do this for you. I did it for my sister."

"She's lucky to have you."

"No, *I'm* lucky to have *her*. I hope we'll get to meet sometime," Jackson said.

"We will," Aspen returned. "You're a hell of a man, and I'd be honored to call you a friend. Anyone who is as smart and loyal to their family as you are is someone I want to know."

Jackson felt a flood of pleasure at the other man's words. He wasn't trying to impress Aspen, but it felt good that he had nonetheless.

"Will you do me a favor?" Aspen asked.

"Maybe."

Aspen chuckled. "Smart man to not agree until you know what the favor is. Can you please delete the voice-mail messages I left for Wendy?"

Jackson stiffened. "What'd you say?"

"Feel free to listen to them," Aspen said, not seeming nervous in the least. "It's just that I want to surprise her on Monday. Don't want to give her any reason to suspect that I'll be seeing her."

"Why would she think that?"

"Because I flat-out told her that if she thought she was blowing me off, now that I got to see how adorable she looked in her scrubs, she was dreaming. I told her I was going to track her down with or without her help, and that she'd be seeing me soon."

Jackson chuckled. "You could do that? I mean, if I didn't give you the name of the place where she worked, you would've been able to find it anyway?"

"Yes. I have some connections from my time in the military who would've been able to look her up and find her within seconds."

Jackson gulped. Shit, that's the last thing they needed. "But you're not going to have anyone look her up now though, right?"

"Is there a reason I shouldn't?"

Jackson tried to answer nonchalantly. "Whatever. Now that you have the info, you don't need to anymore."

"Right. Thanks again, Jack."

"You're welcome."

"Later."

"Later."

Jackson clicked the phone off and immediately pressed the voicemail icon. He wanted to hear for himself what Aspen had said to his sister. If it was mean, then he'd give her a heads-up about what he'd done, and she could arrange to get off work early and miss Aspen's visit.

A couple minutes later, Jackson put the phone back into his sister's purse. The messages were just what Aspen had said they'd be. He could tell the other man was upset that she'd left, but he hadn't yelled at her, had been calm and controlled and had informed her that there was no way he was letting her get away from him now that he'd seen her.

The teenager smiled. He didn't like keeping things from Wendy, and he'd probably tell her all about his conversation with Aspen...*after* she'd met him face-to-face and made up with him.

He settled back at the table to finish up his homework and smiled. He had a feeling Aspen Carlisle would be good for his sister.

CHAPTER FOUR

Three days later, Blade sat in his car and waited for time to pass so he could go inside Cottonwood Estates and finally meet Wendy. It had sucked to let the weekend go by without calling her or hearing her voice, but he'd bided his time so they could talk through what happened in person.

He'd arrived at the facility early, and for a man who could sit in the heat or cold for hours while on a mission, waiting for the perfect moment to strike, he found himself extraordinarily impatient for time to pass. He'd looked at his watch at least twenty times in the past ten minutes...which wasn't making time go by any faster.

Finally, disgusted with himself, he climbed out of his Jeep and headed for the front doors. He carried the same bag of chocolate he'd had on Friday night and was hoping against all hope Wendy wouldn't freak when she saw him.

Blade held the door open for an older woman and what had to be her daughter then entered the facility. He didn't know what he'd expected, but it wasn't the homey, comfortable waiting area that he walked into. Granted, he hadn't been inside many nursing homes, but he'd thought it might smell like a hospital and have plastic chairs and sofas for those waiting to be served.

But instead, the scent of eucalyptus was in the air and the plush rug and leather chairs made the area seem like a living room instead of a waiting room. He walked up to the lady behind a window of glass at a desk wearing a name tag that said "Carol."

"Good afternoon," she said cheerily. "How may I help you?"

"I'm looking for Wendy Tucker," Blade said.

The receptionist looked him up and down for a beat, then said with true apology in her eyes, "I'm sorry, sir, but we can't give out any information about our residents or employees."

Feeling better about the place with every minute that went by, glad that they took safety seriously, Blade said, "I understand that. She's a friend of mine and doesn't know I'm here. We haven't seen each other in a long time and I'm here to surprise her." He pulled out his wallet and took out his military ID and placed it on the counter in front of the woman. "I'm not here to do her any harm, swear. All I want to do is see her."

He turned on the charm even more, not ashamed of doing whatever was necessary to get this woman to help him. He put the bag of chocolate on the counter and leaned in. "If it's okay, I'd like to simply sit out here and wait for her to get off shift. But I don't want to miss her...you know, if she leaves out another door. Do you think you can somehow get her to come out this way? You can watch our reunion and see for yourself that I'm not here to hurt her. I'd *never* hurt her."

For a moment, Blade didn't think his charm was going to work, but after a long second, while the woman looked at his ID then up at him then back to his ID—then wrote his name down on a slip of paper in front of her—the woman finally picked up his ID and held it up to him. "I think I can do that. Sometimes she's late leaving though. If she's in the middle of doing something with the residents, she never just leaves halfway through...unlike some of the other staff."

The last bit was mumbled under her breath, but Blade heard it. He wasn't surprised that Wendy wouldn't be a clock watcher. "Thank you," he said, putting his ID back into his wallet. "This means the world to me."

The receptionist nodded and Blade made his way to the corner of the room and sat in one of the oversized leather chairs. He did his best not to fidget as he waited for his first glimpse of Wendy.

Twenty minutes later, he heard the receptionist talking to someone behind the glass that separated her workstation from the waiting room, and when whoever she was speaking to responded, he stood. He recognized Wendy's voice immediately, which made him realize once more how idiotic he'd been Friday night. Even though it was loud, he should've known from the second the whore opened her mouth that she wasn't Wendy.

He held the bag of chocolate in his hand and waited for Wendy to appear.

She came through the door, but she was looking back at the receptionist. She was smiling, and Blade drank in the sight of her. She was wearing jeans today, and another scrub top. This one had little cartoon dogs and fire hydrants all over it. Her hands were full—she had a bag in one and a small flower pot in the other.

She said goodbye to the other woman and turned to walk through the lobby. But when she saw him standing in front of her, she stopped in her tracks.

"Hi, Wendy," Blade said softly.

Her mouth opened comically and she simply stood there and stared at him in shock.

"Your friend said he wanted to surprise you," the receptionist said, leaning through the sliding glass window. "Are you surprised?"

Wendy licked her lips and, without taking her eyes from him, said, "Yeah, Carol, I'm surprised all right."

"Yay!" Carol said, clapping her hands excitedly.

"Hi, Wen," Blade repeated.

"Uh...hi," she returned.

Remembering the way the bitch had thrown herself into his arms and hugged him, Blade mentally kicked himself again. Wendy wouldn't do that...*wasn't* doing that. She was reserved and cautious, and he had a feeling only part of it was because of what had happened at the bar. Mostly it was just...her.

He stepped toward her and, taking advantage of the fact that her hands were full, leaned into her and gently kissed her on the cheek. She didn't smell like flowers. Nope, she wasn't wearing any kind of artificial scent. He could smell the coconut of what was likely her shampoo, and fried food. Blade smiled as he stepped back. He was so weird...how could he like the smell of food on her?

Because it was Wendy, that's how.

Her dark brown eyes were huge on her face and he took his time drinking in her features. Her brown hair was once again up in a messy bun on the top of her head, except today there were stray tendrils framing her face and neck. The top she had on was V-neck, but she wore a shirt underneath it, so he got absolutely no hint of cleavage or any excess skin. Not that it mattered. Somehow the lack of skin showing was sexier. A tease. In a good way.

The jeans she was wearing were molded to her skin

and he liked the shapeliness of her legs. She had on the same pair of white sneakers that she'd worn at the bar. She looked down-to-earth and friendly, and Blade realized those were among the reasons he was so attracted to her. He didn't want a high-maintenance woman. Someone who would take hours to get ready to go someplace simple like the grocery store.

He wanted to feel as if he could muss his woman up and not have her freak. He wanted to be able to go hiking with her as well as take her out to expensive restaurants. He knew from his chats with Wendy that she enjoyed camping and other outdoor activities, hanging out at home with her brother, and going out for the occasional fancy dinner.

"What are you doing here?" she asked, staring up at him as she bit her lip uncertainly.

"I screwed up on Friday," Blade told her. "I'm here to rectify my mistake."

She immediately began to shake her head. "No, you didn't do anything wrong. I should've—"

"How about we talk about this over a late lunch?" Blade interrupted.

Her brows drew down and she looked confused. "But it's like, two in the afternoon."

Blade smiled. "It is. If you're not hungry, we can do something else. It's not too hot today. We could sit outside in that shaded courtyard I saw on the side of the building if you'd prefer."

He saw the indecision in her eyes. And fear. Perhaps that he was here to berate her for leaving the bar on Friday. Wanting only to reassure her, Blade slowly reached out his hand and placed it on the side of her neck. His thumb brushed the skin near her ear as he leaned in and said quietly, "You've got nothing to worry about, Wen. I'm not upset with you about the other night."

"You aren't?"

He shook his head. "No, sweetheart. I'm pissed off at that bitch who pretended she was you, but I'm not mad at *you*."

"I should've said something."

At her words, the worry Blade hadn't realized he was still carrying around slid off his shoulders like a silk shirt. "I understand why you didn't...well, at least partly why. Will you sit with me and talk?"

Her long lashes lifted and she met his gaze. "Yeah. I'd like that."

He beamed then reached out to take the flowerpot from her. "You always leave work with flowers?"

She giggled. "No. But Mrs. Epson is popular around here. Lots of men like her and she gets at least three or four bouquets a week. This poor thing wasn't doing so well, so she told me to take it home and revive it."

"I didn't know you had a green thumb," Blade said as he steered them toward the front door.

"I don't. I kill any and all flowers that dare to cross the threshold of my apartment door."

Blade looked down at her in confusion for a moment, then his lips quirked. "Flower killer. Got it. I'll keep that in mind. I guess the dozen roses I was going to send you after today are out, huh?"

She looked up at him in shock. "Why on earth would you send me roses? I mean, they're expensive!"

Blade thought she was making a joke at first, but then realized she was serious. "Hasn't anyone ever bought you flowers before, sweetheart?"

"No, but that's beside the point. They're impractical and—"

Blade put a finger over her lips, stopping her words. "Maybe so, but every woman deserves to feel special by having her man give her flowers."

She didn't respond, merely stared at him with those wide, innocent eyes of hers.

"Have fun!" the receptionist called out right before they left the lobby.

Blade gave her a chin lift and held open the door for Wendy.

As they walked toward the shaded area Blade had seen on his way in, she asked, "How's your day been?"

There it was. Her asking about his day. Blade smiled. "Better now that I'm with you."

She rolled her eyes. "Corny," she protested.

"I mean it," Blade said. "I couldn't concentrate at PT this morning and my commander got on my ass. After, Ghost cornered me and made me tell him what was bothering me. I told him all about you, and how I'd screwed up. I told him I was going to come and see you today, and he said to take the afternoon off. I did some paperwork and called my sister, then I went home to change and got here about an hour ago. I ate about three of your chocolates in my nervousness then couldn't make myself wait any longer and went inside about twenty minutes ago."

"*You* were nervous? Why?"

"Seriously?" Blade asked her.

She nodded as she sat on the concrete bench under a large tree. There wasn't any breeze in the air, but the leaves provided a nice shady haven for the two of them. Blade sat down next to her on the bench and rejoiced in the fact that when his leg pressed against her own, she didn't jerk away from him.

She bent over and put her bag on the ground and he did the same with the flowerpot. The chocolates, he put on the bench next to him. Then, with his hands now free, he reached over and took one of her hands in his. He clasped it between his palms and simply held it gently.

"Wendy, I've been talking to you for months. This is the first time we've seen each other, talked to each other in person. Why *wouldn't* I be nervous?"

"Because you could get any woman in a hundred-mile radius?" she asked rhetorically.

"I'm not sure the ladies in my immediate proximity, present company excluded, are my style," he teased. "They're a bit old for me." Then he sobered. "I don't want to be with anyone else but you. I haven't dated in a really long time because I've seen what true love is through my friends' relationships. I want what they have. And hooking up with a chick I meet in a bar isn't in the least attractive to me anymore. I saw you Friday night, you know."

She immediately tried to pull her hand from his at his last words, but he refused to let her.

"Full disclosure and all that, I also talked to Jack later that night when I called you," Blade told her.

If possible, her eyes got even wider. "You did?" she whispered.

"Yeah. I texted you and called and you weren't answering. He picked up the eighty-seventh time I tried calling you." He smiled to let her know he was exaggerating...but only a little bit. "He told me where you worked and what your schedule was."

"That rat," Wendy said under her breath.

"I wasn't happy, Wen," Blade said.

"What?"

"You told him you didn't come over at the bar because you thought I looked happy. I wasn't. That cunt told me a story about something that had supposedly happened to her here at the facility, and I laughed because it sounded sort of like something you'd tell me...but not exactly. I laughed to be polite."

"You put your hand on hers," Wendy countered.

"I put my hand on hers to keep her from touching me inappropriately."

Wendy's eyes widened even as her brows furrowed. "She touched you inappropriately?"

Blade smiled and squeezed her fingers lightly. "She tried. My point is, you told Jack that you didn't interrupt because you thought I was happy, but I wasn't. I don't ever want you to feel weird or awkward about interrupting me again. I don't care where we are or what I'm doing. Besides, I'm going to count on you to save me if another woman gets handsy with me."

"She was pretty," Wendy said, looking down at their entwined hands.

Blade felt a tinge of frustration. He understood her insecurity. He *had* smiled at the fake Wendy, and if their roles had been reversed, he would've been upset at Wendy too. But he needed her to understand where he stood and that *she* was the one he liked. "You know the saying, beauty is only skin deep?" Blade asked.

After Wendy nodded, he reached out and put his finger under her chin and turned her face so she had to look at him. "She might've been pretty on the outside, but inside she was rotten. Anyone who would take advantage of someone like you, who would purposely deceive both of us, is an ugly troll."

Her lips twitched.

Blade went on. "I went to that bar to meet the woman who captured my attention from the very first time she tried to sell me life insurance. I had no expectations about what you looked like, but what I see in front of me right this second blows me away."

Her eyes dropped, but he didn't remove his finger from her chin.

"Someone who's comfortable in her own skin, and someone who cares more about other people's feelings than her own. You smell like fried chicken, which you probably think is embarrassing, but to me it means you care enough to sit with the residents as they eat their lunch. It reminds me of home and makes me want to eat you up. You've exceeded all my expectations, Wendy."

Her eyes came back up his. She took a deep breath then said, "I'm sorry I didn't go up to you at the bar."

"Apology accepted," he said immediately. Blade could see the tension in her shoulders fade away at his words. "If you had stuck around for another five minutes, you would've seen me go off on her ass."

"Yeah?"

"Yeah. She was a prostitute, you know."

"Holy shit, really?" Wendy asked.

Blade reluctantly dropped his finger from her chin

and re-clasped her hand. "Yup. She got just enough information from you to fool me for a bit, but I was suspicious of her almost from the start. She dug her own hole when I asked about 'Josh' and how he was enjoying the fifth grade."

Wendy giggled. "Yeah, I didn't tell her anything about my brother."

"Obviously. But even before that, I knew something was off from the second I met her."

"How?"

"She didn't ask me how my day was."

Wendy cocked her head. "What do you mean?"

"You're very good at turning conversations away from yourself, Wendy. And one of the first things you always ask me is how my day has been. When she didn't do that, I was suspicious."

"Oh."

"Then she tried to grab my junk right there in the bar, and I knew you wouldn't ever do *that* either."

"Oh my God, no!" Wendy exclaimed.

Blade chuckled. "Anyway, I called her on her deception and believe me, she turned from sweet to a bitch in two seconds."

"So, you just left?" Wendy asked.

"First, I talked to the owner of the bar and got her banned for life, so she can't pull that shit with anyone else. Then I looked in every nook and cranny for you...

hoping against hope that you were still there. *Then* I left."

"I couldn't stay," Wendy said quietly.

"I know. Were you really not going to contact me ever again?" Blade asked.

"Darn it, Jackson," Wendy murmured, then shrugged. "Such a blabbermouth. No, I figured you were either enjoying your time with that other woman or you were pissed at me."

"Then it's a good thing I'm stubborn, isn't it?" Blade asked.

Wendy simply nodded.

An hour later, they were still sitting on the bench under the tree talking. Blade glanced at his watch and was amazed at how much time had passed. He'd never felt so at ease with a woman like he did with Wendy. Their conversation never lagged and he'd never laughed so much as he had with her.

She'd explained what had happened on Friday at work and why she'd gone to the bar in her scrubs. While the story was similar to the one the bitch at the bar had told him, Wendy's made much more sense. The fact that she'd put the resident's safety above her comfort, and had allowed him to throw up on her rather than risk him falling, only solidified Blade's thoughts about her compassion.

He hadn't missed the way she'd called her brother "Jackson," rather than "Jack," as she'd originally told

Blade his name was, but he didn't comment on it. It could be nothing. Jack was obviously a nickname...but something about the way she said his full name made him think otherwise.

They talked about her work schedule, some of the residents' antics, and about her telemarketing job. He shared more about his friends and how they were as close as brothers. Blade told her a lot about his sister, Casey, and even went into a bit more detail about her kidnapping in Costa Rica.

Finally, Wendy looked at her watch and said, "I really do need to get going. Jack will be home soon. He—"

"When can I see you again?" Blade asked, brushing his thumb over the top of her hand, which he'd rested on his thigh beneath his own.

"Oh, um...I don't know."

"Tomorrow?"

She flushed and bit her lip.

"What? Are you working?"

"No, but it's a school night."

He smiled. She was so cute sometimes. "I understand." And he did. The last thing he wanted to do was interfere with her routine with her brother.

"But...he's going to some school thing in the afternoon and won't be home until right before dinner. Maybe we could do something then? If you wanted."

"I want to," Blade said with a smile. He brought her

hand up to his mouth and kissed the back, loving the flush that filled her cheeks. "In case it's not obvious, I like you, Wendy Tucker."

"I like you too."

"Do you want to meet me somewhere?" he asked.

"You could...um...come over to my place if you wanted."

Her offer surprised Blade, but he kept his thoughts off his face.

"It's nothing fancy, but I've been meaning to try this new recipe for green beans. I mean, I'll make something to go with it too, but I just thought that maybe you could come over in the afternoon and then we could have dinner. You can meet Jack...but we could also go out if you'd prefer. I don't know what time your boss... or whatever you call him...will let you off work."

Blade never imagined she'd invite him to her place so soon, not to mention meeting her brother. He knew from their conversations that he meant the world to her, so her offering to let him meet Jack was huge. "My commander will let me off a bit early. I'd love to come over, sweetheart. If you're sure it's okay?"

"I have a feeling after I tell Jack how today went, he'll insist on meeting you sooner rather than later. And don't get used to going behind my back and conspiring with him," she warned with a teasing glint in her eye.

Blade smiled. "Never."

"Why don't I trust you?"

He chuckled. "Because you're smart. Come on, I'll walk you to your car."

With that, Blade stood and helped Wendy to her feet. He grabbed the plant and chocolates and she picked up the bag she'd been carrying. They walked to her older-model Chevy Equinox. The small black SUV had seen better days...there was rust on the bumpers and a large dent in the driver's side. The sight of it made Blade clench his teeth. It looked like someone had run into the car at some point, and the thought of Wendy being inside the car when it had happened made him worry about her all the more.

But he didn't say anything as she opened the back door and put the bag inside. She took the plant from him and actually buckled it in with the seat belt in the back, which made him grin. Then he handed her the small bag of chocolate. When she tried to take it, he held on until she looked up at him.

"If I were a different kind of man, I'd insist on taking an IOU for each one of these Kisses," he teased.

As he expected, the blush that had faded away earlier returned.

But instead of ignoring his words, she surprised him by saying, "If I was a different kind of woman, I'd give them all to you right here and now."

It took a moment for her words to register, and when they did, Blade couldn't help but let out a snort of laughter.

"Did you just snort?" Wendy teased.

"Nope," Blade lied. "Men like me don't snort."

"Men like you?"

"Manly men who can open bottles of beer with their teeth."

She giggled, and Blade's heart skipped a beat. This is how he liked to see her. Happy, carefree, not nervous or shy around him. He vowed to do whatever he could to always keep her this way.

"Whatever," she told him, rolling her eyes. She took the chocolate from him and placed the bag on the backseat as well, then shut the door. She opened the driver's side door and stood there, looking unsure once again.

"You want to set a time for me to come over, or do you want to text me when it's convenient?"

"How about three? Jack will get a ride home from one of his friends, so I don't have to pick him up after school. And that'll give me time to get home and make sure I've got everything."

"Do you want me to bring anything?" Blade asked.

She shook her head. "No, I've got this."

"Jack doesn't drive?"

She hesitated before she answered. "Not yet. He's in no hurry to get his license, so for now it works for me to take him where he needs to go."

Blade wouldn't have thought anything about her answer, but she was no longer looking him in the eye. Her gaze had shifted to the left as she'd explained.

Blade didn't have time to delve into why she might be lying about her brother not wanting a driver's license; now wasn't the time or the place.

"Three sounds perfect," Blade told her. "I'm looking forward to spending more time with you."

"Me too," she said with a smile.

Keeping his eyes locked on hers, Blade leaned toward her, watching for any sign he was moving too fast or that she didn't want him kissing her.

When she placed one of her hands on his upper arm and stood on her toes as he got closer, Blade relaxed. He brushed his lips over hers, and even though he wanted nothing more than to plunge his tongue deep inside her mouth and find out how she tasted, he moved his lips to her cheek, kissing her lightly there as well. Then he moved one of his hands to the small of her back and did what he'd wanted to back in the bar Friday night.

He pulled Wendy's body into his taller one. He didn't stop until they were touching from hips to chest, and he sighed in contentment. He wrapped his arms around her and hugged her tight. She was stiff at first, but within seconds, she melted against him. He felt as if she belonged there, fitting against him perfectly.

Every curve of her body was flush against his own. Blade closed his eyes and soaked the experience in. Wendy was soft in all the right places, and he wanted to lift her off her feet and have her straddle him so he could press her against the side of her car and have his way with her.

Surprised, and not a little alarmed at the way his thoughts went from affectionate to passionate in a heartbeat, Blade pulled back. Wendy was staring up at him with the same dazed look he had a feeling was on his own face.

He brushed his fingers over her cheek lightly then took a step back. She stumbled a bit, and he steadied her by holding on to her arm. "You good?"

"Yeah, sorry."

"Drive safe, Wen. Text me your address and I'll see you tomorrow at three. Okay?"

She nodded. "Okay."

"Bye."

"Bye."

Blade forced himself to turn and walk toward his Jeep. He looked back once and saw that Wendy was still standing in the open doorway of her car. He waved and she raised her hand in return, then finally sat down and shut her door.

Blade watched until she started up her car and pulled out of the parking lot. He wanted to follow her. Wanted to talk to her some more. But knew he couldn't.

Instead, he forced himself to start his own vehicle and calmly pull onto the road toward his condo.

That had gone much better than he'd hoped. Most of it was because of Wendy. She was easygoing and she hadn't hesitated to apologize...even though technically he'd been the one to screw up at the bar in the first place.

Blade made a mental note to keep an eye out for when she might be going along with what he wanted just because she didn't like conflict. She needed to learn to speak up when she didn't like something or when she didn't agree with him. Grinning, he decided he'd make it his mission to help her overcome her aversion to disagreeing with people. He hadn't looked forward to something in a long time as much as he looked forward to getting to know Wendy.

CHAPTER FIVE

The next afternoon, Wendy was flitting around her apartment, stressing. After returning home, she'd worried that she'd been stupid in inviting Aspen over so soon, but Jackson had reassured her that it would be fine.

Wendy had been upset at her brother for talking to Aspen behind her back, but in the end, had to admit that it had actually been a good thing. She'd enjoyed talking to him and felt excited about hanging out with a man for the first time in a really long while.

She and Jackson had gone to the grocery store yesterday afternoon before she'd had to leave for her second job and had bought the stuff she needed to make the green bean dish and the rest of the dinner.

As of now, the beans were on the stove simmering

and the pasta casserole she'd made to go with them was in the fridge, and all she had to do was preheat the oven and stick it in.

Aspen had sent a text saying he'd be there in about ten minutes.

So all that was left to do was freak out.

Wendy looked around her apartment and cringed. It wasn't exactly a palace. In fact, it was kind of crappy, but it was cheap and allowed her to purchase things for Jackson that she wouldn't be able to otherwise. Just this year, he'd joined the robotics club, and they were constantly taking trips to the home improvement store so he could get things to make electronics and prototypes.

He was also on the lacrosse team and half a dozen other clubs and programs at the school. He was way more popular than Wendy ever was, but she was as proud of him as she could be. There were many days when she didn't see him more than a few minutes at the beginning or end of the day because their schedules didn't mesh, but Wendy didn't worry too much about him. Jackson was a good kid, and he deserved far more than he'd gotten in his short life so far. She aimed to do whatever it took, to sacrifice everything, so he'd be able to go to college and get the education that had been denied her.

Wendy shook off the morose thoughts. She had a

good life and honestly wouldn't change anything that she'd done. Yeah, she wanted a nicer place for them to live, but Jackson never complained.

But looking around as she waited for Aspen to arrive, Wendy realized just how small their apartment was. They had a little galley kitchen and an equally small dining area. It was just big enough to hold a circular table with three chairs, which she'd scrounged from next to the Dumpsters in their apartment complex.

The living area was just beyond that. It had a beat-up old couch and a recliner. The table had also been thrown away at one point by someone. But Wendy had sanded, painted, and generally spruced it up. They had a flat-screen television that she'd been able to purchase for a song from the retirement home when they were remodeling some of the rooms. She'd bought colorful rugs to put on top of the gross cream carpet that had been there when they'd moved in.

There were two bedrooms down the hallway. Neither was huge, but all they did in them was sleep, so they didn't need to be large. She and Jackson shared a bathroom, which wasn't as bad as it seemed, as she took her shower at night and Jackson showered in the mornings.

All in all, Wendy was proud of the home she'd made for herself and her brother with the little she had...but she didn't know how Aspen would react.

A knock on the door brought her out of her musings and she took a deep breath. If he looked down on her because of where she lived, then she didn't want to be friends with him anyway.

As she walked toward the door, she tried to calm down. Aspen was her friend. Nothing he'd said or done in the past led her to believe he'd turn up his nose at her living quarters.

Pausing for a moment in front of her door, Wendy put a hand on her belly and tried to will the churning to subside. Knowing she was only making herself more nervous by hesitating, she pasted a smile on her face and flung open the door.

Blade scowled as he looked around. Wendy had texted him last night and given him her address, and he'd immediately been concerned. It wasn't in the best part of Temple, and he hated that.

When he'd driven up to the apartment complex, if it could be called that, he was even more worried. The older brick building needed work. Lots of it. Blade could see places where the brick was crumbling right off the side of the building. There were twelve doors, all on the outside, six on the bottom floor and six on the top.

He took a moment to be thankful that her apartment was on the second floor. It wasn't much, but at least it was something. Blade eyed a man leaving one of the apartments on the first floor. He was unshaven and looked like he'd been wearing the same clothes for days. He was also wiping his nose...which could simply mean he'd just sneezed or he had a cold. But the furtive way he looked around as he walked toward his car told a different story.

Blade's hands clenched on the steering wheel. Jesus. He didn't like the thought of Wendy living here, especially not when the signs were pointing to drug activity going on in the apartments around her.

Taking a deep breath, Blade climbed out of his Jeep and locked it...briefly wondering if it would still be there when he left for the evening. He slowly climbed the stairs to the second floor and got upset all over again. The railing was loose, and he knew all it would take was someone stumbling into it and it'd collapse, sending that person tumbling to the ground. The concrete under his feet was chipped and broken as well.

Wendy lived in an absolute shithole, and he couldn't help but be appalled. He didn't want to believe that a woman and a teenager actually chose to live here. It was unacceptable and dangerous—and there wasn't a damn thing Blade could do about it.

He knocked on Wendy's door...and sent a vicious glare toward the man who'd left the downstairs apartment and was now sitting in his car watching him.

Within seconds, the man backed up and peeled out of the small parking area.

Just when Blade lifted his hand to knock again, the door opened and Wendy stood in front of him with a smile on her face. It was strained though; that was easy to see.

"Hi, Wen," Blade said.

"Hey, Aspen," she greeted. "Come in."

He followed her through the door, noting that she immediately locked both the deadbolt and the door-knob after he'd entered. At least that was something.

"It smells wonderful," he told her.

The smile on her face grew, and her shoulders dropped with a decrease in tension. "Thanks. It's the basil on the green beans. You want to come and sit? It's a bit early to put the casserole in, but Jack should be home soon."

"Sure." Blade followed Wendy through the tiny front area and into the living room. The kitchen was attached, and there was a small table and some chairs behind the couch.

"I'm sorry it's not much," Wendy said, shrugging. "But it's home."

And it was. Blade looked around in surprise. The difference between the outside of the building and inside this space was amazing. She'd truly made this a comfortable home.

The bright rugs on the floor lightened up the room. There were photos on almost every available surface and wall. A red blanket was draped over the back of the sofa and the pot of flowers she'd had with her yesterday was now sitting on the small white table in the middle of the living area.

All in all, it looked restful and homey. Blade immediately felt comfortable there, and he was ashamed of his earlier thoughts. Oh, he still didn't like that Wendy and her brother were renting a place in the shitty complex, but this was more of a home than his condo. This was warm and lived in. His place was sterile and cold.

"It's nice," Blade said softly.

"Really?" Wendy asked.

"Really."

"I know the outside is crappy, but the price is right and I've done what I can to make the inside comfortable."

"You've succeeded, sweetheart," Blade told her, turning to her again. He was struck anew at the attraction between them. She was wearing another pair of jeans, but this afternoon she had on a blouse that bared her shoulders. It had sleeves, but it looked like the material on her shoulders had been cut out. It was a light gray color and amazingly brought out the shade of her deep brown eyes more than ever.

Her skin was pale and looked silky smooth. Her hair

was down around her shoulders, the first time he'd seen it that way, and Blade wanted to run his fingers through it to see if it was as soft as it looked. She didn't have any shoes on, and seeing her small painted toenails seemed intimate.

"You look nice," he said belatedly, realizing he'd been staring at her for longer than was appropriate.

"Thanks. You too."

Blade chuckled at that. He was wearing much what he did any time he got home and took off his uniform. Jeans and a T-shirt.

"You want something to drink?"

"Sure."

"I've got beer, coffee, tea, water, and apple juice."

"A beer sounds great. I'll switch to water with dinner." He watched as she walked to the old white fridge and got out a beer for him. She used the bottle opener stuck to the door then handed him the bottle.

"I hope Shiner Bock is all right. It's my favorite."

"It's great," Blade told her. He'd had her pegged as a wine or water girl, but there was something very down-to-earth about her popping the top off her own bottle and taking a long swallow of the yeasty brew.

"You worry about having the beer around your brother?"

She wrinkled her nose. "Why would I?"

"Because he's a teenager? Because he might decide to get drunk one night when you're at work?"

Wendy smiled and shook her head. "No, I'm not worried about that at all."

"Why not?"

"When you meet him, you'll understand. He's an old soul. He'd no sooner get drunk for the sake of getting drunk than I would."

Blade thought she was being a bit naïve, but didn't call her on it. He merely took another drink.

"I can tell you don't believe me," she said. "It might be uncommon, but he's been drinking beer and wine since he was thirteen. I don't mean like chugging beers or doing keg stands every night, but I've let him taste the beer I've brought home, and we even did a wine tasting thing one day when he was fifteen. I figure if he sees what it's all about, and I don't make a big fuss over it, he won't be as interested in going behind my back and getting drunk. I thought about how kids overseas have much more access to beer than kids over here in the US, and I wanted him to have the same 'whatever' attitude about alcohol that they do...or that I imagine they do."

"And is it working?"

"Yup." Wendy beamed at him. "Sometimes he asks to have a beer with dinner, but he mostly sticks to water or juice. I'm aware that it's illegal for me to supply him with it, and some would call it irresponsible, but so far, he hasn't abused the privilege. Believe me, when I was a teenager, I was sneaking out of the house to go to parties and get drunk...I thought it was so grown-up and cool to drink beer. I'm trying to teach him that isn't the case."

Blade shivered with the thought of a teenager sneaking out of the apartment in this part of town. "Does he sneak out?" he asked, gripping his sweaty beer tightly.

"No." Wendy held up a hand as if to forestall the question she thought he wanted to ask. "And before you ask, I know he's not, because for a while I booby-trapped the door. I bought one of those things you put in the doorjamb that make a noise if the seal is broken. Not once did he leave the apartment in the middle of the night."

"Why did you think he might sneak out in the first place?"

Wendy's eyes left his and Blade got a weird feeling in the pit of his stomach. He knew she was about to be dishonest. He'd seen enough people lie in his lifetime to recognize the signs.

"Oh, you know. Because he's a teenager. You know how they are."

"No, not really. Did he give you a reason to think that?"

Wendy shook her head, then shrugged. "I just wanted to make sure."

Blade didn't particularly like her answer. He wasn't going to judge her if her brother snuck out here and there. Hell, he'd done it a few times himself when he was Jack's age. Was she embarrassed? Did she think he'd blame her? Blade wasn't sure what she was hiding, but once again he felt she was keeping things from him.

He tried to blow it off, telling himself they'd just met and there was no reason for her to tell him everything about her life. But a wary feeling remained, even as she continued on as if he hadn't asked the question.

She looked down at her beer and picked at the label on the bottle. "Besides, he knows how dangerous it is out there. He told me once that I didn't need to keep the dinger thing on the door because there was no way he'd ever leave me here in the apartment by myself."

Blade's heart swelled in his chest. Jack sounded a lot like him with Casey. He'd always worried about his sister, even though she was only two years younger than him. He supposed he always would, regardless that she was with one of his Delta teammates now.

"That's great, sweetheart. He sounds like a level-headed, good kid," he told her honestly.

"He is. And he's smart. He's in the robotics club at school. They don't make toys either. Right now, they're working on an artificial arm. It's super cool what this thing can do."

"Wow."

"Yeah." She smiled at him, then looked at her watch. "I'm going to preheat the oven and put the casserole in. It'll be ready when Jack gets home. Is that all right?"

"Of course. Can I help?"

"No, I got it. You can go and sit if you want. We only have a few channels that come in, but we've got lots of DVDs if you want to watch something else."

"I'm okay with talking if you are."

"Sure, although I'm not that interesting."

"Wendy..." Blade drew the word out in disbelief.

"What?"

She stood in the kitchen with one hand on the handle of the refrigerator. Her head was cocked in question.

"We've done nothing but talk over the phone for the last couple months. Why would you think you aren't interesting?"

She shrugged. "I don't know...it seems different now."

Blade set his beer down and walked up to her. He put his hands on either side of her neck and tilted her head up to his. "The only thing that's different now is that I have a face to put to the beautiful voice I've been talking to over the last two months. Everything about you fascinates me, Wen. From the way you've made a shithole of an apartment into a cozy home, to the way you've raised what sounds like a mature, well-rounded brother. Don't ever think you're not interesting. I have a feeling the more I learn about you, the more interesting you'll become. And I want to know everything."

She'd looked relaxed as he'd spoken, but after the last sentence, she tensed under him.

"I'm just like any other woman, Aspen. Don't look too deeply into it."

He stared at her, wishing he could read her mind. Something was bothering her. If he wasn't mistaken, he saw fear lurking in the depths of her eyes. The thought that she was hiding something grew into a certainty. But the fact that he was doing something to scare her was abhorrent. Dropping his hands, Blade immediately took a step away, giving her space. "It's okay, sweetheart," he soothed. "I won't pry."

Wendy closed her eyes and took a deep breath. Then she turned to the fridge, opening it and reaching for the casserole dish. She gave a little forced laugh as she stood. "Of course it's okay. Excuse me, I don't want to drop this."

Blade stepped farther out of her way and picked up his beer once more. He wandered over to the couch and sat on one end. He didn't like the barrier she'd thrown up between them, but he refused to get upset about it. This was truly their first date, and they were still getting to know each other. She'd learn that she could trust him. That he'd never do anything to bring her or her brother harm. Whatever secrets she had would be his secrets too.

Eventually, she ran out of things to fiddle with in the kitchen, and she wandered into the small living area and sat on the other end of the couch. "How was your day?" she asked.

Blade closed his eyes for a brief second then opened them. "I love when you ask me that."

"Why?"

"Because you sound like you truly want to know when you ask. Just as when you ask me how I am, or if I'm feeling okay."

"Of course I want to know. I wouldn't ask if I didn't."

"Most people ask just because it's the socially correct thing to do."

"So? How *was* your day?" Wendy asked again.

"It was good. Got more shit from my friends about taking a few hours off this afternoon."

"They don't want you to see me?"

Blade leaned over and touched Wendy's knee briefly. "No, don't ever think that. They're thrilled as can be that I'm dating. I'm basically the last one in our group to have a steady girlfriend or wife. It's just good-natured teasing, that's all. Besides...even if they didn't approve, I wouldn't give a shit."

"Tell me about them."

"My friends?"

"Yeah. You sound really close with them."

"I am. We've been through a lot of shit together. I'd give my life for them, just as they'd do for me."

"That's awesome," Wendy whispered. She turned

until she was semi-facing him, her knee hiked up on the couch, her beer resting on her knee. "Did you go through basic training together? Is that why you're so close?"

Blade knew he couldn't tell her that they were on the same Special Forces team together, but he could tell her some things. "No, we didn't meet until about five years ago. We're on a specialized team in the Army, and we get sent on missions together. It's not really like a regular platoon, where the guys get shuffled in and out all the time. We're stationed here together for the long haul."

Her brows drew down, and Blade knew she didn't understand. But he went on, hoping she'd be more interested in the details about his friends than the logistics of how his "special team" worked.

"Ghost is the oldest and our captain. His girlfriend's name is Rayne, and they've been together since he helped rescue her from a coup over in Egypt."

"Wow, really?"

"Really. Fletch is married to Emily, and they have an adorable little girl named Annie. I can't wait for you to meet her. She's seriously amazing. They also have a little one on the way as well. Coach is married to Harley, and I have a feeling she and Jack will get along really well. She's also super smart and designs video games for a living. She and Coach met when she went skydiving, and he was assigned to be her jumpmaster for the day."

"Why is that funny?" Wendy asked, obviously noting his smirk.

"It's not really funny, but Coach was knocked unconscious by a bird during the jump, and Harley had to safely get his ass back to the ground."

Wendy inhaled. "Oh my God, that's not funny at all!" she exclaimed.

"It is if you know Coach. He's super protective, and he'd told her over and over that she had nothing to worry about, that he'd get her safely to the ground."

"Still not funny," Wendy insisted.

Blade couldn't help but smile wider. "Yeah, I guess it's not...but it's funny every time we jump now. We all give him shit and tell him to 'duck'."

"Men and their senses of humor," Wendy said, rolling her eyes. "Is that all on your team?"

"Nope. Hollywood is married to Kassie. She's also very close to her sister, but their parents are still in the picture, so it's not exactly the same as you and Jack. She's also pregnant. Fish is a de facto member of our group, but he now lives out in Idaho with his wife. She's a genius. And I don't mean that she's simply smart. She's literally a genius. Truck is unofficially officially with Mary. We know it, but for some reason, they're playing this game where they act like they don't like each other or something. It's weird, but Truck loves that woman with everything in him."

"So, she's playing him?"

"No," Blade said immediately. "She likes him back... it's complicated."

"Sounds like it," Wendy muttered.

"Then there's Beatle and my sister, Casey."

"Your sister is with one of your friends? Isn't that against some sort of man code or something?"

Blade immediately shook his head. "Who the hell knows, but I was ecstatic when he told me he was interested in her. Of course, he told me when we were in the middle of the jungle as we were going to rescue her from the assholes who kidnapped her, but it wouldn't have mattered if we were sitting in the middle of my living room. I know Beatle as well as I know myself. He'll move heaven and earth to make her happy and to ensure she's safe. Why *wouldn't* I want him with one of the people who mean the most to me?"

"Gosh, when you put it that way...not all men think like you though."

"That's the truth," Blade said with a nod. "I've seen some bad shit in my lifetime," he told her. "Shit that no one should have to see or experience. The only reason I'm able to deal with it is because of the six men I work with. They're all amazing. The one thing we have most in common is a deep desire to make the loved ones in our lives happy. To make sure they're safe. There's something in our DNA that won't allow us to settle when it comes to our life partners. In just about every case, the second my friends saw their current girlfriends or wives, they knew they were it for them."

Blade didn't look away from Wendy's wide-eyed gaze, willing her to understand.

"We fight hard, we play hard, and we love hard. That's just the way it is. Beatle loving my sister is like we both won the lottery. He's always been my brother-in-arms, but eventually, he'll be my brother legally as well."

"You're lucky," Wendy said quietly.

"I am," Blade agreed immediately. "I figure as a reward for doing what I do for a living, and seeing what I see, I was given this amazing group of men, and now women, to be friends with. I'm blessed."

"I like that for you."

"Thanks. What about you?"

"What about me?"

"What about your friends?"

Once again, Wendy looked away from him, and Blade knew she was going to deflect the question. Frustration welled inside him.

"I've been really busy with Jackson. I haven't really had time for friends."

"Everyone has time for friends," Blade chastised gently. "What about the parents of *his* friends? Or people at your work?"

"I'm younger than most of the other parents, and

because I'm just an aide, I don't have much in common with the nurses at the home."

"How old are you?" Blade asked.

"Does it matter?"

She still wouldn't look up at him.

"No, I guess not," Blade said, knowing he wouldn't get any answers from her right now.

"Can I ask something?" she asked.

Blade knew she was going to change the subject, and he let her. He didn't want to push. He was enjoying spending time with her and didn't want to rock the boat as far as their relationship went. He'd have plenty of other chances to get to know her. Once she felt more comfortable with him, she'd open up more. He hoped.

"Of course you can. Ask me anything. I'll tell you everything, I don't have any secrets—although you should know, I can't promise to always be able to answer all your questions about my job. Not because I don't want to but because I'm literally not allowed. A lot of what I do is top secret. I can't tell my sister, or you, or anyone else. I don't want you to take it personally if I tell you I'm not able to talk about something."

"Oh...okay. All I was going to ask was about your friends' names. They're a little unusual."

Blade laughed so hard another snort escaped, which in turn made Wendy smile at him. "They're nicknames, sweetheart. Ghost because he can move freaky quietly. Fletch because his last name is Fletcher. Coach got his nickname in basic because he was always coaching others. Hollywood is the pretty boy of the group. Could've easily been an actor, but instead, he joined the Army. Fish because he was always the best swimmer; Beatle because his last name is Lennon. However, he also can't stand bugs, which is hilarious and makes his nickname that much funnier. Truck...you'll understand when you meet him."

"And yours? Do you have a nickname?"

Blade nodded.

"Are you going to tell me? Or is it top secret?"

He was slightly uncomfortable. His friends all had names that could easily be passed off as something funny or non-threatening. His wasn't. He debated telling her, but in the end, decided that he didn't want to keep anything from Wendy. He wanted a relationship with her. A long one. And if they both started off by keeping secrets, it didn't bode well for that relationship.

"It's Blade."

"Like that movie with Wesley Snipes?"

"Not exactly. I used to just be called by my last name, Carlisle...I didn't have a fancy nickname. But after a particularly nasty fight overseas, I earned the nickname Blade. We were pinned down and had run out of bullets. We had to resort to hand-to-hand fighting, and I guess my...skills...with a knife impressed my captain at the time."

Blade didn't take his gaze from Wendy's. He wasn't

ashamed of his nickname, it just wasn't something that he thought would endear him to the woman sitting next to him.

"Hmmm," she murmured. "I suppose that's better than 'Tree' or something, especially considering what you do for a living. The bad guys wouldn't exactly quake in their boots if they heard 'Tree' was on their heels, would they?"

It took a second for the fact that she wasn't turned off or made uneasy by his nickname to register, but once it did, he couldn't help but laugh. He laughed so hard he was snorting almost nonstop, but the best part was that Wendy joined in. She was giggling so much she had to put her beer on the table in front of them so she didn't spill it.

When Blade got himself under control, he said, "Yeah, I think I'll keep Blade. 'Tree' just doesn't have the same ring to it. But you aren't allowed to *ever* suggest that as a nickname around the guys. They'll immediately decide it's perfect and refuse to call me Blade again."

"What's it worth to you?" Wendy teased.

"Are you blackmailing me?" Blade asked, his eyebrows raised.

She coyly smiled. "Maybe."

Blade slowly leaned forward and put his beer on the small table and angled his body toward her. If she knew him better, she might've realized he was readying to pounce, but she didn't. "Soldiers like me don't do well when blackmailed or threatened," he said—then lunged.

Wendy shrieked as he threw himself at her, but then giggled when he grabbed her around the waist and turned, carefully throwing her onto her back on the cushions of the couch. Blade kneeled over her, holding her wrists in his hands.

He loved how she remained boneless in his grip. How she wasn't freaking out and didn't seem to be scared of him in the least. He'd probably gone too far, but he couldn't help it.

"Let me up, Aspen!" she said, finally squirming under him.

And just like that, the atmosphere went from casual and teasing to charged and erotic. Blade was straddling her hips, and the second she shifted under him, he got hard. Looking down, he could see her nipples pressing against her blouse and her breathing had increased.

"Aspen," she said breathlessly, and just his name on her lips made him harder.

He lifted his hips so he wasn't grinding himself between her thighs and stared down at her. He wanted her. Wanted the right to move his hand from her wrists down her body. Wanted to take her tits in his hands and tease them until her nipples were hard little spikes. Wanted the privilege to make her explode with passion before pressing inside her body.

Blade's hands tightened on her wrists to keep

himself from doing everything he'd just fantasized about.

He opened his mouth to say something, he wasn't sure what, when the door to the apartment slammed open with a loud bang, effectively interrupting the sexually charged moment and changing the mood from mellow to intense in a heartbeat.

CHAPTER SIX

Wendy had barely heard the door slamming against the wall before Aspen had moved. He was kneeling next to the sofa with one hand resting protectively on her shoulder—the other was holding a knife.

She had no idea where he'd gotten the knife, but with a nickname like "Blade," she supposed she shouldn't be surprised. She *should* be more freaked out about the fact he had a knife on him, but for some reason, she wasn't. In a weird way, it made her feel protected. He hadn't threatened *her* with the knife, and it was more than obvious he knew how to handle it.

Almost as soon as she saw it in his hand, he'd put it away after seeing who was at the door.

What she *had* been surprised about was the chemistry between them. One second she was teasing him and the next she was lying under him, feeling his erection pressing against her core. As soon as she'd felt his excitement, he'd lifted his hips to a respectable distance, but that didn't make the sudden flare of lust she'd felt at being held down by him go away.

She liked Aspen. A lot. And if she wasn't mistaken, he liked her back. She didn't like keeping things from him, but there was no way she could tell him she didn't have any friends because she didn't trust herself not to spill too many things about her past that might get her, and Jackson, in trouble. He'd been frustrated with her, she knew that, but he hadn't pushed, which she appreciated.

There were still a lot of things she didn't know about Aspen as well, but what she did know she liked. A hell of a lot. She liked that he was protective of his sister. Liked that he had friends who were as close as brothers. Liked that he seemed to be interested in hearing about Jackson.

She'd been out with men in the past who didn't give one little shit about her brother. In fact, had seemed annoyed that she even wanted to talk about him. Those relationships didn't last, because anyone who couldn't accept the fact that Jackson was one of the most important people in her life, wasn't someone she wanted to be around.

Wendy moved slowly, scooting up on the couch until she could see who had burst into the apartment.

Her brother was standing in the doorway, glaring at Aspen. Jackson looked extremely put out and irritated.

"Jackson?" she asked, as Aspen moved away from her and slowly stood.

He didn't answer her, but grabbed the door and slammed it closed.

Wendy winced. She hadn't seen her brother in a mood like this in a long time. He was generally very even-keeled. She couldn't help but worry he was upset with her, but he'd told her earlier that he liked Aspen. That he was happy for her. So her being on the couch with him couldn't really have upset Jackson this much...could it?

She stood and eyed her brother warily. "What's wrong?"

He mumbled something under his breath as he wandered into the kitchen.

"Jackson, what's wrong?" Wendy repeated.

Her brother let out a sigh and slumped against the counter. "Nothing you can help with," he said finally.

Frowning, Wendy started to head into the kitchen, but was stopped by Aspen's hand on her arm.

"Do you want me to leave?"

She didn't. But Jackson didn't look happy at all. She looked from Aspen to her brother helplessly, biting her lip in indecision.

"He can stay," Jackson answered for her. "I'm just

upset about something that happened this afternoon after lacrosse practice."

"If you want to talk to your sister, I can go take a walk," Aspen volunteered.

Wendy's eyes went to his. She was somewhat shocked that he'd do something like that.

Jackson snorted. "Taking a walk in this neighborhood wouldn't be the best idea," he said. Then he sighed and repeated, "You can stay."

"I might be able to help. I probably have a different perspective than you or your sister," Aspen offered.

Wendy wanted to go to her brother and comfort him. Obviously, whatever happened wasn't good. She hadn't seen him this agitated in a very long time. He usually didn't let things bother him.

She felt Aspen's thumb caress her arm for a moment before he let her go. She looked up at him, but his attention was all on her brother. She liked having his support. It felt...nice.

She shook herself out of the fog she'd been in and headed for Jackson. Deciding to let him talk in his own good time, she stood between him and Aspen.

"Jack, I'd like you to officially meet Aspen. Aspen, this is my little brother, Jack." It was a little late for introductions, but better late than never.

"He doesn't look so little to me," Aspen said with a slight grin as he came forward and held his hand out to Jackson.

The two shook hands and Wendy took the time to study her brother. Aspen was right, he wasn't the little boy she'd taken under her wing a decade ago. He was taller than her five-eight by a couple inches, and she had a feeling he wasn't done growing yet. He ate as if he had a bottomless pit inside him and every couple months, she had to shell out the money for new pants as he was still outgrowing the ones he had. Jackson was lean where she was...fluffy. He had a five o'clock shadow on his face, and that reminded Wendy of the day she'd had to show him how to shave.

He was definitely growing up, and the thought that he'd soon be moving out and getting on with his life was almost depressing. She'd spent the last decade raising him, spending every free minute she had with him, and she suddenly understood how moms could get so weepy when their kids graduated from high school and moved on.

"Dinner should be ready before too long," Wendy told the men sizing each other up in the kitchen.

"I was serious about listening," Aspen said, as if he hadn't heard Wendy's inane comment about dinner.

Jackson took a long swallow of the water he'd retrieved from the fridge then nodded.

Wendy was surprised. Well, maybe not. Aspen was extremely easy to talk to. She supposed that Jackson innately knew that as well as she did.

Her brother walked over to the table and collapsed

into one of the chairs. She followed slowly and stood next to the chair to his right. She felt Aspen's hand on the small of her back, and knowing he was there somehow made this easier. Made her not worry as much.

He held out her chair and she sank into it. Aspen sat next to her and looked at ease...as if he hung out with them all the time.

"What's up?" she asked Jackson.

"I really shouldn't be so upset," he began, "but those guys made me so mad."

"What guys?" Wendy asked.

"The assholes who decided it would be fun to show up and harass us as we practiced today."

"Start at the beginning," Wendy ordered, completely lost. She wanted to reprimand him for his language, but he was getting to the age where it was a little silly.

Jackson took a deep breath before starting on his tale. "We were on the field as usual, when a group of guys peeled into the parking lot of the school. They revved their engines and basically made asses of themselves. Then they got out and came over to the field. They sat in the bleachers for the rest of practice, heckling us. It was honestly more annoying than anything else. Coach told us to ignore them. After practice, we headed to our cars and were getting ready to leave when the theater club's practice got out. The assholes decided since they weren't getting a rise out of us, they'd start in on *them*."

Jackson ran his hand through his hair in agitation. His leg was bouncing up and down and he fidgeted with the water bottle in front of him.

"What'd they do?" Wendy asked.

"They surrounded a group of three freshman girls. They were saying all sorts of crap to them. Telling them how pretty they were and how they bet they were great in bed...that sort of shit. Me and a couple of the other guys on the team decided enough was enough and went over there. Two of the bigger guys were touching the girls. Running their hands up and down their arms and stuff. They were saying they wanted them to come to a party. The girls were scared to death."

"Assholes," Aspen muttered.

"Yeah. Anyway, so me, David, and Patrick told them to knock it off. They immediately turned on us, taunting us, asking if we were their boyfriends, shit like that. We got between them and the girls. I told Jenny to run inside and get a teacher. That set off the guys even more. They were pretending to cry, telling us we were pussies and crap."

"Oh my God, Jackson," Wendy said. "What happened?"

He shrugged. "A couple teachers came out, along with Coach, and the guys left."

"Just like that?" she asked.

"Just like that," Jackson confirmed.

"Who were they?" Aspen asked.

"I think they graduated a couple years ago," Jackson told him. "I think one guy's name is Charles, although his friends were calling him Chuck. They're losers who have nothing better to do than scare a bunch of freshmen."

"Are the girls okay?" Wendy asked.

The look on her brother's face changed. The irritation he'd been expressing shifted to concern. "Yeah. They were pretty shaken up. After everyone else had been picked up, Jenny was scared Chuck and the others would come back and hurt her since her mom was running late. So, me and Patrick talked with her for a while, making sure she was all right. Then her mom finally showed up and we left."

"What did Coach say about the guys?"

Jackson shrugged. "Not much. Just warned us that if we got in a fight, even if we didn't start it, that we'd be benched for at least two games."

"That's not fair," Wendy protested. "Especially if you don't start it and are protecting others."

"Those are his rules," Jackson said.

"You give Jenny your number?" Aspen asked. He'd been quiet throughout Jackson's story, so his question surprised Wendy.

"No."

"You should."

"Really?"

Wendy stared at her brother. She thought he'd protest Aspen's suggestion and tell him he wasn't interested in the freshman that way. Or that it wasn't necessary. But instead, Jackson looked pensive.

"Really," Aspen confirmed. "I don't like the sound of what happened. Those guys were looking for someone to harass, and when you and your friends stepped up to protect the girls, they got their targets."

"Me or them?" Jackson asked.

"Not sure. But either way, it's not good. You don't want Jenny to be in a situation where she's vulnerable again, not like that. If you give her your number, she can call you if she sees the guys again, or if she's scared."

"She didn't want to admit it, but I saw how freaked she was when the one guy was touching her," Jackson said.

"No one has the right to touch a woman without her permission," Aspen said, his voice steely hard. "Those assholes would probably argue that they weren't hurting her. That all they were doing was touching her arm, but that's not the point."

"I didn't like the look in their eyes," Jackson admitted. "It was as if they enjoyed scaring them. They got off on it or something."

"They probably did," Aspen agreed.

"If you see them again, you need to let the principal know," Wendy said.

"I know."

"And your coach."

"I will."

"And any grown-up who's around."

"I *know*, sis," Jackson growled. "I'm not an idiot. But if they come around again, I'm not going to run away like a coward to find an adult. They're not going to touch Jenny or her friends again. Not if I can help it."

Wendy now felt as agitated as her brother had looked when he first got home. "Don't do anything that will get you hurt," she warned. "I couldn't take it if something happened to you."

"Nothing is going to happen to me," he said. "It's people like Jenny and the others those assholes decide to harass that I worry about. It sucks. I don't get it. Chuck and his friends are older; why aren't they in college or working? Why do they have to come back and pick on people younger and more vulnerable than them?"

"Because they can," Aspen said. "I've seen it over and over throughout my time in the service. Picking on those who can't fight back gives them power."

"So, what can I do about it?" Jackson asked.

Aspen shrugged. "I'm not advocating fighting them, but if that's what they want, they aren't going to stop until they get it."

Wendy gasped. "Aspen!"

He went on. "Hopefully, they were just bored and

you won't see them again. Maybe they got what they wanted this afternoon and it was a one-off."

"But you don't think so," Jackson said.

Aspen shrugged. "Unfortunately, no. Men like them get off on scaring others. Now that they've found an audience who they have power over, they're going to want it more and more. It's like a drug."

"So...I should fight them."

"Jackson, no!" Wendy exclaimed again.

Aspen reached a hand over and rested it on hers. He squeezed, but didn't look at her. His eyes stayed glued to Jackson's. "Not if you can help it. They won't fight fair. They'll gang up on you and it won't end well for you. The best thing you can do is not give them a chance to exert their power. They probably showed up when they did because they knew there wouldn't be a lot of teachers there, and they probably also knew there would be clubs and sports ending around that time. You said they were older than you and that you think they went to school there, so they know the routines. Get with the students in the clubs, make sure no one travels by themselves. Make sure the principal is aware of what's happening. That might not stop their harassment, it might make them sneakier, but if you take away their ability to get to people, eventually they'll move on."

Wendy looked from her brother to Aspen. What he was saying made sense, but that didn't mean she had to like it. She could tell that Jackson was drinking it in though. Not for the first time she felt a pang of sorrow deep inside. She'd done her best to be a mother, sister, friend, and disciplinarian to her brother. But she knew there were times he craved a masculine influence in his life, and that was the one thing she couldn't give him no matter how hard she tried.

"I'll find Jenny tomorrow and give her my number and talk to her about the situation. She can hopefully talk to the teacher in charge of the theater club. I'm not sure the principal will do much, but at least he'll know about it."

Aspen nodded. "Again, I don't want to scare you, but hopefully they'll lose interest in harassing you guys."

"Thanks, Aspen," Jackson said.

"Anytime. I'm sorry that happened to you today."

Jackson shrugged. "I just hate bullies. I don't get why they're such assholes. Why can't people just live their lives and leave the rest of us alone?"

"I don't know, buddy. I just don't know."

There was silence around the table for a beat, then Jackson said with a smirk, "So...I interrupted you and Wen making out, didn't I?"

"Jackson!" Wendy protested, knowing she was blushing furiously.

Aspen merely chuckled. "Actually, no. It's only our first real date and I'd never disrespect your sister like that...by making out when I knew you'd be coming home soon."

"But you like her, right?"

Wendy rolled her eyes and pushed back from the table. "That's it, I'm going to check on dinner."

Both men laughed. Wendy could still hear them talking as the kitchen was right next to the table.

"Yeah, Jack, I like your sister. What's not to like?"

"Well, she takes forever in the shower. That's why she started showering at night. She hits the snooze four hundred times in a row then has to rush to get ready so she's not late to work. It's a good thing I'm a morning person because I would've been late to school every day of my life if I wasn't. She also doesn't like science fiction. I don't know about you, but that would be a deal breaker in any girl I dated. She also doesn't like cops. Any kind of police officer. So, she drives like a granny. It's annoying."

Wendy leaned over and laid her head on the counter in exasperation. "Kill me now," she mumbled. She heard a chair scoot back on the floor, but didn't lift her head to see who had moved.

A warm hand rested on her upper back and rubbed in small circles. Aspen.

"None of those things make me *not* want to get to know your sister better...but, Jack, you're embarrassing her, which isn't cool."

At the rebuke to her brother, Wendy raised her head to defend him, but Jack spoke before she could.

"You're right. Sorry, Wen. Do I have time for a shower before dinner? I stink from practice."

Wendy looked from her brother to Aspen. His hand had moved to her lower back when she stood, and she could feel his thumb gently caressing her through her shirt. "Uh...sure."

"Cool." Then Jack got up and headed for his room without looking back.

Wendy glanced up at Aspen. "I'm not sure if that went well or if I should be worried."

"That went well," he declared firmly.

"I'm still worried about him," Wendy said.

"He seems like a good kid. He didn't hesitate to stand up for those girls and he's worried about them."

"Do you think those guys are going to come back?"

He eyed her for a long moment before bringing his free hand up to her face and brushing a lock of hair behind her ear. "Yeah, sweetheart. I think they will."

Wendy closed her eyes in frustration. "Darn it."

"He's a good kid," Aspen repeated. "He can handle it."

"I hope so."

"So...you drive like a granny?"

Wendy groaned. "I'm gonna kill him."

Aspen chuckled.

"And no, I don't drive like a grandma. I'm cautious.

Too many people don't think twice about the fact they're riding around in something that could easily kill or hurt someone else."

"You should know something..."

Wendy furrowed her brow. He sounded so serious, but his thumb on her lower back never stopped its rhythmic caress. "What?"

Aspen pulled her close until she was flush against him. His warm breath feathered over the skin at her ear as he whispered, "I'm okay with you driving like a granny, I'd rather you did that than have a lead foot and have to flash your tits at an officer to try to get out of a ticket. I don't want you flashing those beautiful tits at anyone but me. And I'm perfectly okay with you wanting to stay in bed as long as possible. It's my favorite piece of furniture."

His words sent a carnal image rushing through her head. The two of them entwined in a large king-size bed, his hips thrusting as he stared down at her, his hands on either side of her head as they made love.

Wendy looked up at him and licked her lips.

"God, sweetheart. Don't look at me like that," he begged. "You're making it really hard to remember, or care, that your little brother is right down the hall and will be back out here any second."

Wendy fought with herself. She never did this. Never threw herself at men. Never felt as though if she didn't feel his lips on hers, she'd spontaneously combust.

But then again, Aspen wasn't just any man. He was the guy she'd gotten to know over the last couple months. The man who made her laugh when she felt like shit after being hung up on and yelled at eight hundred and thirty-two times in a row. He was the man she texted just to ask how his day was going. And he was the man who made her brother feel better about his crappy day much more easily than she ever could've.

"Why don't you like cops?" he asked.

She licked her lips and looked away from him. She wasn't going to tell him that she was scared a cop would ask for her identification and then look her up in a database.

She felt him sigh and knew she'd disappointed him again. She hated doing it, but she couldn't stop herself.

"Kiss me," she whispered, looking back up at him, trying to change the subject.

Aspen groaned but didn't hesitate. His hands came up to her face and he tilted it toward his. He didn't look down the hall to see if Jackson was coming. He didn't act like he was in a big hurry. The fire in his eyes burned into her own as his head slowly lowered.

Wendy closed her eyes in anticipation and latched onto the shirt at his sides. A second later, his warm lips were on hers.

He didn't kiss her hesitantly or ease into it either. His tongue swiped along the seam of her lips and she immediately opened to him.

He swept inside as if he'd been kissing her his entire life.

Wendy moaned softly and dug her nails into his sides as he tilted her head to a better angle. She'd never felt anything like this in her life. Her fingers and toes tingled and she couldn't get enough of him. Wendy opened her mouth wider, twining her tongue with his.

After the initial onslaught, his kiss gentled. He teased her tongue with his own and took his time getting to know what she liked.

Way too soon, he pulled back and rested his forehead on hers. His breaths came out in short pants, making her feel much better about her own unsteady breathing.

She licked her lips again, tasting him once more. "Wow," Wendy said after a moment when he didn't speak.

One of his hands moved up to her hair and smoothed it back from her face. "Wow, indeed," Aspen said quietly. He pulled back but didn't take his hands from her. "You okay, sweetheart?"

"Yeah."

His eyes stared into hers with an intensity that would've scared her if she hadn't been feeling as off-center as she was. He moved the hand on her head and his thumb brushed over her lips, smearing the wetness from their kiss. She couldn't help it; her tongue came out and licked him as he caressed her.

His pupils dilated, and it was a heady feeling knowing she could affect him as easily as he did her.

"God, this mouth," he said in a low, rumbly voice that went straight to her clit.

Wendy shifted where she stood, uncomfortable with the lust coursing through her body. This wasn't like her. She enjoyed sex, but never felt as if she was missing anything when she didn't get it. But with one kiss, Aspen had gotten her body primed and ready...for him.

"Don't look at me like that, Wen."

"Like what?" she asked, playing coy. She had a feeling she knew exactly how she was looking at him...as if she wanted him to throw her on the floor and fuck her hard and fast.

He smirked. "Like you want me hard and deep inside your sweet body."

A small sound of need escaped her throat.

With that, Aspen wrapped his arms around her and hugged her. Wendy moved her hands so she was clutching his back. She buried her nose into his shoulder and held on. They stood like that for several moments, enjoying the feel of each other, before Aspen finally pulled back and held her at arm's length.

"Jesus, Wen. I haven't been that close to losing my cool in a very long time. I want you," he said without pretense.

"I want you too," Wendy replied shyly.

"Don't get me wrong," he went on. "I want you in

my bed, under me, over me, and any other way I can get you. But I also want you sitting next to me when we eat, while we watch TV, and when we're sitting in the stands watching Jackson play lacrosse or compete with his robotics club."

Wendy's eyes got big and she stared up at him, lost for words.

"I want a relationship. An exclusive one. I feel as if I know you better than any woman I've ever dated. There's something to be said for getting to know someone via the phone. Something good. I knew we had chemistry, but I didn't realize how explosive it would be in person. I know I'm moving fast, but I can't help it. And you're not saying anything...am I freaking you out?" he asked.

Wendy couldn't believe he was nervous. "I'd like that...a relationship, I mean. It's...it's been a while for me."

His nostrils flared at her words, and he opened his mouth to speak, when Jackson asked, "Am I interrupting you not making out again?"

Wendy closed her eyes in embarrassment, but Aspen didn't pull away from her.

"Nope, you're just interrupting a little after-kiss cuddle."

Wendy's eyes popped open at that. She smacked him on the shoulder. "Aspen!"

"What?" he asked not so innocently.

"Let go of me so I can get the casserole out of the oven," she told him, even as she blushed.

Aspen and Jackson chuckled at her expense, but Wendy couldn't be upset with them. Sometimes when Jackson had come home from school in a funk, he'd gone to his room and hadn't reappeared until the next morning. The fact that he was there now, laughing and teasing her, was amazing. And she was thankful for Aspen's help in making that happen.

She couldn't think about the kiss they'd shared or what "seeing each other exclusively" really meant. She needed to get dinner on the table and wanted to enjoy being with the two people who currently meant the world to her. She'd figure out everything else later.

CHAPTER SEVEN

A week later, Blade was at PT when Truck questioned him about the situation with Wendy.

"So...what's up with this chick, Blade?"

"Her name is Wendy. And we're dating," Blade responded. He wasn't ashamed of Wendy or how they'd met. He'd told the guys all about her initial phone call to him and how she'd tried to sell him life insurance. They'd all gotten a good chuckle out of that.

The fact that she lived right there in Temple was a fucking miracle as far as he was concerned. He probably would've continued being her friend but trying to make a long-distance relationship work wasn't something he had any interest in. It was hard enough to have a girl-friend as a Special Forces soldier; it was almost impossible to have a meaningful, true relationship when they were never in the same place except for booty calls.

So far, he loved everything about her—except her increased penchant for avoiding his questions. It was starting to really get to him. He'd gone out of his way to be open and honest with her, hoping she'd feel comfortable enough to reciprocate, but often she hadn't. He could tell something was going on with her. Something big. Though he was clueless because she wasn't giving him anything to go on. He wanted to put her at ease. Wipe the wary look from her eyes when he asked the littlest things, like where she grew up or what her major had been in college.

He wanted to be with her all the time. Get to know every little thing about her, but his frustration was increasing. His feelings were growing, and with every question she avoided answering, it made him feel as if she wasn't as into him as he was her.

"When do we get to meet her?" Beatle asked.

Blade shook off his morose thoughts and eyed the men around him. They'd just gotten done running their usual five miles and were on their way to the weight room for the second part of their workout.

"I'm not sure. Are you going to behave if I introduce you?"

The guys all chuckled.

"What? You think we're going to scare her away or something?" Hollywood asked.

"Not on purpose, no," Blade told them. "But I know you guys. She'll say something that amuses you and you'll start teasing her and she won't understand that you're kidding. Or you'll sic your women on her."

"Is that a bad thing?" Ghost asked. "I know the second I tell Rayne that you're dating someone, she'll want to meet her."

"And if your sister hears from *me* that you're officially dating, she might never forgive you," Beatle said.

Blade sighed. He knew he needed to bring Wendy into the fold of his friends, but he was enjoying getting to know her and having her all to himself. "It's early, guys," he told them.

Fletch clapped him on the shoulder. "Don't listen to these assholes. Take your time. The girls are gonna love her."

"How do you know?" Blade asked.

"Because you do," Fletch said immediately.

"I've only officially known her a week," Blade protested. "It's too early to know if I love her."

"Bullshit," Truck said in a serious tone. "It might be love with a healthy dose of lust thrown in there, but I've seen you on the phone with the woman. You get this intense look on your face as if you're using every one of your senses to listen to her. You block everything and everyone else out. And last week? After that fuckup at the bar and you went and saw her? You were different, man. In a good way."

"Yeah," Coach added. "When we went to that family organizational day and helped out with the obstacle course, you didn't even notice the single soldiers there checkin' you out...and usually you do."

"And the last time you saw Annie, you looked at her differently," Fletch said. "You want to share what *that's* about?"

Blade sighed. He knew his friends were right. But love?

He couldn't deny he liked Wendy a hell of a lot and thought about her all the time, but he wasn't sure that was love.

"Wendy's raising her brother. Has been since he was young...about Annie's age. I've just been thinking about how tough that had to be on her...on both of them. I can't imagine what she's been through. She gave up a hell of a lot to take that on."

Fletch whistled. "Wow. That's serious devotion right there. How old was she?"

Blade frowned, then admitted, "I'm not sure. I've asked, but she didn't really answer. Jackson is sixteen. I'm guessing she had to be in her early twenties when she took him in?"

"So, you're dating an older woman, huh?" Hollywood teased. "Now I *really* can't wait to meet this cougar of yours."

Blade shoved his friend and everyone laughed. "See? That's why I don't want you assholes meeting her yet. Saying shit like that will make her skittish and uncomfortable."

"You want to make sure she's as into you as you're into her," Truck concluded. "Makes sense."

"No, I just..." Blade's words trailed off. Yeah, that was exactly it. He loved these men, but he was scared to death that someone would say something that rubbed Wendy the wrong way and she'd bolt. He could tell she was skittish, and that she hadn't been completely open with him about something. He wanted to break down those barriers before she met his rowdy and somewhat uncouth friends.

"It's okay," Hollywood said, clapping Blade on the back. "But you might want to work on tying her to you faster because Fish and Bryn are coming to town in a couple months."

"They are?" Blade asked in surprise. "Why?"

"He's got an appointment at the VA hospital. Bryn talked him into getting fitted for a fancier arm. He said he might as well come back here to the doctors who originally worked on his arm since they already know him."

"That's awesome," Blade exclaimed. They hadn't seen Fish or his wife since the shit Bryn had found herself in the middle of back in Idaho and then their wedding. "Do the girls know?"

"Yup," Fletch said. "We're going to have a barbeque at the house."

Blade eyed him. "How's the construction going?" Fletch's house had recently been halfway destroyed by a man who'd used a rocket-propelled grenade to flush out the object of his obsession. Rayne's brother had saved Sadie, and they were now an item. Poor Fletch's house hadn't fared as well.

"It's going," Fletch said. "The apartment over the garage is way too small for all of us, but we're managing."

There was something in the other man's tone that Blade couldn't read. "Em and the baby okay?" he asked.

"Yes. They're great. The little whippersnapper has been kicking up a storm. Emily's still got a few months to go, but I know she's ready to bring that little one into the world *now*."

"Still don't know if it's a boy or a girl?" Truck asked.

"Nope. We talked to Annie, and although she really wants a little brother, she agreed that it would be fun to keep it a mystery until he or she is born," Fletch said.

"So, a barbeque at your place in a couple months... will the house be ready?" Coach asked.

"The contractor claims it will."

Blade smiled. He had a feeling the contractor would see the deadly Delta Force soldier come out in Fletch if the house wasn't done on time.

"So, you'll bring Wendy? And her brother is invited," Fletch said. "Oh, and if he's dating anyone, he can bring her along too, or he can bring a friend to make him more comfortable, being the only teenager there. The more the merrier."

Blade thought about all the good times the team had experienced at Fletch's house. Barbecues, Fletch and Emily's wedding, and countless other get-togethers. He could see himself hanging out in the backyard with Wendy on his lap, laughing and having a good time with all his friends.

"I'll bring her," he told them. "As of right now, Jackson isn't dating anyone, but I'll let him know he can bring a friend if he wants."

"Awesome," Fletch said.

"If you want to introduce Wendy to the girls one on one before then, just let us know," Ghost said. "You know the girls would love nothing more than to meet the woman who finally caught your eye."

Blade rolled his eyes at his friend's not-so-subtle order to introduce Wendy to Rayne and the other women. "Yes, Sir," he said cheekily.

Everyone laughed.

As they settled into the routine of lifting weights and doing the circuit they'd set up in the weight room, Blade thought about Wendy. Was Truck right? Did he already love her? He wasn't sure, but he did think about her all the time. Receiving texts from her was akin to winning the lottery. And when he thought about her brother having more run-ins with the thugs who were still harassing him and the other kids at the school, his blood boiled.

He might not know everything there was to know

about Wendy and Jackson, but what he did know was that he wanted to do everything possible to make their lives better. More fun, easier, and safer.

Was that love? Maybe.

The only other people he'd felt that way about were Casey and his parents. He'd dated other women before but didn't think about them while he was running, doing hand-to-hand combat training, or while innocently making his dinner. The sound of his phone ringing or the ding of a text made his heart beat faster and gave him butterflies. He was acting like a teenager with his first crush, but he didn't care.

It was the thought of something happening to her that made Blade admit to himself that Truck was right. He was well on his way to loving Wendy. Getting to know her via phone had been the foundation for their relationship. A strong, sturdy one. This wasn't a fling. He wasn't casually dating her. He wanted her in his bed *and* his life.

Mentally, Blade vowed to do everything possible to get Wendy to open up to him. To answer his questions. To show her that she could trust him with all her secrets. To slowly integrate her and Jackson into his world. Once she met the other women, and little Annie of course, there was no way she'd be able to walk away. He hoped.

By the time Fish arrived with Bryn and they all gathered around the fire pit at the back of Fletch's newly repaired house, Blade vowed that Wendy would love him back.

He was nothing if not stubborn, and once he set his mind to something, he always achieved it.

———

Wendy was running late, again.

It wasn't exactly a surprise. She'd hit her snooze button too many times this morning, but this time it wasn't because she'd wanted more sleep. Well, it was, sorta. She'd been dreaming of Aspen. They were lying together in bed and he was running his hands all over her body. He was gentle and loving and everywhere his lips touched her skin, she tingled.

It had been so long since she'd been with a man, she'd almost forgotten what it felt like. She had great orgasms with her vibrator, but it wasn't the same as feeling a man's rough hands on her skin or being filled by a nice hard dick. She'd been a bit wild as a freshman; her poor parents had the worst time with her, and Wendy was now ashamed of how irresponsible and bratty she'd been.

She'd snuck out, drank more than she should, and slept with too many boys. When Aspen had asked her why she thought Jackson might sneak out, she didn't want to admit it was because she'd done just that. All the time. It was embarrassing, and she had a feeling answering him honestly would lead to other uncomfortable questions.

He'd been asking her questions she couldn't, and wouldn't, answer for a while now. Wendy hated avoiding them, and she had a feeling Aspen was getting increasingly frustrated with her, but she couldn't answer him. She had to think about her brother.

Her dream this morning had been unexpected, but definitely enjoyable. There had only been two men in her bed since she'd taken responsibility for Jackson, and they'd been nice but hadn't exactly made her see stars.

Her dreams of Aspen turned her on more than those past men ever had in person. Just the thought of Aspen in her bed, inside her body, made her wetter and hornier than she could ever remember being.

The one kiss they'd shared played over and over in her head like a broken record. He'd devoured her as if he couldn't get enough. No one had made her feel like that, ever. Kisses had always been pleasant and merely a precursor to the "good stuff." But Aspen's lips on hers had been almost orgasmic all by themselves.

So that morning, she'd been dreaming of Aspen in her bed, both of them naked, and him looking at her with the same intensity he'd brought to their kiss. She kept hitting snooze so she could continue with her dream.

But her brother knew her all too well. When he'd

first knocked on her door, telling her to get up, and she'd told him she was, he rightly didn't believe her.

He came back ten minutes later, entering her room without knocking, and physically dragged her out of bed toward the bathroom.

They were now on their way to school. Wendy would drop her brother off then head to Cottonwood Estates for her shift.

"You want to practice driving tonight?" she asked, then yawned hugely behind her hand.

Jackson smirked over at her. "You gonna be able to stay awake until after I get home from my robotics club meeting?"

Wendy smacked him on the arm. "Shut it. Drive?"

"You could get in trouble if we're caught."

Wendy glanced over at her brother and smiled. "We aren't going to go drag racing down the streets of Temple or anything. It'll be fine. I hate that you can't get your learner's permit or license right now. I know you want it."

Jackson shrugged. "We can't risk it."

Wendy sighed. "You'll be eighteen in less than a year. It'll be here before you know it."

"Sis?" Jackson asked.

"Yeah, bro?"

"Do you regret it?"

Wendy knew exactly what he was talking about. "Never. Not for one second."

"But when I think about how you were younger than I am right now when Mom and Dad died, and all you gave up, I can't help but—"

"Stop right there," Wendy interrupted firmly. "I don't regret one thing that I did. I regret that you have to lie about your age. I regret that I can't throw you the biggest, baddest eighteenth birthday party this town has ever seen *on* your actual eighteenth birthday. I regret that I wasn't able to get you everything you deserved growing up. There are a lot of things I regret, Jackson, but every single one has to do with the life *you've* led, not about my own situation."

He was quiet for a long moment before saying, "Have I ever thanked you?"

Wendy's eyes filled with tears, but she refused to shed them in front of her brother. "Yeah, you have."

"No, I don't think I have. It sucks that I have to pretend I'm younger than I am, and it sucks that I can't get my license until I'm over eighteen just to be sure I can't be sent back to foster care. But I can deal. Thank you for doing what you did, Wen. Thank you for getting me out of that house."

They hadn't really talked about what had happened ten years ago, and this wasn't exactly the time or the place, but Wendy wasn't going to shut Jackson down now. "Do you remember much of it?"

"I remember every second," Jackson said harshly. "I've never been so scared in my life. You absolutely made the right decision in getting me out of there. I hate that you've had to fly under the radar since then and that you could never get a degree or finish high school, but I want you to know that I won't ever do anything that will make you regret what you did. I'm going to get my diploma, then get a scholarship and my college degree. I won't let all those nights you went hungry so I could eat, or the money you spent on clothes and shit for me, go to waste."

Fuck. Now she was crying. Wendy wiped the tears from her face and concentrated on not wrecking the car before she could get to the high school safely.

"It was absolutely my pleasure," she told her brother softly once she had control of her emotions. "I would sooner have died than leave you in there, not after I found out what was going on. I'm so proud of you, bud. You have no idea. I thought for sure I was going to screw you up. That everything Mom and Dad had done to make you the amazing seven-year-old kid you were would get flushed right down the toilet. Thank *you* for being as amazing at seventeen as you were at seven. And if you don't get your diploma or your college degree, I'm gonna kick your ass. Someone has to look after me when I'm old and gray, you know."

And with that, the heavy atmosphere in the car lightened.

"I wouldn't mind driving a bit tonight," Jackson told her, answering her earlier question.

"Great. Will Rob be able to drive you home after robotics?"

"I'm sure he will. If not, I'll get a ride from someone else or call you."

"Cool. We'll eat, then head out and maybe work on some parallel parking."

Jackson groaned. "I hate parallel parking."

"Which is why we need to work on it some more," Wendy returned easily.

"Sis?"

"Yeah?"

"When is Aspen coming over again?"

Wendy's heart beat faster at the mere mention of his name. "I'm not sure. Why?"

"I like him."

"Me too."

Brother and sister smiled at each other.

"You deserve someone like him."

"What do you mean?"

"Someone who will stand up for you when you won't do it for yourself."

Wendy rolled her eyes. "I'm fine, Jackson."

"I know you are. I just think with him around, people would be less likely to take advantage of you like that bitch in the bar."

Wendy refused to take the bait. Jackson had been complaining about how she'd let the other woman almost steal Aspen right from under her nose. She didn't like to think about it.

"You've been talking to him every night, right?" Jackson asked.

Wendy nodded. "Just about."

"I want the best for you, Wen. You weren't able to have a real relationship when I was younger; it wasn't safe for either of us. But I'm almost eighteen now. It's time. I don't want you to be alone when I go off to college."

The pesky tears threatened again. "I'm not going to hook up with the first guy who asks just so I don't have to be alone," she told her brother. "I'm okay with being by myself. I've never been on my own, you know." She said it in an upbeat, happy tone, when in actuality she was dreading the day Jackson would leave. She didn't *want* to be alone, but she wasn't going to go out and marry the first guy she saw just so she didn't have to be. She'd just have to get used to it.

"I didn't mean that you should. I just…I worry about you. You've never had a lot of friends because you were worried about someone finding out about me."

"That's not the only reason why," Wendy protested.

"Yeah, that, and you were working two jobs to try to make sure we had enough money to eat and a roof over our heads," Jackson said. "Look, I'm more thankful than I can say for everything you've done for me, but after Aspen left the other night, I started thinking."

"Jackson—" Wendy started, but he didn't let her continue.

"No, don't 'Jackson' me. Let me say this."

Wendy pressed her lips together and nodded.

"He's exactly the kind of man I would love to see you end up with. He's in the military, so he has a steady paycheck and health insurance. He's not a deadbeat and he looks strong enough to deal with any shit anyone tries to throw your way. You told me he's got a tight circle of friends who are also in the Army. They all have girlfriends or wives, so you could have an immediate group of friends. He's close to his sister, which you know is a plus because of the kind of relationship we have. If you were with him, you could probably quit that stupid telemarketing job that you hate. You could even go back and get your GED and possibly even start on your degree, so you could do more at the old folks' home. You're still young...almost twenty-seven. You've got your whole life ahead of you, and I want you to get out there and *live* it."

"And you think Aspen could help me do that?"

"Yeah."

Wendy tried to come up with something to say that would discourage her brother from matchmaking, but she couldn't. Every single word out of his mouth was something she'd already thought about herself. He hadn't mentioned regular sex and having someone to share her worries about the law catching up to her, but she wasn't going to bring those up.

Wendy pulled up to the curb at the high school and turned to her brother. "He might not end up liking me back. Besides, we just started dating."

"He likes you," Jackson said, meeting her stare straight on.

"I know, but that doesn't mean we're gonna get married or anything."

"I'm not an idiot, Wen, but it's been a long time since I've seen you so happy with someone. I saw how he couldn't take his hands off you the other night. Every chance he got, he was touching you. Your hand, your arm. Even when you weren't looking at him, he had his eyes on you. Not to mention the way I interrupted you guys...twice. Once on the couch when I got home and once in the kitchen."

"I admit that we have good chemistry. But, Jackson, you'll learn this as you get older, sometimes it's just about sex."

"Don't do that," Jackson said, the disappointment easy to hear in his voice. "Don't blow this off as if you just want to have sex with him. I know the difference between lusting after someone and really liking them. Wanting to get to know them better, liking them for who they are. You like him back, sis. I know you do."

She wanted to question him about who he liked and how he knew the difference, but right now wasn't the time. Wendy'd had the sex talk with Jackson about four years ago. She'd told him all about condoms and even demonstrated how they worked. They'd both been embarrassed, but it had to be done. The last thing she wanted was for him to get a girl pregnant. She'd help him however he needed help, but a baby would definitely change his life, *their* lives, in a huge way.

"I do like him," Wendy admitted. "A lot."

Jackson grinned and reached for the handle of the car. "Then don't hold back. Go after what you want for once, Wen. And get him to introduce you to his friends, get in tight with them. It'll be harder for him to dump you."

Wendy rolled her eyes at her brother's teasing. She looked for something to throw at him, but he was already out of the car before she could find anything handy. He leaned in through the open door. "All kidding aside, Wen, he seems like a good man. I'm perfectly okay with you spending time with him. I'm almost eighteen, you can leave me home alone without fear that I'm going to drown in the bathtub or something."

"Shhhh, you're only sixteen, remember?" Wendy said, old habits hard to break as she glanced around furtively.

"I know." He went to shut the door, then thought better of it. He leaned back inside and said quickly, "I invited Jenny over for dinner tomorrow night. Hope that's all right."

"Jenny? The freshman from the theater club?"

"The one and the same," Jackson said with a smirk, then slammed the door and waved before jogging toward the front doors of the high school

Wendy chuckled to herself. "You go, Jackson," she murmured, before pulling away from the curb and heading for work.

CHAPTER EIGHT

"Are you sure you're okay with coming over to my place tonight?" Blade asked Wendy four days later.

"Yes," she told him, then reached over and put her hand on his shoulder as he drove. "I'm looking forward to meeting your sister and her boyfriend."

"I wish they'd get married already," Blade grumped.

"You anxious to have him make an honest woman out of her?" Wendy teased.

"Nope. I want her to make an honest man out of *him*," Blade returned immediately. He reached up and took her hand in his, kissed her palm, then laid it on his thigh as he drove. "Casey doesn't need a man to make her life complete. She's got an amazing career, and she makes friends wherever she goes. But together, those two just work. Even though Beatle hates bugs and Case loves them, it doesn't matter. Their differences somehow make them closer. I know he worries about her when we go on missions. He'd feel so much better if he was married to her already, then he'd know she'd be protected and taken care of if something happened to him."

"Is that how you feel?"

Blade looked over at Wendy and didn't even worry when he felt his heart rate increase. Her hair was down tonight and she was wearing a T-shirt and a pair of jeans. He'd told her to be casual, and he loved that she'd taken him at his word. Even though she'd be meeting his sister and Beatle for the first time, she was herself, didn't try to put on airs at all. She was wearing a bit more makeup than usual, and he liked the fact that, while dressed down, she'd still put in the effort to look nice for his friend and sister.

"I can't lie, I do. There are some things I haven't told you about what I do for the Army. What me and my buddies do is dangerous. There's always a possibility that we'll get hurt or killed when we're gone. Money doesn't solve the world's problems, but it certainly does help. Having health insurance, the life insurance payout, and more importantly, someone from the Army to assist the ones left behind through the weeks after the passing of a loved one is comforting. To me, Beatle, and to the rest of my friends."

"That's kind of morbid," Wendy observed.

"No. It's a fact of life. It sucks, no doubt about it, but if Beatle dies without marrying my sister, she'll still mourn the same amount, but won't have any benefits."

"I guess I can see your point."

Blade squeezed her hand. "I realize that too many GIs marry for the wrong reasons, but since Casey and Beatle love each other, and have no intention of ever being with anyone else, why not go ahead and get married?"

"When you put it that way, I don't know."

"Don't even get me started on Rayne and Ghost," Blade murmured.

"What about them?"

"They aren't married either. Ghost wants his ring on her finger worse than anyone I've met...maybe except for Truck with Mary."

"Rayne doesn't want to get married?"

"Oh, she wants to, but she's waiting for Mary. She's her best friend, and I guess a long time ago they agreed to have a double wedding ceremony. So now Rayne refuses to get married without her."

Blade looked over and saw Wendy's forehead crinkled in confusion. "But I thought Truck and Mary were together."

"They are and they aren't. Truck loves Mary, and it's pretty obvious that Mary cares about him right back, but she's stubborn. For some reason, she's resisting truly being with him."

"Wow, that's crazy. I mean, what if Mary *wasn't* with Truck? Would Rayne wait forever to get married? That's not really fair to her or Ghost."

"I agree. It seems silly to me too. But I don't actually think Rayne would wait if Truck wasn't in the picture. I think she's hoping that reminding Mary about their pact will help spur her into giving Truck a chance."

"Hmmm. Still seems crazy to me," Wendy said.

"You don't know the half of it," Blade agreed. Then, changing the subject, asked, "How's Jackson? Anything else going on with those assholes who were bothering him?"

Wendy sighed. "Same old crap. They're still hanging around. They've moved to parking across the street in the huge lot for that shopping center after the principal called the cops on them one day for loitering on school property. They're still scaring the girls, but Jackson has tried to arrange for every girl who leaves the building after school hours to have at least one boy with her."

"Good for him."

"Yeah, except now those guys have it out for him."

"What?" Blade asked, his voice hard.

"I guess they've made him their main target now."

"That's not good."

"No, but he says he's handling it. He claims that he doesn't give a shit what they say to or about him. He just ignores them," Wendy said, squeezing his hand harder than normal.

"He could always put a complaint in with the cops. That might help."

"No!" Wendy protested immediately. "No cops."

Her swift reaction assured Blade there was more to her reticence than a simple dislike of police officers, but he knew by now if he pushed, she'd deflect and not answer his question anyway.

The more time he spent around her, and the more Wendy refused to open up, the more discouraged he was starting to become. He wanted to take her in his arms and comfort her, tell her that she didn't need to be afraid to tell him anything, but he couldn't exactly do that while he was driving.

"Oh, but I have other news about him," Wendy said.

"What's that?" Blade was clenching his teeth together at the thought of Jackson being targeted by bullies. He hated that the kid was going through that, but was also impressed with his maturity in dealing with them. He'd said brief hellos to her brother over the phone in the last few days, but hadn't seen him again.

"Jenny came over for dinner the other night."

Blade's head swung her way and he stared at her in surprise. "Really? You didn't tell me that last night when we talked."

She smiled at him. "Nope. Figured I'd spring it on you when I saw you today."

"Wow. This is the Jenny from theater class, right?" Blade asked.

"Good memory," Wendy praised. "Yes. That Jenny. She's a lot younger than him, but he seems really taken with her."

"She's a freshman, right? So, he's only, what...a year or so older than her? That's not so much."

He glanced over as Wendy bit her lip then looked out the side window before answering him. "Yeah, but he *seems* a lot older than her."

Blade's eyes narrowed. He could spot deception a mile away—the night at the bar with the whore notwithstanding—and he wasn't happy that Wendy was still lying to him about something. Her brother's age? But that made no sense. His frustration level rose a notch and he ran a hand through his hair in agitation.

"You like her?" he asked, keeping a close eye on Wendy's reactions.

Her shoulders relaxed, and she looked back at him. "Oh, yeah. She's polite and down-to-earth, and she really seems to like Jackson. All good things in my book. I wasn't sure she should come over to our apartment, since it's not in the best part of town and her parents are loaded, but Jackson was amazing. He said that she'd be safe with him. I swear, I almost melted." She smiled. "When I left tonight, he was talking to her on the phone, helping with her algebra homework. He's so good at math. I certainly didn't get any math genes from our parents. But it's a good thing he enjoys it, and is good at it, because he uses math all the time in the robotics club. Their current project is so complicated, the second he started telling me about it, my eyes crossed."

"Are they still working on the robotic arm?"

"Yeah."

Setting aside what she might be lying about for a second, Blade said, "Our friend, Fish, is missing part of his arm."

"Really?"

"Yup. He lost it overseas. He'll be in town in a month or so to see the doctors about getting a new one."

"I'm sorry that happened to him."

"You think Jackson would want to meet him? Maybe Fish could go to a club meeting and talk to the guys."

"Oh my God, seriously? You think he'd do that?" Wendy asked, bouncing up and down on her seat in her excitement.

Blade chuckled. "I don't know. But I'd be happy to ask him."

"That would be amazing. Oh, but Jackson and his friends would ask him a million questions. He might not be comfortable with that."

Blade's smile grew, and he laughed until he snorted.

"What's so funny?" she asked.

"Wait until you meet his wife, Bryn. She asks more questions and is the least politically correct person I've ever met. I guarantee there's nothing your brother and his friends could ask that would embarrass him or make him uncomfortable. His wife has gotten him so used to all sorts of off-the-wall questions, he won't even blink at whatever a bunch of high schoolers could ask."

"Well, I'm not going to even tell Jackson about it until you get your friend's approval."

"That sounds good." Blade pulled into the parking lot of his condo and parked. He saw Wendy taking in his place with big eyes.

"It looks fancier than it is," he told her.

"It's really nice."

Blade thought he heard a note of envy in her words. He hated that she and her brother were living in the shithole they were, but at the moment, he wasn't in a position to do anything about it. He would've loved to have volunteered Fletch's garage apartment for them to live in, but since Fletch and his family were currently living in it, it wasn't possible anyway. Blade didn't think she'd agree even if it was available.

"It looks nice and homey on the outside, but as my sister keeps telling me, it's completely boring and devoid of any comforting touches on the inside. Although I refuse to let her mess with it. She'd put flowers and shit all over the place. Come on," he said after he'd cut the engine. "Case and Beatle are already here."

They climbed out of the Jeep and Blade met her at the front of the vehicle. He immediately took her hand in his, loving how it fit so perfectly in his own and how smooth her palm was. Whenever he touched her, he seemed to forget all about her evasiveness...and how uneasy it made him.

They walked hand in hand to the door of his condo and he opened it for her.

"I'm back!" Aspen yelled as soon as they were inside, and Wendy flinched at the loudness of his voice.

A woman about her height, with dirty-blonde hair, appeared around a corner and smiled at them. Wendy could immediately see the family resemblance between her and Aspen.

"Hi!" she said with a bright, warm smile on her face. "I'm Casey, this reprobate's sister. It's so good to meet you. Aspen has done nothing but talk about you every time we've gotten together." She held out her hand and Wendy shook it.

They smiled at each other for a moment before a man stepped up beside Casey and put his hand on her opposite hip. He also held out a hand. "I'm Beatle. It's nice to meet you, Wendy. Blade's been keeping you to himself a bit too much."

"Oh, but we only met a short time ago," Wendy said after she'd shaken his hand.

"Like I said, keeping you to himself."

Wendy smiled at him and felt goosebumps race up her arms when Aspen put his arm around her waist much as his friend had done to Casey.

"Shut it, Beatle. Don't embarrass her."

Wendy teasingly shoved against Aspen. "He's not embarrassing me. I have a teenage brother, remember? Not much makes me uncomfortable."

"See, Blade? I'm not embarrassing her. Now, wait until I tell her the story about the time in Djibouti when you had to piss so badly you almost wet your pants and—"

His words were cut short when Aspen moved faster than Wendy had ever seen him move before. He had his friend in a headlock and was dragging him backward toward what Wendy assumed was the kitchen. "Excuse us, sweetheart. Beatle and I are gonna go check out the steaks on the grill. I'm sure he screwed them up while I was gone..."

Wendy looked at Casey with wide eyes, and when she began to giggle, Wendy relaxed.

"I swear to God they act like they're twelve years old sometimes," the other woman said with a huge smile. "Come on, you can keep me company as I get the rest of dinner ready."

"Can I help?" Wendy asked.

"Oh no, I got this. Aspen would have my head if he came inside and saw you slaving over dinner."

"Really, let me help. I don't do well with just sitting

around," Wendy insisted.

Casey's smile widened. "Okay, if you insist."

They entered the beautiful chef's kitchen and Wendy barely kept herself from drooling. She wasn't the best cook, though she got by. But looking at this kitchen made her suddenly want to crack open a cookbook and try something new and different.

There was a six-burner gas stove. The appliance looked like it belonged in a fancy magazine, not in a condo. The fridge, dishwasher, and stove were all stainless steel and obviously top of the line. There were two ovens, a luxury Wendy would've killed for, and a gorgeous farmhouse sink.

"Fancy, isn't it?" Casey asked.

"Uh, understatement of the year," Wendy quipped.

"Yeah, way too hoity-toity for my brother, that's for sure," Casey told her. "He bought this place for a song and had it gutted and remodeled. I told him that if he was doing it, he might as well do it right. He knows if he ever wants to sell this place that the kitchen and bathrooms will make or break it. You've seen those house-hunting shows on TV, right? I realize they're totally fake and the people have already bought one of the houses before the show's filmed, but the first thing people do is bitch about the kitchen being outdated or the fact that there aren't granite countertops. And don't get me started on the bathrooms."

Wendy smiled and accepted the head of lettuce the

other woman was holding out to her. "If the kitchen looks like this, I can't wait to see the bathrooms."

"Trust me, they're to die for," Casey said. "Although the place needs a woman's touch. It's so... plain. I keep telling him he needs to paint an accent wall or throw some pillows around, but he won't listen to me."

The two women chatted about nothing in particular until Aspen and Beatle came back inside with a plate of steaks and a few vegetable kabobs.

Aspen put the platter on the counter then immediately came to her side. He leaned over and kissed her on the cheek. "My sister made you her kitchen slave already?"

Flustered at the easy and nonchalant way he'd kissed her in front of his friend and sister, Wendy said, "I think I could move into this kitchen and be happy for the rest of my days."

He chuckled. "I always figured my good looks and charming personality would win the chicks. Who knew all it would take was a fancy kitchen?"

Wendy smiled at him. "This is more than a fancy kitchen, Aspen. It's amazing."

"I'm glad you like it, sweetheart. Wait until you see the master bathroom."

Feeling her tummy flip in summersaults, Wendy merely said, "I can't wait."

"Me either," Aspen whispered back, then kissed the

side of her head and turned to the others. "How're your classes going, sis?"

Brother and sister talked about her work as they all helped get the food placed on the wood table in the dining area.

By the time they sat down to eat, Wendy had learned that Casey taught at Baylor University and had transferred from Florida to move in with Beatle not too long ago.

"This looks delicious," Wendy said before they all started eating.

"I'm sorry Jackson is missing it," Aspen said.

Wendy tried not to wince. She and her brother had agreed that he'd be "Jack" to everyone but them. It was purely a cautionary measure, and one they'd both been really good at doing for almost ten years. But she'd felt so comfortable with Aspen that she'd forgotten to be cautious and had called her brother by his real name since they'd started dating. Aspen had obviously picked that up.

"Yeah, but Jenny invited him over to her house for dinner and there was no way he was going to miss it."

"He's that into her?" Aspen asked.

Wendy nodded. "Yeah, I think so. She seems really sweet. They don't have any classes together since she's a freshman and he's a sophomore, but they hang out at lunch and he makes sure he always waits with her after school until her mom or dad can pick her up."

"That's fast," Beatle observed. "Blade said they met, what, just over a week ago?"

Wendy shrugged. "Yeah, but he's always been so into school and activities, I'm actually glad he's showing an interest in a girl for once. Although I have no clue how he's going to fit dating in with all his other activities... but I suppose if she's important to him, he'll make the time."

Everyone agreed.

"So, Blade says that you work at the old folks' home south of town. What do you do there?" Beatle asked.

"It's not really an old folks' home," Wendy rebuked gently. "There are a lot of residents who don't need any kind of medical care. It's a retirement community with a rehabilitation section, as well as a full-time care section. Many of the people there don't need any help, but they like it because they can be around others their age. Then when they need more care, they move to the assisted-living apartments. As their health needs change, they transition to more full-time care. It's a wonderful place for people to live out their lives. It's not like the nursing homes, where everyone is lying around waiting to die."

"I didn't mean to hit a nerve," Beatle said earnestly. "You're obviously passionate about what you do."

"No, I'm sorry," Wendy said, embarrassed. "I didn't mean to go off."

Beatle laughed. "You didn't, Wendy. You rightly

corrected me on my incorrect assumptions. If you want to see someone go off, you should be around when our commander yells at us for being slackers during PT."

Wendy smiled back at him, happy she hadn't put her foot in her mouth this early in the evening. The last thing she wanted was to cause conflict.

"What do you do there?" Casey asked.

"I'm an aide. Which means I'm a jack of all trades. I visit with the residents, help them change the channels on their TVs if they need it, get water, and talk to the relatives. I hold hands when it's needed and sit with people when they're feeling lonely at meals, that sort of thing."

Once upon a time, Wendy had been embarrassed by her job. It wasn't as if she was a nurse and actually helped heal anyone. She was merely there to assist with the little things. It was one of the few jobs she'd been able to get without an education. But now she loved it.

"She also gets puked on, yelled at, and ignored," Aspen put in.

"That doesn't sound so fun," Casey said.

Wendy shrugged. "All part of the job."

"When did you move here?" Beatle asked.

Wendy tried not to tense, but she couldn't help it. She didn't do well with questions about her past. Never had. "A few years ago," she said and tried to smile as she spoke.

"Where were you before that?" Casey asked.

"Somewhere dark and cold," she said dramatically. "The Texas weather suits me so much better."

"I hear ya, sister," Casey agreed. "I loved Florida and swore to myself that I wasn't ever going to live somewhere it snowed. Luckily, Beatle lived in Texas, otherwise I wouldn't have agreed to move in with him. There's only so much a girl can deal with."

"Hey!" Beatle griped.

Everyone chuckled.

Wendy felt Aspen's hand move to her lap. The weight of his hand was heavy on her thigh. She looked over at him. He wasn't smiling and was staring at her in concern.

"You all right?" he mouthed.

She nodded. She was a little discomfited that he could read her so well. Most women would be rejoicing in the fact that the man they were dating could tell when they were upset, but not her. The last thing she wanted was for him to ask why she wasn't comfortable talking about her past. Jackson turning eighteen would protect *him*, but would do nothing to keep *her* from getting in trouble. It was best if no one ever found out what had happened a decade ago. What she'd done.

"Do you want to go on to be a nurse?" Casey asked. "It seems like being an aide would be a good first step toward getting your degree."

"Oh, um...I hadn't really thought about it." But she had. Wendy would love to be a nurse, but it wasn't in the cards for her. The second she tried to apply for college somewhere, she'd have to give them her social security number. It was bad enough she'd had to give it to human resources for payroll. The fewer ways she made herself trackable, the better.

"If you want information about the program at Baylor, let me know. I'm happy to set up a meeting with an academic advisor for you to talk about your choices."

Wendy cleared her throat twice, trying to keep the tears threatening from becoming a real thing. "Thanks. I appreciate it." She could've used a friend like this ten years ago. But back then, all her so-called friends seemed to disappear when she'd needed them the most.

"How are *you* doing, Case?" Aspen asked, taking the spotlight from her to his sister.

Wendy didn't know if he'd done it on purpose or if he was just moving the conversation along to something more interesting. But when his thumb began to brush back and forth on the outside of her thigh, she had a feeling he'd deflected the conversation to give her a break.

She tried to add up in her head how long it had been since that fateful evening when she'd gone to meet Aspen for the first time in that bar and was surprised to realize that it had only been about two weeks. It felt as if she'd known him forever, although she supposed that was because of all their phone calls and texts before that night, and the fact that they'd spoken every night on the phone since he'd been at her house a week and a half ago.

She connected with Aspen like she'd never done to anyone before in her life. It was weird and scary...and right.

"Are you still seeing Doctor Martin?" Aspen asked Casey.

Wendy's attention was jerked back to the conversation going on around her.

"Yeah, but only once every two weeks or so now. I'm getting better with the dark too, aren't I, Beatle?" Casey asked.

Wendy frowned.

Casey saw her expression and asked, "Aspen didn't tell you what happened to me?"

"Not really. I mean, I know the basics, but not everything."

"I was kidnapped in Costa Rica and thrown into a hole in the ground for over a week with nothing to eat and only a trickle of water from a hose to keep me alive."

Wendy stared at the other woman in disbelief. She'd said that as if she was recounting a trip she'd made down the street to the grocery store.

"Holy crap."

Casey looked at the man next to her. He didn't look happy, but it was obvious he was trying to keep his cool. Then she looked back at Wendy. "Turns out a woman I worked with at the university in Florida wanted research on how having a positive attitude during a traumatic situation could help keep a person alive. Of course, when I was rescued by Beatle, my brother, and their team, she got nervous and didn't want me to remember anything I might've seen or heard during my ordeal. When I was back in the States, she drugged me, and I almost jumped out a window when I was on one hell of a bad trip."

Wendy could only continue to stare at the other woman in horror.

"She's okay now, sweetheart," Aspen said in her ear. He'd leaned in and had his arm around her shoulders.

Wendy realized she was holding her fork and knife in midair. She slowly put down the utensils and asked, "Are you really okay?"

Casey smiled a huge smile and gestured to herself. "As you can see, I'm good. I'm a bit afraid of the dark now, but I'm working on it."

Wendy's thoughts were all over the place. "But...did they catch the person who did that to you?"

"Yup," Casey said brightly. "She was in custody, but died."

"Thank fuck," Beatle grumbled under his breath.

At the same time, Aspen said, "Fucking bitch."

Wendy's gaze met Casey's—and suddenly they were both giggling.

When she had herself under control, Wendy said, "If

anyone did something like that to my brother, I'd kill them myself."

"Don't think that didn't go through my mind," Aspen said then asked Beatle a question about something related to their friend, Fish, and Wendy was drawn into a conversation about the man and his wife.

Twenty minutes later, after she'd eaten every morsel of food on her plate, and after her stomach hurt from hearing stories about little Annie and her handmade tank, Wendy sat back as Aspen and Beatle carried their used dishes into the kitchen and put them in the sink.

"You want me to take care of those?" she asked when Aspen came back into the dining room.

He looked appalled. "No. I'll take care of them after everyone leaves."

"It's no trouble," she insisted.

Aspen leaned over and kissed her, the warmth of his lips making her want to open under them, to encourage him to kiss her the way he had when they were standing in her kitchen.

"I said *no*," he replied as he hovered over her. "You aren't going to do the dishes the first time you're at my house. Not gonna happen."

"But maybe the second time?" she teased.

Aspen was still leaning over her, one hand on the table and the other on the back of her chair. She was half turned so she was facing him and felt totally encompassed by the man.

"Maybe."

She gazed up at him and forgot for a moment they weren't alone. Her eyes went to Aspen's lips and she licked her own, wanting him to kiss her once again. He groaned quietly, and just as she lifted her chin to make the first move, Casey said, "Why don't you give her the grand tour, bro? Me and Beatle have to get going anyway."

"We do? I thought we—"

Wendy heard his grunt as if his words were cut off because of an elbow to his stomach. When she turned to look, he was rubbing his belly, so she knew she'd been right.

Embarrassed, and knowing she was probably beet red, as Casey wasn't exactly being subtle, Wendy opened her mouth to protest. To say she wouldn't mind if they stayed longer, but Aspen beat her to it.

"That's a great idea. It was great to see you guys. I'll see you tomorrow, Beatle. And Casey, don't be a stranger." And with that, he took hold of Wendy's hand and hauled her to her feet.

She stumbled into him and his arm went around her waist to hold her steady. She could feel the bulge of his erection against her belly, but she didn't pull away. It was a relief to know he was as affected by her as she was by him.

With effort, she turned from Aspen's intense gaze to his sister and Beatle. "It was wonderful to meet you."

"Same," Casey said. "I can't wait to meet your brother. He sounds amazing."

"He is," Wendy replied, beaming.

Beatle came forward and, ignoring the way Aspen was scowling at him, tugged Wendy out of his arms and gave her a hug. "It was good to meet you, Wendy. Welcome to the family."

"Oh, um. Thanks," Wendy stammered as she awkwardly patted the other man on the back.

Casey laughed and pulled at her boyfriend. "Come on, Romeo, you're freaking her out."

The second Beatle let go of her, Aspen claimed her again, pulling her against his side. "Drive safe," Aspen told the couple as they walked toward the front door.

"Always do," Beatle returned.

Then Wendy was alone with Aspen. Without a word, he moved her until she was in front of him once again then leaned down.

Eager for his lips on hers, Wendy didn't protest and went up on her tiptoes to meet him.

As in her kitchen, the kiss was immediately intense and carnal. How long they stood there, making out in his dining room, Wendy didn't know. All she knew was, when he finally pulled back, they were both breathing hard.

She licked her lips, tasting Aspen on them, and pressed against him harder. This time the bulge in his pants was longer and thicker than before. But he didn't make any obscene moves against her. Didn't pick her up and throw her down on the comfortable-looking couch in the other room. He simply kissed the palm of her hand and took a step away, not letting go of the hand he'd kissed.

"Want the grand tour?"

Swallowing her disappointment, Wendy nodded.

A hand came up to brush her hair behind her ear. "Don't look at me like that, sweetheart."

"Like what?"

"Like you're wondering why I stopped. Or if I really want you. Because I do. Badly. But I want more than a fling, Wendy. I want to slay all those dragons I see behind your eyes. I want to be the kind of man your brother can be proud to introduce to his friends. I want you to trust me with all your secrets—and to trust that I'll never betray you."

She looked up at him in shock. She'd thought maybe she'd deflected his questions successfully before tonight when he never pressed and had gotten away with changing the subject when it had gotten too close for comfort. Obviously, she'd drastically underestimated this man.

He smiled ruefully. "Yeah, I know you've got secrets, but I won't push. We're still getting to know each other. But you should know, I *do* want you. I want you spread out naked as the day you were born on my bed. I want to see you squirming under me as I find out how delicious you taste. I want you to come apart under and around me as I lose myself inside your body. But I want *all* of you, Wendy. The good, bad, and ugly. Not just your body. Until you can give that to me, I'm going to try to control myself and be good."

The dream she'd had the other morning rushed back into her brain. But his words scared her. She couldn't tell anyone about her past. About Jackson's. Couldn't risk it.

"Jesus, Wen, don't look at me like that. It'll be okay. Swear." Aspen gathered her into his embrace and they stood like that in the middle of his dining room for almost a full minute, neither saying a word, just soaking in the moment.

Finally, he pulled back. "Come on. Let me show you a bathroom so amazing you'll weep with joy...or so Case tells me."

Wendy gave him a weak smile and let him pull her through his condo.

It was an amazing place. Four bedrooms, an extra multipurpose room—which currently held workout equipment—three full bathrooms, plus the half-bath on the first floor near the kitchen.

The master bedroom was on the third floor, and it took up the entire space. Hardwood covered the floor, but there was a huge gray rug softening up the space. There wasn't a lot of color, as Casey had warned, but Wendy liked it just the way it was. The king-size bed drew her attention, and Wendy wanted to curl up in the middle of it and sleep for days. It was unmade, and seeing the mussed sheets and comforter made Wendy want to drag Aspen down onto it with her and muss them up some more. She could practically see him lying there sleeping. Maybe only wearing a pair of boxers, or maybe naked.

Wendy felt her nipples harden under her shirt at the erotic thought, and quickly glanced around the room trying to divert her attention to something safer than the thought of Aspen's naked body.

There was a huge leather armchair in a corner next to a window, which looked just as comfortable as the bed. She could imagine herself sitting there reading a book as she watched Aspen sleep.

Shaking those thoughts out of her head, Wendy followed him into the en-suite bathroom.

Gasping, she looked around with eyes she knew were as big as saucers. Casey was right—this bathroom was to die for.

"Casey helped me design it. And by 'helped,' I mean she told me what to have done."

"Holy crap, Aspen. It's..." Wendy was at a loss for words.

Big. It was *big*. There was a walk-in shower off to the right. When she peeked inside, she saw there were two rain-shower heads attached to the ceiling across from one another, and another two coming from the sides of the walls. Three people could easily shower in there without touching, maybe even four or five people. The tile was done in various muted shades of gray, creating an intimate space of serenity.

The Jacuzzi tub was also large enough to hold a few people as well. Circular, with a window above it looking out over a small treed piece of land. Wendy knew without a doubt the stars would be amazing from the vantage point of that tub.

There were two sinks in the long granite counter, as well as a door that she figured led to a toilet.

"Come look at his," Aspen urged, grabbing her hand and towing her out of the amazing bathroom back into the main bedroom. He pulled her over to another door. Gesturing to it, he bowed and said, "After you, my lady."

Wendy smiled at him and turned the knob and pushed the door open. Another gasp left her mouth.

She stepped inside a closet...no, that was too tame a word for where she was standing. It was a room. As big as her bedroom in her crappy apartment on the other side of town. Aspen had obviously had someone professionally design the space because there were cubbies for shoes, shelves for shirts and pants, and room for hanging clothes as well. Aspen's clothes only took up a third of the space. There were a couple pairs of shoes littering the floor, not in their designated spaces, but that didn't detract from the amazingness of the room.

Wendy turned to face Aspen. "Holy crap," she whispered.

"A little over the top, isn't it?"

She immediately shook her head. "No, absolutely not. It's beautiful. And wonderful. And overwhelming. Will you marry me so I can live inside this closet, only coming out to spend time in the equally amazing bathroom?"

Aspen laughed so hard he started snorting again. When he got himself under control, he said, "So I take it you like it."

"No, Aspen," Wendy told him. "I love it. You aren't going to have any problems ever selling this place. All you have to do is get a woman to look at this place and she'll be throwing money at you."

"I'm glad you love it, sweetheart," he said softly.

And just like that, the mood in the room went from teasing to intense.

His eyes bored into hers, and Wendy would swear he could see inside her heart. That he knew how badly she wanted to confide in him.

"Come on," he said quietly. "You want to watch TV for a while before I need to take you home?"

"Yeah, I'd like that," she said, squeezing his hand.

They walked back down the two flights of stairs to the living room with the big TV and comfortable-looking couch. "Why do you have a house this big if it's just you?" she asked as she settled on the sofa while Aspen looked through the DVDs.

Without turning around, he said, "Because I've always wanted a big family. Because I loved this place when I first saw it. Because it gives my friends a place to crash if they want it." He shrugged. "Everything about this condo appealed to me."

Putting a DVD in the player, Aspen picked up a remote before coming over to where she was sitting. As if it was the most natural thing in the world, he sat right next to her and pulled her into his side.

Wendy settled deeper into Aspen's side and looked at the screen. When the movie began, she chuckled. "*Deadpool?*"

"It's a romance," Aspen said, even as the actor on the screen shot someone in the face.

"Really?" Wendy asked skeptically.

"Yup. Now hush and watch."

Wendy smiled and did as ordered. And by the time the end credits rolled, she had to admit that Aspen was right. It *was* a romance. It was bloody, gory, violent, and crude, but in the end, the hero and heroine got their happily ever after, so she supposed it was a romance after all.

CHAPTER NINE

Two weeks later, Wendy was sitting at the small table in her apartment when she heard the door open. She looked up, her mouth open to ask Jackson how his day had gone, but instead, she let out a horrified gasp.

Jackson's shirt was torn, and he had the beginnings of a black eye forming.

Jumping up, ignoring the way the chair landed on the floor, she rushed to his side. "Oh my God, what happened?"

"Those assholes are what happened," Jackson said grumpily, dropping his backpack on the floor just inside the door.

"I thought you hadn't seen them in a while," Wendy said, hovering around her brother as he walked into the kitchen. She wasn't sure where to touch him to make sure he was all right.

"I hadn't. But they obviously didn't get tired of being bullies," Jackson said as he opened the fridge and grabbed a bottle of water. He lifted it to his mouth and drank.

Wendy tried not to be impatient, but it was tough. "Talk to me, Jackson," she ordered. "We need to report this to the principal again. This has gone on long enough."

Sighing as he recapped the bottle, he went over to the table and picked up the chair lying on the floor, then sagged into it. Resting an elbow on the table, he leaned on it and told her what happened.

"There's nothing the principal can do. Besides, this didn't happen on school property."

"Quit stalling and tell me what happened," Wendy said sternly.

Jackson smirked. "I recognize your 'tough sister' face. I'm not sure it works on me now like it did when I was ten."

"Jackson," Wendy warned.

He held up both hands in capitulation. "Okay, okay. They were across the street when Jenny and her friends left play practice again today. They were whistling and honking their horns at them and I yelled at them to knock it off, that they were immature little assholes who were obviously compensating for the minuscule size of their penises by harassing kids younger than they were."

Wendy gasped. "You didn't."

Her brother sighed. "I did. I know you always say to ignore bullies, that they want a reaction to validate themselves and to make themselves feel powerful, but, Wen, you should've seen Jenny. She was so scared of them, even with them being across the street, and it pissed me off so badly."

"I know," Wendy soothed. "How did they get to you?"

"Me and Rob made sure Jenny and her friends got their rides, and then we went over to where the guys were hanging out near their cars. They said some shit and we said some shit. They said if we were so tough, why didn't we meet them at the ball fields in the city park."

"You didn't!" Wendy exclaimed.

"Of course not. It would've been like five against two. They would've beaten us to a pulp," Jackson said.

Wendy breathed out a sigh of relief.

"We warned them to stay away from the school, that we had their license plate numbers and I was going to find out where they lived. Apparently, that freaked two of them out because they backed off immediately. I heard one guy say if his dad found out he wasn't taking classes at Temple College like he was supposed to, he'd whoop his ass and kick him out of their house on post."

"His dad is in the Army?" Wendy questioned.

Jackson shrugged. "I guess so. Anyway, so the leader, Lars, told them to shut the fuck up. He glared at me, and I swear to God I didn't see one ounce of remorse or humanity in his eyes. The other guys probably would've given up harassing us a long time ago if it wasn't for Lars running the show. He didn't say anything, simply stared at me for the longest time. It was creepy as all get out. Then he snapped his fingers, and all his little cronies got back in their cars and they took off."

"Wait, I thought Chuck was the leader?"

Jackson rolled his eyes at his sister. "No. He's a dick, and he was the one touching Jenny that first time, but Lars is definitely the one who's in charge of those douchebags."

"So, how'd you get hurt?" Wendy asked impatiently.

"Me and Rob left and were on our way here. Lars had to have been waiting because as soon as we got off school property, he was on our ass. He even nudged Rob's car at a stoplight, which freaked him out because he was in his dad's car. We pulled off at the Walmart to let him by, but he followed us.

"We all got out, me and Rob, and Lars and his buddy, Tyrell. I was pissed but still knew better than to start something. Then Lars started talking shit about Jenny again. Telling me she looked like she'd be a good fuck and he couldn't wait to get between her legs... whether she wanted him there or not.

"I saw red and went right up to him. Warned him if he ever touched her, I'd make sure he never touched another girl without her permission again. That's when he hit me. I swear, Wen, I didn't even see it coming. He knocked me on my ass, but I was immediately up and swinging. I caught him twice in the face before Tyrell grabbed my shirt and pulled me away. That's how it ripped.

"The weird thing is that Lars wasn't even trying to hit me back again. He just stood there smirking at me. He and Tyrell left after that, but I didn't like the look in Lars's eyes. There's something seriously wrong with him, sis."

"Damn, Jackson. I don't like this," Wendy said.

He chuckled, but the sound didn't have any humor in it. "Me neither."

"What are you going to tell Jenny?"

"That she can't ever go anywhere by herself. Seriously. He might try to get to her at the mall or something. It sucks! No one should feel threatened like that. I can take care of myself, but Lars is strong. He's an asshole, but he's also biding his time, I can tell. He didn't lose his shit when I hit him back, he just stood there and took it. I have a feeling he's planning something...and it scares me."

Jackson slumped into his chair at the table then and looked up at Wendy with an expression so scared, it reminded her of when he was seven years old all over again. "I don't know what I'd do if something happened to Jenny. I know he's only picking on her because of me."

Wendy kneeled in front of her brother and put her hand on his knee. "It's not because of you. If it wasn't her, it would be someone else. It sucks that it's the girl you like, but I know you. You'll do everything in your power to make sure she's safe."

"Do you think Aspen would teach me some self-defense moves? I mean, I know how to hit, but if Tyrell decides to join in or something, I need to know how to fight two people at once."

Wendy inhaled and thought about her answer—she remembered a conversation she'd had with Aspen a while ago when he told her that he was on a specialized team and that he didn't get moved from post to post. She also recalled that he and his friends were sent on a mission to rescue Casey in Costa Rica. She could only think of one reason that made sense...Aspen and his friends were Special Forces.

If Aspen was a Special Forces soldier, he would definitely be able to teach Jackson how to defend himself. She didn't like it, not in the least. Not the fact that he wanted to defend himself, but that he had to in the first place. Didn't like that he couldn't have a normal first-time relationship and definitely didn't like that Aspen was probably in a lot more danger than she'd ever know every time he and his friends were sent on a mission.

"I think that's a great idea," she told her brother after a while. "But...you can't just go off on this guy. You need to do what you can to work within the parameters of the law. The last thing we want is some cop doing a background search on you and finding out about our past."

"I know. And I don't want to fight Lars or his friends. I just want them to go away. But maybe if I show him that I'm not a pushover, he'll find someone else to pick on."

Wendy couldn't deny that most bullies chose vulnerable victims, that they didn't like to pick on those who stood up to them. "Maybe you could give the license plates of the vehicles to Aspen. If their parents are military, then maybe something can be done on that end. I know you don't like to tattle, but it might be the best thing in this case."

Jackson didn't look happy at the prospect. His brows were drawn down and he was frowning as he picked at his jeans. "I normally would say absolutely not. I'm not a snitch and going through their parents seems like such a fourth-grade thing to do." He looked at his sister then. "But they've targeted Jenny now. And I can't, and won't, let anything happen to her. So yeah, I'll give them to Aspen."

"I'll call him later and let you talk to him," Wendy told her brother.

He shrugged. "I have his number. I'll call him."

"You do? Since when?"

Jackson smirked. "Since he gave it to me."

Wendy frowned in confusion. "Oh."

"Don't look like that," Jackson told her. "He gave it to me the last time we talked. I was telling him about Lars and how he was still hanging around. He said that if something happened, or if I needed a ride somewhere and I couldn't get in touch with you, that he wanted me to have another option of someone to call. It's cool."

Wendy wasn't sure what to think about it. She was happy that her brother was getting along with Aspen, but she sort of felt usurped.

"Don't be mad at him," Jackson said perceptively.

"I'm not mad," Wendy denied immediately. "I'm just not sure why he didn't tell me."

"Because it's not a big deal," her brother retorted. "I swear, girls make everything so much more complicated than it is. He gave me his number as a backup, not because he wants to be my dad or because we're going to start being best friends and text each other day and night or something. Sheesh."

Wendy's lips quirked upward. Yeah, it was safe to say her brother was something special. She stood and rolled her eyes at him. "Whatever. And now that you and Aspen have exchanged numbers...can he come to Jenny's performance next week?"

"Of course."

"You want to invite him, or should I?"

Jackson stood and stalked over to his sister. He grabbed her and had her in a headlock before she could squirm away.

"Hey!" she complained. "Let me go."

He gave her a noogie. Wendy did everything she could think of to get out of his hold or get him to stop, but she was no match for him.

"Say, 'Jackson is the strongest and smartest Tucker living in this apartment' and I'll let you go."

"No!" Wendy said between giggles.

"Say it," her brother threatened, using his knuckle to press harder into the top of her head.

Wendy was laughing so hard she almost couldn't talk. "Fine! Jackson is the smartest and strongest Tucker living in this apartment, but if he doesn't stop messing up my hair, he's also going to be the hungriest!"

He let go of her so quickly, Wendy almost fell to the floor. The second he withdrew his arm from around her, Wendy turned and did her best to tickle his sides. She knew Jackson was extremely ticklish, and he was always helpless when she managed to get to him.

He laughed and tried to fend her off, but Wendy ducked and tried again.

Finally, when they were both exhausted from laughing, they collapsed onto the couch.

Wendy glanced over at him and winced at the sight of his darkening eye. She wasn't happy about the situation with Lars, but she was proud of Jackson for being the better man. "I love you, Jackson."

"Love you too, sis. You're working at that stupid telemarking job tonight, right?"

"Unfortunately, yeah."

"Why don't you quit?"

"Because you like to eat."

"I'm serious."

"So am I," Wendy countered. "It's not a big deal. It's not hard and it gives us an extra couple hundred dollars every month."

"But everyone is so mean to you," Jackson protested.

"I can deal with it. I've learned not to take it personally."

"Maybe when I go to college you can quit. I'm going to apply for every scholarship under the sun so you don't have to pay for any of it either. So...what's for dinner?"

Wendy chuckled and was glad he'd changed the subject. She didn't want to think about him leaving. "Hamburgers. That okay?"

"Only if you make me three. I'm starving."

"I'd already planned on it."

"Do I have time to call Jenny before it's ready?"

Wendy nodded. "Yeah. You gonna tell her about what happened today?"

"Yeah. She needs to know to be extra careful. That Lars isn't messing around and that he has it out for her."

"Don't scare her," Wendy warned.

Jackson rolled his eyes. "Give me some credit, sis."

Wendy held up her hands. "Sorry! You've got this."

"That's right. I do. I'll call Aspen after dinner and ask him about the self-defense lessons and give him the license plate numbers."

"Tell him I'm working tonight," Wendy said. "And that if it's okay, I'll call when I get home."

"So now I'm your messenger?" he asked with a grin, and with that, Jackson got off the couch and headed down the hallway to his room.

"That's right," she called after him.

Wendy shut her eyes for a moment. She wished she knew what advice to give Jackson that would help him deal with the bullying situation. But she wasn't sure what to tell him that he hadn't already thought about. The situation definitely sucked, and she couldn't help but feel as if Jackson was right...that this Lars person was planning something.

She liked that Jackson was taking responsibility for Jenny's safety though. It proved that he'd become the kind of man their parents would be proud of. Wendy wasn't sure it was because of anything she'd done or not done as she'd raised him, but she was more grateful than she could express that he wasn't a thug like Lars and his friends.

Not for the first time she regretted the teenager she'd been. She'd felt as if the world owed her something and that she was entitled to whatever she wanted...clothes, electronics, boys, alcohol...it didn't matter. "Sorry, Mom and Dad," she whispered before taking a deep breath and standing up.

She had dinner to make. Then had to get to her crappy job that she hated as much as Jackson did... although she'd never tell him that.

It was going to suck when Jackson left for college, but she'd cross that bridge when she got to it. Right now, she had to feed him, then help see him through this bout with bullying. She loved watching him with Jenny and was excited to see her act in the high school's performance of *The Little Mermaid*. Jenny was Ursula, and Jackson said her costume was "sick." Whatever that meant.

Smiling, Wendy headed into the kitchen, mostly happy with her life. Jackson was thriving, she had a kick-ass boyfriend, and they had food in the cupboards.

It was more than she ever would've guessed ten years ago when she'd kidnapped her little brother from his foster home and hitchhiked with him across the country.

CHAPTER TEN

L ate that night, Wendy snuggled in her bed. She was exhausted. But not too tired to talk to Aspen. She'd texted, asking if it was still all right to call, and he'd immediately texted back and said of course.

So, after locking up the apartment and checking on Jackson, who was fast asleep, Wendy had changed into her pajamas and crawled under her covers. She'd plumped the pillows behind her head and dialed Aspen's number.

He picked up before the second ring. "Hey, sweetheart."

"Hi, Aspen. How are you?"

"I'm good. Better now that I'm talking to you."

"Flatterer."

"To you? Always. How'd the calls go tonight? What were you selling this time?"

"Razor blades."

"Seriously?"

"Yup. It was actually a subscription-service thing. They get a new pack of razors every three weeks. I had this whole spiel about how much cheaper it is and how the blades are sharper than the ones they get in the stores."

"Did you sell any?"

"One. To a guy who sounded a bit too excited to be getting extremely sharp blades in the mail." Wendy sighed. "I'll probably be the one on the news saying, 'Yeah, I sold him the razors, but I had no idea he'd use them to chop his kidnapping victims into little pieces... he seemed so nice.'"

Aspen chuckled. "You sound tired."

"Yeah."

"I hate that you're burning the candle at both ends, sweetheart."

"You sound like Jackson. He wants me to quit."

"I knew I liked that brother of yours," Aspen quipped. "But I know you need the money the job brings in. I don't like that you're tired, but I understand doing what you have to do in order to make sure you and he have what you need."

Wendy closed her eyes and took a deep breath. It meant a lot that he didn't harp on her to quit, or that he didn't try to push her to do something she simply couldn't do. "Thanks. I figure there are a lot of other people doing a lot worse jobs to put food on their tables. I get to sit in a room and talk on the phone for a few hours a couple times a week. I don't have to take my clothes off, work out in the heat, or do something dangerous, like work night shifts in a gas station."

"That's a good way to look at it. Although, I have to say...if you took your clothes off for a job, I'd be in the front row every time."

Wendy could feel herself blushing. "Thanks...I think?"

He chuckled again. "Although I'd probably beat the shit out of anyone who looked at you, so that wouldn't actually do much for your ability to earn money as a stripper."

It was Wendy's turn to laugh now. "You're crazy."

"Nah, just worried about you. You okay after what happened with Jackson?"

The question came out of left field and it threw Wendy for a moment. "You mean about him getting in that fight today?"

"Yeah, that."

"No. But there's not much I can do about it. He's almost an adult, and I need to start treating him like one."

"He's got a couple years to go before he's an adult, Wen."

She fisted her free hand and mentally berated herself. The more she spoke with Aspen, and the more time she spent with him, the lower her guard was around him. She didn't think he'd run straight to the cops or family services if he knew the truth; it was just hard to talk about the secret she'd held so close to her chest for so long. "Figure of speech," she said in what she hoped was an airy tone.

"He asked me if I would teach him some self-defense moves."

"I know, he told me he was going to."

"And?"

"And what?"

"Are you okay with that? I told him I wasn't going to do anything that you didn't approve of. The last thing I want is to do something that will chase you away and make you pissed off at me."

"Like giving your number to Jackson without telling me about it?"

There was silence on the other end of the phone, and Wendy shook her head in exasperation.

"Sorry, forget I said that."

"Jackson said you were concerned about it."

"No, I'm really not. It's a good idea, and I'm glad you thought about it. The thought of that Lars guy or his buddies getting their hands on Jackson, and him not being able to get ahold of me if he needs me, is awful. I'm glad you reached out."

"I didn't mean to overstep my bounds. I know we're new, and I wouldn't want to do anything without your permission. I wasn't thinking. It won't happen again."

"Aspen, it's fine," Wendy said forcefully. "It's just hard for me to go from the person Jackson turns to for everything to being just his sister."

"You'll never be 'just' his sister, Wen. He loves you, it's easy to see. It's not like we're going to be best friends and texting and shit all the time."

"That's exactly what he said," Wendy told him.

"Right. So, me teaching him some defensive moves is okay?"

"Yeah. I think at this point, it's the smart thing to do. I don't like the sound of this Lars guy."

"Me either," Aspen agreed. "I got the license plate info and I'll give it to my commander tomorrow. I'm not sure anything can be done because as Jackson has said, they haven't exactly broken the law...yet."

"But Lars hit him."

"Yeah, he did. But it's Jackson's word against Lars's. I told your brother that if Lars did turn out to be the son of someone here on post, that I would be glad to talk to his father, but of course he vetoed that idea."

"Not surprised. I wanted to talk to the principal and he wouldn't let me do that either."

"He also invited me to Jenny's play next week."

Wendy's stomach churned. She would love for him to come with her; she hated sitting alone at things like that, but it also seemed like a big step. Especially since they hadn't done anything but kiss. Wasn't watching your girlfriend's brother's girlfriend sing and dance in a high school play something that people who had been a couple for more than a month did?

"Wendy?" Aspen asked. "Are you still there?"

"Sorry, yeah, I'm here. What did you tell him?"

Aspen paused as if considering his answer. Then said, "I told him I was thrilled to be asked to go. But if you don't want me there..." He let his words trail off.

"No," she said immediately. "It's not that. I just...are you sure you want to go? There will be singing and dancing and stuff. Not exactly your sort of thing."

"Are you going to be there?" he asked.

"Of course."

"Then it's my sort of thing," he said definitively.

Wendy felt all soft and mushy inside at his response.

"I like your brother, Wendy. I think he's a good man, and the fact that he feels comfortable enough to invite me to something like this means the world to me. I told you before and I'll tell you again, this isn't a fling for me. I want to know everything about your life. I want to get to know Jackson better. Want to be the kind of man he can look up to, and who he can go to when he wants or needs to ask another man something. I know our relationship is moving fast, and I'm okay with that. But I need to know if *you're* okay with it. If not, I'll slow down. I won't come to the play and I'll back off."

"No!" Wendy exclaimed. "I like having you in my...

our...life. I feel as if I've known you forever. If anything, it almost feels like we're moving too slow."

"When can I see you again?" Aspen asked abruptly.

"Um...tomorrow, me and Jackson are shopping for some parts he needs for his robotics projects."

"Friday?"

"I work at the call center. What about Saturday?"

He sighed. "I can't. I've got training at the post all day and into the late evening. Sunday?"

"What are we doing?" Wendy asked sadly. "Neither of us have time to actually date. I'm always either working or doing something with Jackson."

"We'll make it work," Aspen insisted. "Next Tuesday night is Jenny's thing, right?"

"Yeah."

"We'll see each other then for sure. What about next weekend?"

"Oh, um...well, it's my birthday, and me and Jackson were going out to celebrate."

"It's your birthday?" Aspen asked. "Were you going to tell me?"

She hated that he sounded upset. "Probably not. It doesn't have anything to do with you, I just don't like celebrating my birthday much at all." She never made much of a fuss over her own birthday; in fact, she hated thinking about her age.

"I see."

He didn't sound like he understood.

"Are you mad at me?" Wendy asked.

Aspen sighed. "I'm not mad. I'm frustrated. I've told you things about me, about my life, that not many people know. I want to move our relationship to the next level, but I feel as if you're constantly putting up a wall between us. I hate that."

"Aspen," Wendy protested, not sure what to say to his statement. In many ways, he was right. But she couldn't tell him the full truth about her. Not about her age. Not about Jackson's age. Not about her background. It wasn't that she didn't want to. It was just that she'd kept the true details of her life secret for so long, she was uncomfortable sharing them now. Even with him.

"For now, I can deal with your secrets. But eventually, I'm gonna want to know everything. I can tell you're holding back, not telling me things, and all I want is for you to feel safe enough with me that you can open up. I'm not going to hurt you, Wen. I'd never do anything to hurt you."

"Even if I did something really horrible?" Wendy asked.

There was silence on the phone for a long moment, and Wendy felt like kicking herself for saying even that much.

"I will never believe you could do something truly bad," Aspen finally said. "The woman I know is too good-hearted."

Her heart sank at his words. She wasn't sure he'd understand if she did tell him. He might even feel like he had to turn her in.

She heard him sigh. "We don't need to discuss it now. Where are you?" Aspen asked.

Wendy knew he was purposely changing the subject, and she was grateful. She hated disappointing him. "Um...in bed?"

"What are you wearing?"

Wendy smiled and sighed in relief that he didn't sound irritated or disappointed anymore. "Why? Where are you and what are *you* wearing?"

"I'm in bed and naked. I was thinking about you before you called and interrupted me."

Wendy swallowed hard. Was he saying what it sounded like he was saying?

"I was masturbating when you called," he confirmed, as if he could read her mind.

"Aspen," Wendy whispered.

"Are you embarrassed?" he asked, the humor easy to hear in his voice.

"I think so, yeah."

"Don't be. What are you wearing?"

"Um...a tank top and a pair of boy shorts."

"Take 'em off," Aspen ordered.

Shivering at his take-charge tone, she protested, "But Jackson's here. And if he needs something, I don't exactly want to be naked when he comes in here."

"Then lose the shorts. Keep the tank on."

Wendy rolled her eyes at his bossiness, but did as he asked, awkwardly shoving down her sleep shorts with one hand. "I can't believe I'm doing this."

"*We're* doing this," Aspen corrected. "And you did say that you thought we were moving too slowly. I'm just pushing our relationship to the next level a little faster than I'd planned, is all."

She liked that. "Okay. Now what?"

"Lie back and close your eyes. I'm going to tell you exactly what I was thinking about earlier before you called. Feel free to touch yourself however you want."

She giggled. "Why thank you so much, Lord and Master."

Chuckling, he said, "That did come out a bit high-handed. Sorry. All I meant was that I want you to feel as good as I am as I tell you what I've fantasized about doing to you. If this truly makes you uncomfortable, we can stop. I won't be offended."

"No...I've had fantasies of my own," Wendy admitted.

"Oh, sweetheart. I can't wait to hear every single one. Are you comfortable, and are your eyes shut?"

"Yes, and yes."

"I was lying here thinking about how you'd look in my tub. Covered with bubbles up to your chin. I fantasized about walking in and seeing you there and asking if I could join you. You lifted your hand and held it out to me. I stripped out of my clothes and eased into the water. It was hot. As soon as I got settled, you shifted until you were straddling me. Your beautiful tits in my face. You held one up to me and I sucked on it, hard. You moaned and threw your head back, bracing yourself on my drawn-up knees. I used both hands to hold your tits and alternated sucking one, then the other. Soon you began to grind on me, and I swear I could feel the difference between the heat between your legs and the warmth of the water around us. The water began sloshing back and forth with your movements as you got more and more excited."

The image Aspen was describing was so vivid in her mind, Wendy couldn't help but touch herself.

"When I thought I was going to come right there, before I got inside your hot, wet body, I gripped your hips and forced you to stop. I scooted you back and stood, lifting you out of the tub. Without bothering to dry either of us off, I picked you up and brought you here to my bed. I've thought about you on my sheets ever since I gave you the tour. I wanted to lay you back on them then, and I want to even more now. In my fantasy, you arch your back and put your arms over your head. You smile at me so seductively and coyly, it's all I can do not to shove your legs apart and drive inside you. But since this is my fantasy, I have the control I need to slowly part your legs and hold them there with my hands on your thighs. You're glistening with the water from the tub, but also from your own excitement. I feel your hands grip my head as I lean in and taste you for the first time. You taste fucking delicious."

Wendy moaned then, not able to hold it back. Her fingers between her legs were soaked and the longer Aspen spoke, the closer and closer she got to orgasm.

"I'm not a patient man, Wendy, you should know this. When I want something, I go after it with everything I have. And what I want from you is your orgasm. I want to feel you quaking in my hands and under my tongue. So, in my fantasy, I latch onto your clit and suck hard, whipping my tongue back and forth over that sensitive little button until you're gushing for me. Your hips are pumping up into my face, searching for something to fill you up. But I don't let go of your thighs, simply keep you wide open for my mouth. Within a minute, you go over the edge, shaking and whimpering in my grip. I smile and don't let up, wanting to feel and watch you go over one more time before I fuck you long and hard."

"Aspen," Wendy moaned as she frantically rubbed her clit, wanting to feel the same ecstasy that Dream Wendy was getting from him.

"That's it, sweetheart. Make yourself come for me. Are you wet? I can't wait to feel your juices all over my dick. I'm gonna fuck you so good, you're going to wonder where I've been all your life. I have a feeling once I get you in my bed, I'm never going to want to let you go."

His words were enough to push her over the edge, and every muscle in Wendy's body tightened as she came. Hard. She heard Aspen talking in the background, but couldn't focus on his words. All she could do was feel and experience the utter bliss that momentarily took over her body.

When she came back to herself, Wendy realized she'd dropped the phone and she could still hear Aspen talking. She quickly fumbled with it and put it to her ear again.

"...come that hard in a long time."

"Sorry," she whispered. "I dropped the phone. What?"

"I said I haven't come that hard in a long time."

"You came too?"

"Fuck yeah," Aspen said in a low, gravelly voice that made her nipples tighten once more. "Hearing you moaning in my ear, and knowing you trusted me enough to let go and make yourself come while you were on the phone with me, was more than enough to send me over with you."

"Aspen," she murmured, curling onto her side and pulling the comforter tight around her.

"I wish I was there to cuddle with you."

"How do you know I'm cuddling?" Wendy asked.

"Because I heard the sheets rustling, and because if

I was there with you, you'd definitely be cuddling. I'd get behind you and wrap you in my arms as we both came down from our orgasmic highs."

Wendy sighed. "That sounds nice."

"Yeah, it does, doesn't it?" After a moment of silence, Aspen said, "I'm going to let you go, sweetheart. I have a mess to clean up here and you need to get some sleep. You have your alarm set?"

"Yeah, but it's not like I'll actually get up when it goes off."

Aspen chuckled. "Things will be interesting with us since I'm a morning person."

"Just don't make me get up when you leave and we'll be good," Wendy retorted.

"Deal. Sleep well, Wendy. I'll talk to you tomorrow. Tell Jackson I'm looking forward to meeting his girl and seeing her play."

"I will. Bye."

"Bye, sweetheart."

Wendy clicked off her phone and thought about what they'd done. She supposed she should be embarrassed about it, but she simply couldn't be. Aspen was amazing, and he'd made the entire experience easy and sexy at the same time. She hated that she couldn't see him until Tuesday. She'd just have to make do with talking over the phone.

The thought went through her head that if they lived together, she'd be able to see him every night no matter what their schedules were like, but she dismissed the idea immediately. It was way too frickin' early to be thinking about moving in together. He didn't know that she was probably wanted by the California police, or that she was younger than he thought she was.

Frustrated, Wendy closed her eyes. It wasn't as if Aspen was going to ask her to move in anytime soon. What man would want a woman and her kid brother moving in?

A little voice inside said that Aspen would welcome them both with open arms, but she ignored it.

"One day at a time," she whispered into her empty room. "Don't put the cart before the horse." She racked her brain to think of any more idioms, but couldn't. "He might not even want to be with you once he finds out what you did."

And with that depressing thought, Wendy closed her eyes, and her exhausted and physically sated body eventually fell asleep.

CHAPTER ELEVEN

"I appreciate you coming tonight," Jackson told Blade the following Tuesday as he pulled into the parking lot at the high school. He'd picked up Jackson and Wendy at their apartment fifteen minutes ago and announced that he was driving.

Wendy didn't seem to care, which Blade was grateful for. Her driving was all right, but the one time she'd insisted on driving and he relented, he'd held his breath the entire trip, wondering if they'd make it to wherever they were going because her car was obviously on its last leg.

"No problem," Blade told him. "I'm looking forward to meeting Jenny, and the fact that I get to spend time with you and your sister is a bonus."

The teenager smiled at him from the backseat. "And one of your friends is coming too?"

"Yup. Fletch and his wife, Emily, and their seven-and-a-half-year-old daughter, Annie. And if you happen to mention her age, make sure you add on that half year, because she's very particular about that."

He looked over at Wendy and saw that she was smiling. Ever since they'd both gotten off while they were on the phone, she'd acted shy, as if she wasn't sure what they'd done was acceptable. When he got her alone later, he'd make sure she knew it absolutely was, and that she had nothing to be ashamed, shy, or worried about.

"Is this the girl with the tank?" Jackson asked.

"The one and the same. We all helped Fletch make it and she spends hours in the thing, tooling around their yard. She talks to herself the entire time, telling stories, starring herself as the heroine and her boyfriend as the hero in whatever scenario she's thought up. It's super adorable."

"Her boyfriend?" Wendy asked.

Blade nodded. "Yup. His name is Frankie, and lives out in California. Annie's declared she's going to marry him someday. She is definitely going to be a handful when she's a teenager."

"Hopefully not like Wen was when she was fifteen," Jackson said with a laugh.

Out of the corner of his eye, Blade saw Wendy tense in her seat, but before he could say anything, Jackson was continuing his teasing.

"You snuck out so many times, sis, I thought Mom and Dad were going to nail your window shut. Remember that one time you came home at two in the morning drunk? I was up because I was sick, and you stumbled into the house. I thought Mom was going to have a heart attack. You just smirked and told them to lighten up. You were at some boy's house—I don't remember his name now—the whole time. That didn't make them feel any better." Jackson laughed at his recounting of the situation.

"Ha, ha," Wendy said, with almost no inflection in her voice. "You always were a brat, spying on me all the time."

Blade reached over and grabbed Wendy's hand, holding it on his leg. He could feel her trembling and knew he needed to change the subject, quick.

He opened his mouth to tell the siblings another story about Annie...when something caught his attention across the street.

It was a group of three trucks. They were parked with their lights on. It was late enough, and dark enough, that Blade couldn't make out the license plates or tell how many people were in each truck.

Blade pulled the Jeep into a parking space and looked back at Jackson. He gestured to the trucks with his head and asked, "That them?"

Jackson's face lost all humor and he nodded. "Yeah. That's where they like to hang out."

"Wendy, go inside with Jackson. I'm going to talk to them."

"No!" Wendy said, gripping his leg where her hand was resting. "First, it's stupid to confront them by yourself. And two, let's just go and enjoy the play."

Blade clenched his teeth. He could handle himself with the punks, even if there were several of them. But Wendy didn't know that because he hadn't told her what he did in the Army. Hadn't told her he'd killed people with his bare hands. Hadn't told her that he'd been trained to fight up to five men at the same time. Hadn't told her he was one of the most lethal and powerful fighting machines the Army had, with or without his knives.

He took a deep breath and looked into the rearview mirror at Jackson. The boy was alternating between looking at the thugs and his sister. Blade could tell he was torn between wanting to confront the bullies with him and making a run for it.

It was then that Blade realized the guys had probably been harassing Jackson far more than he'd shared with his sister.

Making a mental note to meet with Jackson and start his self-defense lessons sooner rather than later, Blade said, "Okay, sweetheart. We'll go inside."

"Thank you," she said quietly. "I know you want to teach them a lesson, but I haven't seen you in several days and I'd prefer not to have to clean up blood right before a nice relaxing night of watching my brother's girlfriend wow us with her Ursula impression."

Blade couldn't help but smile. He ran a finger down her nose playfully. "Got it. No blood. Come on, let's go see if Fletch and his family are here yet."

They exited the Jeep and quickly walked toward the front doors of the school. Blade looked back once, but no one got out of the trucks and they didn't make any move toward the school.

Breathing a sigh of relief—and frustration that he couldn't deal with the punks—Blade held the door open for Wendy and nodded at Jackson reassuringly as he entered the building.

"Blade!"

He turned and saw Fletch standing off to the side with Emily and Annie. Emily looked as beautiful as ever. She had one hand resting on her rounded belly and was smiling down at Annie.

The little girl saw them and came running over. She flung her arms around Blade's waist and said dramatically, "Thank goodness you're here! We've been waiting for-ev-er! There've been hundreds of people going inside and Daddy Fletch wouldn't let us go in until you got here. I bet all the goodest seats are probably taken by now!"

"Hi, Annie," Blade said, smirking at her dramatics. "Would you like to meet my friend and her brother?"

Her head popped up and she turned to face Wendy

and Jackson. "Yeah! Any friend of yours is a friend of mine."

"Annie, this is Wendy, and her brother—"

"Jack. This is Jack," Wendy interrupted.

Blade nodded subtly at her. He understood. He was going to introduce him as Jackson. He'd been around Wendy and her brother so much, he'd gotten used to calling the teenager Jackson, not Jack.

Making a mental note to have a serious talk with Wendy soon, he continued the introductions.

"Jack, Wendy, this little sprite is Annie."

Jackson, proving he was one day going to be an awesome father, squatted down on his haunches and held out a hand. "Hi, Annie. I hear that you're seven-and-a-half. You're practically a grown-up."

Annie beamed at him and shook his hand enthusiastically. "I am! And I'm in the second grade, but I can read on a fifth-grade level. I'm learning sign language because my boyfriend is deaf and I'm getting really good at it. I tried to tell Mommy I should just skip the other grades, but she won't let me because I have to learn math and history and science stuff. Ugh."

"Math is fun," Jackson told her.

She wrinkled her nose at him. "No, it's not."

"I'll have to tell you what my robotics club is making sometime. We use math to get everything just right. But maybe it's over your head anyway..." He let his voice trail off and stood.

Annie tugged on his shirt. "No, tell me! I'm not that tall, but it's not over my head. Tellmetellmetellmetellme!"

Blade loved the tinkle of Wendy's laughter next to him. How anyone could be in a bad mood around Annie or resist her, he had no clue.

"Okay, but you have to keep it hush-hush," Jackson said, pretending to look around to see if anyone was listening.

Annie mock-zipped her mouth closed and threw away the key.

"We're making a robotic arm."

Annie's eyes got big. "Like for a person?"

"Yup. And it's going to be able to be moved when the person wearing it simply *thinks* about moving it. It's super cool."

"Fish needs that!" Annie declared. Then turned and yelled at her parents, "Jack is making an arm for Fish!"

"We're right here," Emily said. "There's no need to yell."

"So much for her keeping it hush-hush," Wendy whispered to Blade.

He smirked.

"Oh!" Annie said in surprise, not having seen her parents come closer as she was talking to Jack. "Daddy, Jack is making an arm in his robot class and Fish needs an arm. They need to get together. Make it happen!"

It was Blade's turn to lean into Wendy and whisper, "She's a little demanding."

Wendy smiled. "All seven-year-olds are."

"Seven-and-a-half," Blade reminded her.

He loved the happiness and humor he saw in Wendy's eyes. He turned to his friend. "Fletch, I'd like for you to meet Wendy Tucker and her brother, Jack. Wendy, this is Fletch and his wife, Emily."

"It's nice to meet you," Emily said, shaking Wendy's hand.

"Same," she replied.

Fletch shook both Wendy and Jackson's hands and smiled at them. "We've heard a lot about you," he said.

"Fletch," Blade warned.

The other man held up his hands in capitulation. "I'll be good."

"Uh, thanks," Wendy said.

"So, your girlfriend is going to be playing Ursula tonight?" Emily asked Jack.

Blade saw the teenager's chest inflate with pride. "Yeah. And she's good. Really good. She's only a freshman, but I have no doubt that if she wants to be an actress when she gets older, she could. Although she says she wants to get her degree in chemistry and not major in drama in college. So, we'll see."

"Ursula!" Annie cried excitedly. Then began to sing "Poor Unfortunate Souls" at the top of her lungs.

Fletch reached out and put a hand over Annie's

mouth, chuckling. "How about we save that for the actors on the stage, huh, squirt?"

Annie laughed and nodded. Fletch removed his hand and put it on his daughter's shoulder.

"Can we go in now and get seats?" the little girl asked. "Canwecanwecanwe?"

"You guys ready?" Fletch asked.

"How about we let the girls go in and find us some seats," Blade said, catching Fletch's eye and giving him a chin lift.

Fletch immediately understood that Blade wanted to talk to him about something and agreed. "Sounds good. Go on, Annie, find the best seats in the house and we'll be in there in a second."

"Aspen?" Wendy asked with a hand on his arm.

"It's okay, sweetheart. I just want to talk to Fletch for a second. Go on in."

She frowned a little, but nodded.

Blade leaned down and kissed her on the lips lightly. "Thank you," he said softly.

Wendy squeezed his arm, then followed the excited Annie and her mother toward the entrance to the theater.

"What's up?" Fletch asked as soon as they were out of earshot.

Blade gestured to Jackson. "The guys I told you about, who are harassing Jack and others here at the school?"

"Yeah?"

"They're across the street in the parking lot right now."

Fletch's jaw tightened and he looked toward the front doors. "The trucks with their lights on," Fletch concluded. After Blade and Jack nodded, he said, "We going over there to confront them?"

Blade's lips quirked upward. "I told Wendy that I wouldn't."

"You told her you wouldn't right then," Jackson cut in. "What if we went out during intermission?"

"Smart kid," Fletch observed. "Blade?"

Blade looked at Jackson. He looked stressed. Not only had he brought his sister to watch his very new girlfriend perform, he now had to worry about the bullies who'd been on his ass. He understood that the teen would do whatever it took to get them to back off, but for some reason, Blade hesitated. Finally, he said, "I think getting into an altercation in the middle of your girlfriend's play isn't the best idea."

Jackson's shoulders slumped. "Yeah, I guess."

"I'm sorry you're going through this," Blade told the boy. "It's not right or cool. You've got a lot of pressure on you to protect Jenny and the others, while at the same time keeping yourself safe. I'm sorry I haven't reached out before now to start those self-defense lessons. We'll do that this weekend if you have the time."

"Saturday, me and Wen are celebrating her birthday," Jackson said.

"That's right. What about Friday after school? Your sister is working at the call center, isn't she? What if we did it then?"

"That should work. I have a robotics club meeting, but we'll be done by four," Jackson said eagerly.

"Great. You think the guys'll want to come help?" Blade asked Fletch.

"Absolutely."

"Perfect. We'll talk to your sister and see if that'll work. Okay?"

"Okay."

"And after the performance is over tonight, we'll all walk out together just in case those assholes want to try something. Yeah?"

Jackson's shoulders dropped even more with the release in tension. "Thanks."

"Anytime. I gave you my number and told you to call if you needed anything. I was serious about that. Any. Time. Got me?" Blade asked.

"Yeah. I appreciate it. Wendy's awesome, but she literally can't do anything about this. We both know it, and it sucks. If you can help me figure out what to do if they decide to jump me and my friends one day, I'd appreciate it."

"Violence doesn't solve problems," Fletch pointed out. "But when you don't have a choice, it can help get you out of a dangerous situation long enough to get help."

Jackson nodded then turned to Blade again. "Wendy's amazing. She gave up literally everything to look after me. I'd do the same for her, no questions asked. I like you, Aspen. Thank you for treating her right. She needs someone to look after her for once in her life."

Blade knew there was a lot about the siblings' situation that he didn't know yet, but he'd never doubted their close bond. "She's a hard person to look after, but I'm giving it my best shot," he told the teenager.

"Don't give up on her," Jackson said. "She has reason to be tight-lipped about a lot of stuff."

Blade nodded. Getting confirmation that something big was up with Wendy was good. He just wished she would trust him enough to share what that something was. He could help her, he knew it. But not if he didn't know what was up.

Jackson seemed relieved. He looked at his watch. "It's almost time for the play to start."

"Go on in," Blade said. "We're right behind you."

The second Jackson was out of earshot, Fletch asked, "How old is that kid again?"

"Sixteen."

Fletch shook his head. "He seems older."

Blade considered that for a second, then agreed. "Yeah, he does. Look, I don't like the situation with those assholes across the street at all. Do you know if the commander found out anything about the license plates we gave him?"

"Last I heard, no."

Blade frowned. "I'm going to have to ask him to speed it up. If their parents live on post, I want to talk to them."

"I'll go with you," Fletch agreed. "Now, come on. Let's do this."

"You ready for Annie to sing *Little Mermaid* songs for the next month or so?"

Fletch grinned. "No. But that doesn't mean I'm not going to love every second of it."

***

Three hours later, Blade stood in the hallway outside the theater with Jackson, Wendy, Fletch, Emily, and Annie as they waited for Jenny to emerge from backstage.

She'd been fantastic as Ursula. Her voice was amazing, and she was able to put just the right amount of evilness into her character. Annie had been chattering nonstop ever since the play had ended and Emily was leaning into Fletch tiredly.

"Here come Jenny's parents," Jackson said.

Looking over, Blade saw a middle-aged couple approaching their little group from the right. Jenny's mom was wearing a black sheath dress with several thousand dollars' worth of jewelry on her wrists, ears, and around her neck. She had on high heels and her hair and makeup were beautifully done. Blade estimated her to be in her mid-forties, and she'd aged extremely well. Jenny's father was wearing a suit and tie and he was beaming with pride.

"Jack!" the older man said, reaching out to shake the teenager's hand. "So good to see you tonight. Wasn't Jenny great?"

"Yes, sir," Jackson replied immediately. "She was." He turned to Jenny's mom. "It's good to see you again, Mrs. Stewart."

"You too, Jack. Have you seen Jenny yet?"

"No, ma'am. She told me earlier that it might take a while, as she had to get all the purple makeup off her face and arms before she could leave."

"Right," the older woman agreed.

Jack turned and gestured at Wendy. "This is my sister, Wendy. Wen, these are Jenny's parents, Monroe and Elizabeth Stewart."

Wendy held out her hand and shyly said, "It's nice to meet you."

"You too. Jack told us all about you when he was over at our house for dinner the other night. You've raised a fine young man."

Blade saw Wendy blush, but she smiled and thanked the older man.

"And this is Aspen, Wendy's boyfriend," Jack continued, finishing up the introductions.

Blade shook the couple's hands and had to admit he was relieved they were so open and friendly. Wendy had told him that Jenny's parents were very wealthy, and she'd worried they'd look down on Jackson as a result. But they seemed gracious and welcoming. Blade was glad for both Jackson and Wendy.

"And I'm Annie Fletcher," the little girl next to them said. "I belong to my mommy and Daddy Fletch. I like playing soldier. I don't sing good, but Daddy says that there's nothing wrong with pressing myself however I feel the need."

"*Ex*pressing yourself," Fletch corrected with a smile. There were more handshakes all around.

"That's what I said!" Annie protested, and everyone chuckled.

"Mom! Dad!"

Everyone turned and saw Jenny heading toward them. She had a huge smile on her face and the sheen of a blush on her cheeks, probably from where she'd scrubbed off the purple makeup.

Blade and the others watched as she hugged her parents, then immediately turned to Jackson. "Hi," she said shyly, the flush on her face deepening.

Inwardly, Blade smiled. The girl was extremely outgoing onstage, but as soon as she was around Jackson, she turned into a blushing, shy teenager.

"Hey," he said, and without seeming awkward, reached out and pulled Jenny into a hug. "You were amazing, as I told you you'd be."

Jenny relaxed the second Jackson touched her. When he pulled back, he twined their fingers and the teenagers stood with the group of adults, holding hands. They had an easy kind of connection that was easy to see.

"Let me introduce you to everyone," Jackson said, and thus another round of introductions commenced.

"Wow," Annie said. "You aren't so fat anymore."

Everyone laughed, and Emily explained that it was the costume Jenny was wearing that made her look like Ursula.

Blade put his arm around Wendy's waist in an easy embrace as everyone talked about the performance and praised Jenny. He could tell Wendy was tired as she leaned against him a bit more with every minute that passed.

"It's getting late," Mr. Stewart said. "You've got school in the morning, kiddo. Say goodbye to Jack and we'll meet you at the car. Okay?"

"Okay, Dad," Jenny said.

Blade took the opportunity to let the young couple know he and Wendy would go wait in the car as well. He wanted to give Jackson the time and space to talk to his girlfriend alone...and maybe steal a congratulatory kiss or two.

He intertwined his fingers with Wendy's and walked toward the doors with Fletch and his family. Fletch was parked on the opposite side of the parking lot, and as they began to part ways, he asked, "You want me to stick around?" and gestured toward where the trucks were still sitting across the street, their lights now turned off. Blade had no idea if the boys had hung out there the entire time they were inside watching the play, or if they'd taken off to do something else and returned. Either way, it seemed a bit obsessive for them to be there that late at all.

"Nah, it's cool. Thanks though. I'll see you tomorrow at PT."

Blade leaned over and kissed a sleepy Annie, who had her head resting on her dad's shoulder. "See you later, squirt."

"Bye, Blade," she mumbled.

"It was nice to meet you, Wendy," Emily said. "You're coming to the barbeque we're having in a few weeks, right?"

Wendy looked up at him and Blade nodded encouragingly.

"If you want me to. I wasn't sure, since Aspen and I are so new."

"Doesn't matter if you've been dating a day or a decade. You're welcome," Fletch said definitively.

"Then I guess I'm going," Wendy said with a smile.

"Good. See you then," Emily said.

"Bye."

Blade was ridiculously pleased to have Wendy for himself for the first time that night. He put his arm back around her waist and led her to his Jeep. When he reached the passenger side, he didn't open the door, but instead backed Wendy against it and turned her to face him.

"So...you used to sneak out to see boys, huh?"

She groaned and shook her head. "Figures you wouldn't let that go by without a comment."

"No way. Is that why you rigged the door to make sure Jackson wasn't sneaking out? Because you'd done that exact thing?"

For a second, he thought she was going to brush off his question, like usual. If she did, Blade was going to call her on it. He was tired of her deflecting. Especially when her brother had already spilled the beans. He clenched his fists to try to control his impatience. He didn't want to scare her, but he really, *really* wanted her to talk to him.

"Yeah. I know how easy it can be and I didn't want to risk that he'd sneak out and get hurt because of where we live."

Blade unclenched his fists in relief. She hadn't told him anything he didn't already know, but at least she hadn't flat-out lied or refused to answer. He tried to lighten the conversation and reward her for being honest. "While I can't deny I'm benefiting from all that experience when you were younger, I think I'm jealous."

"You have nothing to be jealous about," Wendy said firmly. "You are head and shoulders better than the slobbering kisses I used to think were heavenly."

"I am, huh?" he teased, rubbing his nose against hers.

"Yeah."

"I've been wanting to do this all night," Blade said in a voice husky with desire. Then he leaned down to kiss her.

Wendy immediately put her arms around him and stood on her tiptoes as she welcomed his lips on hers. Instead of consuming her like he did almost every other time they'd kissed, Blade took his time. Nibbled on her bottom lip, teased her with his tongue, sipping and caressing her lips with his own.

She protested his teasing touches. "Aspen," she whined.

"What?" he asked, his warm breath feathering over her glistening lips.

"Kiss me."

"I am."

"I mean, *really* kiss me. Jackson is going to be back any second."

Taking her warning to heart, Blade did as he'd wanted from the first second he'd seen her that night. She was wearing a pair of black slacks and a light purple top that had some sort of sparkles in it. She was a breath of fresh air, and he'd immediately wanted to corrupt her. Bend her over a handy piece of furniture and take her from behind. Ever since their phone sex the other night, he'd had more and more erotic fantasies of making love with her. It was becoming an obsession. *She* was becoming an obsession.

Blade leaned down again, and this time didn't hesitate to kiss her the way they both needed. Deep and rough. He felt Wendy step toward him, and he gathered her to him, loving how she fit against him. Tilting his head so he could get a better angle and so he could better twine his tongue with hers, Blade continued their carnal kiss.

They were interrupted a moment later by harsh words coming from somewhere in the parking lot. Lifting his head, Blade saw that Jackson and Jenny were surrounded by a group of men.

Swearing under his breath, Blade immediately let go of Wendy and headed for her brother.

He heard Wendy hurrying after him, and wished she'd stay by the Jeep, but knew she'd never agree to it. He couldn't blame her. If it was his kid, or Casey, he wouldn't stand by either.

The area was mostly empty of people. Their waiting for Jenny to get changed after the play had given most of the attendees time to leave. Blade heard the taunting before he reached the group. He knew the principal had already forced the men to park off the school property, and that they shouldn't be there now, but obviously, these guys thought they were above following the law.

"Your girlfriend looks mighty nice tonight, Jackie boy. Think we can borrow her for a while?" The guy was touching Jenny's arm as he spoke.

Jackson shifted Jenny until she was standing at his back, but unfortunately, there was another boy behind him who took up the harassment.

"She looks confused. Haven't you taught her how to take your dick, Jack?"

Jenny squeaked in terror when the boy nearest her reached out and touched her hair.

"Get your hands off her," Jackson growled, turning to face the newest threat.

The problem was that he was surrounded by the four older men. There was no way he could protect Jenny from all of them at the same time.

He stalked up and grabbed a fistful of one of the boy's T-shirts and flung him away from Jackson and Jenny. "Why don't you boys move on?" he suggested in a low, lethal voice.

Immediately, the other three boys backed up, showing that they truly were cowards at heart. The one who seemed to be in charge held up his hands as if in capitulation. But Blade could see the gleam of excitement in his eyes, as if he was enjoying terrorizing Jenny and pissing off Jack.

"Whoa, man. Everything's good here. I'm Lars, and we're friends of Jack's. We were just messing around."

"You're not my friends," Jackson said immediately. "You don't even go to this school anymore. Why are you hanging around here bothering everyone? The principal already told you to bug off. Don't you have a life?"

Blade winced, as he figured taunting these guys probably wasn't the best course of action; it would only piss them off more.

"Fuck you," Lars said, glaring at Jackson.

"No, fuck *you*," Jackson retorted, pushing Jenny behind him and holding an arm out, as if that could shield her from the bully's words and actions.

Blade could see her fingers digging into Jackson's sides, but he didn't even seem to notice. He felt more than saw Wendy come up next to him. She put a hand on his back. Her tension easily transmitted to him. He wanted to tell her to step back, to give him room in case he needed to take these assholes down, or get to the knife in a holster at the small of his back, but he didn't want to warn the boys that he was anything other than just a random guy...just in case.

"Why don't we all just head on home?" Blade asked softly.

"Yeah, man, we're doin' just that," Lars said, backing away with his hands still up. He turned to look at Jackson. "We'll see you soon, Jack."

It was the way the words were said that made the

hair on the back of Blade's neck stand up. He'd been in many ugly situations before. Faced down the worst of the worst. And something about Lars's words made him extremely uneasy.

"Don't do anything stupid, boy," he warned. "You have no idea who I am and what I can do."

Lars turned his sneer to Blade. "I don't give a shit who you are. You can't do anything to me. I'm just a kid. If you fuck with me, a boy younger than your old ass, *you'll* be the one in trouble."

"Don't count on it," Blade returned. "You're over eighteen, legally an adult. You're in way over your head. Go home, get a job, and move on with your life. Stop hanging out in high school parking lots."

Lars's eyes narrowed. "You can't tell me what to do," he told Blade. "No one tells *me* what to do."

"Go home," Blade said again, turning with the movements of the boys, making sure no one was sneaking around behind him.

With one more smirk and a mocking bow, Lars turned his back on them and walked toward the trucks as if he didn't have a care in the world.

Blade immediately turned to Jackson. "That guy is seriously bad news."

Jackson nodded his head as he turned and brought Jenny into his embrace. He wrapped his arms around her and said, "They were touching my girl. No one touches Jenny without her permission. I appreciate your help."

"Aspen?" Wendy asked, and he felt her hand on his arm. He turned and wrapped it around her shoulders. He was pissed that their kiss had been interrupted. He was pissed that the punks felt it was okay to threaten and touch Jenny. He was pissed that they were messing with Jackson. He cared about the boy and hated that he was dealing with this shit. And finally, he was pissed that Lars didn't seem to give one little shit that he'd just threatened a grown man.

"I'm okay," he told Wendy, even though he didn't feel okay in the least. "Jackson, go ahead and walk Jenny to her parents' car. I'll keep my eye out and we'll meet you back at the Jeep. That okay?"

"Yeah, thanks."

Blade nodded at the boy and turned in time to see, and hear, Lars and his crew rev their motors and peel out of the parking lot.

As he walked Wendy back to his Jeep, she asked, "Is Jackson in danger?"

"Honestly? I'm not sure. I'd like to say no, that those jackholes are all talk and no action."

"But you don't believe that."

"Unfortunately, no. You're going to have to be really careful anytime you pick him up or drop him off somewhere. Those guys don't care who they hurt and the last thing I want is you getting stuck in the crossfire of their irritation with your brother."

"Well, I don't want Jackson to be in their line of fire," she retorted. "Just let those assholes try something with me around. I'll Tase their asses if they do anything."

Blade couldn't help but smile at her. "You have a Taser?"

"I'm a single woman. Of course I have a Taser."

"You ever use it?"

She looked at him. "No. But I test-fired it at a dummy before I bought it."

"Not the same thing."

She shrugged. "Whatever. All I'm saying is that I'm not afraid of those guys."

Blade turned her to face him and put a finger under her chin, forcing her to look him in the eyes. "Don't underestimate them. Just because they're younger than you by a decade or so doesn't make them any less dangerous."

Something went through her eyes that he didn't understand, but she nodded. "I know. I'm just mad."

"Me too, sweetheart. Me too."

Blade moved until he had his arm around her shoulders again. Wendy had one arm wrapped around his back and the other on his stomach. They stood like that watching as Jackson consoled Jenny, and then as he walked her over to where her parents were waiting.

They were parked around the other side of the school and hadn't seen anything that happened.

"I'm worried about him," Wendy said quietly as her brother finally came toward the Jeep.

"He'll be okay," Blade said, the conviction in his tone easy to hear. "Me and the guys'll teach him how to protect himself."

"Even if he's surrounded again like he was tonight?"

"Even then," Blade vowed.

Previously, he'd planned on going easy on Jackson. Showing him simple moves and not getting into anything too deep. But tonight changed that. He was going to put Jackson through the wringer this weekend. He'd put him in full pads and would tell the others not to go easy on him. If the kid was going to learn how to protect himself, and Jenny, he needed to be prepared to do whatever it took.

Because if there was one thing Blade had learned, bullies like Lars didn't fight fair. He'd do whatever was necessary to take Jackson down, no matter who got hurt in the process.

CHAPTER TWELVE

"How's Jackson?" Aspen asked after he'd kissed Wendy hello. She'd met him in the parking lot of her complex. She'd been anxious to see him and was too impatient to wait for him to come up to the apartment itself. He'd frowned at her and scolded her for not letting him escort her to his Jeep, but she'd merely rolled her eyes at him.

"We worked him pretty hard Friday night." It was Sunday, and they had the entire day to themselves. Jackson was spending the day with Jenny and her family. Things between the teenagers had gotten serious quickly, but Wendy didn't worry about him too much. She trusted her brother and knew he'd make an excellent boyfriend...the night of Jenny's play had proved that. He'd done what he could to keep her safe.

On Saturday, she and Jackson had celebrated her

birthday as planned. They'd gone out for pizza, but instead of going to the putt-putt place like usual, because Jackson was still super sore, they'd chosen to see the latest superhero movie at the theater.

They celebrated her turning twenty-seven just like they'd celebrated every other birthday...pretending she was five years older than she was. She'd explained to Jackson when he was eight that it was important people think she was twenty-one when their parents had died. That way, no one would try to separate them again because she was too young.

Wendy sighed. "Hurting," she said, answering Aspen's question. "But he hasn't complained. In fact, he was super excited to show me the bruises on his sides and legs. Have I thanked you for teaching him self-defense? I don't like why he wants to learn, but I have to admire him for it all the same."

Aspen wrapped his arms around her in a warm hug. "It's my pleasure, sweetheart. And I won't lie to you and say that he probably won't ever have to use what we're teaching him because I think you're smarter than that. You were there last week. You saw that Lars guy and his friends. Most bullies back off when their victims won't give in to their taunts. But not Lars."

Wendy sighed and pulled back a bit. "I know. That's why I'm not asking you to take it easy on him. I hate that he's going through this, but I actually feel relieved you're here to help."

"I'll be there for him no matter what. If for some reason things between us don't work out, I'll still be his friend. I hope you both know that. But that being said...I'm going to do everything in my power to make sure that things *do* work out between us."

Wendy smiled up at him. "Me too. I like you, Aspen."

"I like you too. Now...what do you want to do for your birthday today?"

Wendy bit her lip. That was totally a loaded question. She knew what she wanted. She wanted Aspen to make love to her. Then fuck her so hard and deep, she didn't know where he ended and she began. She'd loved sex when she was younger, and it had been a long time since she'd been with anyone. Too busy with Jackson, tired from working two jobs, and too afraid to get close to anyone.

"Wow, those are some deep thoughts," Aspen commented, smirking.

"What I'd really like is to spend time with you at your place. Just the two of us. Jackson will be at Jenny's until after dinner."

Aspen looked at his watch, then back at her, his eyebrows raised suggestively. "So, we have five hours all to ourselves?"

"Yup."

"Are you sure you want to go to my condo? We can

go out to eat, or I can take you to a movie, or shopping for something you've always wanted."

"Lately, all I want is you."

Aspen licked his lips and took a deep breath before answering. "Are you sure?"

"Yes. Absolutely. One hundred percent."

He smiled then leaned down and kissed her gently and affectionately. "The birthday girl should always get what she wants."

Then he turned and, a little too quickly, hustled her into his Jeep. The parking lot was quiet, as it was a Sunday afternoon and most of the questionable people who lived there were probably still sleeping. He jogged around the front to the driver's side.

He started the Jeep and was headed toward his condo without any other commentary. Wendy appreciated it. The last thing she wanted was him to ask a million times if she was sure. Of course she was. She was an adult. She wouldn't have suggested it and told him she wanted him if she didn't.

Aspen had a habit of being overly cautious, and she realized a couple nights ago that she was going to have to make the first move toward changing their relationship from brief kissing or making out here and there, to a more physical one.

Yes, they'd had phone sex that one time, but instead of moving them toward having sex faster, it seemed to have stalled it. For her birthday, Wendy wanted to go after what she wanted for once. She was horny, and Aspen was hot. Not only that, but he was a genuinely nice guy. She needed more of those in her life.

She was so lost in her head, Wendy didn't realize they were at his place until he'd turned off the engine.

"Having second thoughts?" he asked quietly.

"Absolutely not. You?"

He chuckled. "You're funny."

Wendy beamed.

"Wait there," Aspen ordered.

Wendy did as he asked and watched as he went around the front of the Jeep to her side. He scooped her up out of the seat and she squealed as she threw an arm around his neck to hold on. He used his ass to shut the door and immediately strode up to his condo. He had to set her down to put the key in the lock, but afterward, picked her up again.

Wendy giggled as he shut the front door with his foot.

"Are you hungry?"

"No."

"Want something to drink?"

"No."

"We could watch TV."

Wendy reached up and palmed the side of his face. "I don't want to watch television. I don't need to use the restroom. I don't want to play a board game. I want you inside me, Aspen. So hard and deep, I can't remember a time when we weren't together."

She watched his pupils dilate at her carnal words.

"I'm not sure I can be slow the first time," he said, his words rough with emotion. "I want you too badly."

"Good."

Without another word, he headed for the stairs. Carrying her as if she weighed no more than a child, when Wendy knew for a fact that wasn't the case, he walked up to the third-floor master bedroom without breathing hard at all. He strode into his room, the sight of his once again unmade bed making Wendy lick her lips in anticipation. He put her down on the edge of the mattress and leaned over her.

Wendy went back on her elbows and stared up at Aspen. His face was as intense as she'd ever seen it. "Aspen," she whispered, not sure what she was saying with that one word.

"Last chance to back out," he practically growled.

Instead of answering him, Wendy reached for the hem of his shirt and slowly drew it up his body.

The second he realized what she was doing, he stood and brushed her hands away. He grabbed hold of the shirt and tore it over his head.

"Get naked," he ordered as his hands went to the fastening of his jeans.

With a little giggle, Wendy did as he asked. She unzipped her own jeans and pushed them over her hips.

She was unbuttoning her blouse when Aspen's hands moved hers out of the way again and he took over.

Looking up, Wendy blinked. He was standing over her, already butt naked. Aspen's cock was hard and jutted out from black curls between his legs. It bobbed and dipped as he moved, and she couldn't take her eyes from it.

He pushed her shirt down her arms, and even as she was still struggling out of the sleeves, he'd unhooked the clasp of her bra and was pushing that down her arms as well. Then his hands went to her hips and he yanked her to the very edge of the mattress. Wendy fell back with an *umph* and grinned as he pulled her panties over her ass. He stepped back long enough for her to kick them off, then he was back, hovering over her.

She felt his cock brush against her belly, leaving a wet, cold smear of precome. Wendy wrapped her legs around his hips and reached up for him at the same time his mouth lowered to hers.

If she thought the kisses they'd shared in the past were hot, this one left all the others in the dust. She could feel his cock pulsing between their bodies. Her nipples were hard from the chilly air in the room and with excitement. Every time they brushed against the hair on Aspen's chest, it was as if a jolt of electricity went straight to her pussy.

The wetness between her legs was almost obscene.

Wendy couldn't remember ever wanting a man more than she wanted Aspen right that second.

He pulled back and his gaze went from her face to her chest. Then he pushed himself up onto his hands so he could see more of her. By the time his gaze came back to her face, the intense look in his eyes made her feel that much more beautiful...and turned on.

"You are so fucking beautiful. I can't believe you're here. In my bed. With me."

"Less talk and more action," Wendy gasped, needing him inside her more than she needed to breathe.

He took one hand and flattened it against her collarbone. Then he slowly, ever so slowly, ran it down her body, his calluses scratching her erect nipple as his hand moved over it. She sucked in a breath as he practically covered her not-so-flat belly. But it was when he ran his fingers through the short hairs covering her pussy that she flat-out forgot to breathe.

"So wet," he murmured. "You want me."

"Duh."

He smiled and moved his hand to his cock, squeezing the base and closing his eyes for a second. Then he said, "This is gonna be hard and fast, sweetheart. You okay with that?"

"After you put on a condom, yes."

Aspen froze, then swore long and low even as he was bending down to grab his pants. He was mumbling to himself. "Shit. Fuck. Get it together, Carlisle."

Wendy giggled and relaxed. She'd been ready to shove him away if he refused to use a rubber, but she should've known better. Aspen wasn't that man. He wasn't an asshole. He'd given her plenty of chances to back out and had been over-the-top careful about making sure she really wanted this. Wanted *him*.

He dropped his pants back on the floor and ripped open the packet with his teeth. Watching him roll the condom down his rock-hard dick was almost as arousing as anything else he'd done.

When he was all gloved up, he leaned over her again. "Sorry about that. I'd never take you bare without your permission. But you should know, I'm clean. I get tested every couple of months by the Army. A full physical."

"I am too...but I'm not on anything."

The gleam in his eyes at her admission made her insides quiver. "A lot of women your age are on some sort of birth control," he fished.

Wendy gave him what he was looking for. "There's no need for me to be since I haven't had sex in years. My periods are regular and relatively pain-free."

"I can't claim years, but it's been a while. Ever since I started talking to this fascinating woman on the phone who tried to sell me life insurance, I haven't been able to think about anyone but her."

"Fuck me, Aspen," Wendy said softly.

"Oh, I'm going to," Aspen said, leaning over her

once again. "Then I'm going to make love to you. After, I want to put you in that tub in my bathroom and fulfill that fantasy I had of you in there."

Wendy could only nod as images flooded her brain of the two of them in the tub together...and what they'd do afterward.

Moving slowly, Aspen notched the head of his cock at her opening. Then, using his thumb to rub slow circles over her clit, he slowly pushed inside.

Wendy tensed at first, then relaxed when she realized he wasn't just going to slam himself inside her.

As if he could read her mind, he explained, "You said it's been a while. I refuse to fuck you properly until you're good and ready for me."

He slipped in another inch. He never stopped his thumb's movements as he eased farther and farther inside her. When she thought he was in as far as he could go, he put one hand under her ass, lifting her a couple inches, at the same time shifting closer to the bed.

Wendy inhaled deeply. She could feel the hair on his legs brush against the inside of her thighs. She'd missed this. The feeling of being connected to another human being. Of being one with them. But with Aspen it was different. Bigger.

Her inner muscles contracted, and she was fascinated by the way Aspen groaned as a result.

"You okay?" he asked.

"More than."

He experimentally shifted backward, then pushed inside her once again. "Sure?"

"Fuck me, Aspen. I need it. I need *you*."

"Tell me if I hurt you," he warned.

Wendy nodded.

And with that, Aspen got down to business. He pulled almost all the way out of her, then slammed back in with a force he hadn't used before. Then he did it again. And again. He had one hand on her hip and the other rubbed firmly over her clit as he fucked her.

Wendy knew her boobs were bouncing up and down with each thrust, but it just added to the carnality of the experience. Aspen wasn't being gentle, but he absolutely wasn't hurting her. She needed the friction and feeling of his body hitting hers to help her get off.

"God, Aspen. Yes!"

"Rub your clit," he ordered.

Mindless with lust, Wendy did as he asked, moving her hand down her body to stimulate herself.

Both hands now free, Aspen grabbed her butt and held her a couple inches off the mattress, pulling her into him with each thrust of his hips.

The position was slightly uncomfortable for her, but Wendy didn't care. It was hot, and Aspen was using her how he needed to in order to get off. She continued to frantically rub her clit even as she kept her eyes open and on the man between her legs.

She didn't want to miss one second of this. She hadn't felt this womanly and feminine in a long time.

"Fuck, this feels good," Aspen murmured, his gaze meeting hers. "*You* feel good. I've dreamed about this, but the reality is so much better than my fantasy."

Wendy used her free hand to pinch one of her nipples even as she tried to spread her legs wider, to get Aspen deeper inside her.

"You like this, don't you," Aspen said. "You like being taken hard and fast."

"Yesssssss," Wendy panted. "You feel so good."

"You need to make yourself come," Aspen warned. "I'm not going to last. You're too slick. Too tight. I haven't had pussy like this *ever*."

His words were crude, but they turned her on even more.

"Do it, Wen. Come all over my cock. Let me feel it."

Closing her eyes for the first time, Wendy concentrated on coming. She wanted this. More than she could articulate. Using two fingers now, she wasn't gentle and fingered herself roughly until her legs began to tremble with her pending orgasm.

"That's it. Fuck, you're beautiful. Laid out for me, open for whatever I want to give you. That's it, sweetheart. I've got you. Let go."

And with his words echoing in her mind, she did just that. Every muscle in her lower body tightened and she came. Long and hard. She vaguely heard

Aspen moan in appreciation even as he fucked her harder.

Then, as she was coming down from her orgasmic high, he pressed inside her as far as he could and threw his head back. He groaned even as he shook with his release.

How long they stayed connected like that, Wendy didn't know, but when he finally opened his eyes and looked down at her, she almost gasped at the intensity of his gaze.

He didn't say anything, simply let go of her ass and propped himself over her, then leaned down and kissed her. It wasn't sweet, it wasn't loving—it was a claiming. He devoured her mouth as if he'd never get enough.

Wendy opened wider for him, letting him take what he wanted. When he finally pulled back, he was breathing as hard as she was.

"That was the most amazing experience I've ever had in my life," he said quietly, and so earnestly, Wendy couldn't help but believe him. "Thank you for giving me that gift, although since it's your birthday, I'm supposed to be the one giving and not taking."

"Oh, you gave all right," Wendy assured him. "And I'm hoping you give that to me again soon."

He chuckled, and Wendy felt his cock slip out of her soaked folds.

"Damn," he said. "That sucks."

She smiled up at him, loving how at ease he was

with his body. It made this after-loving part not so awkward.

"I'm going to go take care of this condom. I'll be back. Climb under the sheet, sweetheart."

But he didn't move. Instead, his eyes raked over her face, as if he was memorizing it. He brushed a lock of hair off her sweaty forehead and his lips quirked up in a secretive smile.

"Thought you were going to clean up."

"I am," he said, but still didn't move.

Wendy relaxed under him and caressed his sides with her fingers. Finally, after another minute of quiet contemplation, he sighed and eased up from his position over her.

He turned and walked toward the bathroom, not at all concerned about his nudity. Wendy didn't think she'd ever be that nonchalant about being naked in front of him, but then, she didn't have an ass that looked like she could bounce quarters on it all day long.

The afternoon sun shone through the window and Wendy wasn't at all tired. But she did as Aspen asked and got under the sheet. Pulling it up to her chest, she smiled at the feeling of wetness between her legs. It was a bit uncomfortable, but she didn't mind.

In less than a minute, Aspen appeared back in the room and came straight to the bed. She didn't get to look at him long, as he was moving fast, but what she was able to see, she liked.

He had a bit of chest hair, but she had to look hard to see it. His arms bulged with muscles, and he had those delicious V-muscles as well. The skin around his hips was lighter than the rest of him, proving that he worked out in the sun quite a bit without a shirt on. The five o'clock shadow on his chin made him look even more rugged and masculine. All in all, there wasn't one thing about his body that she didn't like.

Heck, there wasn't much about him as a person she didn't like. He was just about perfect—and that scared the shit out of Wendy. Because she wasn't. Not even close.

He was at her side, sliding under the covers before she had the wherewithal to open her mouth and compliment him on his looks. He slid one arm under her shoulders and tugged her into him. When she rolled to her side next to him, he reached down and grabbed one of her legs, pulling it over his thighs.

"Snuggle in, sweetheart," he ordered.

Wendy smiled. "I thought men didn't snuggle."

"Fuck that. Whoever said that never had a warm, sated woman like you in his bed." Aspen kissed her forehead. "Take a nap, sweetheart."

"I'm not all that tired," she told him.

Before the words were even out of her mouth, she found herself on her back with Aspen looming over her. "I thought all women were exhausted after coming as hard as you did?"

She narrowed her eyes up at him and dug her finger-nails into his biceps. "Reaaaaally?"

He had the grace to look a little abashed. "Although my experience isn't all that vast. You want more?"

Wendy was embarrassed by her desires. She shrugged and looked away from him. "You said you were going to fuck me then make love to me. We don't have that much time before I have to leave."

"Look at me," Aspen ordered.

Wendy brought her eyes back to his.

"Don't ever be scared or ashamed to tell me what you want or need. You want my cock again, sweetheart?"

Wendy nodded.

"How about my mouth on your pussy?"

She nodded again, shifting under him in anticipation. "I...uh...have a pretty high sex drive."

Aspen smiled then. A big, wide smile that lit up his face and made him look a little evil at the same time. "We're a match made in heaven then, because I'm not nearly done with you. If you need a break, just say something. I could fuck you all afternoon and still be ready to go all night. I only have two more condoms though...we'll have to get inventive today. Tomorrow, I'll make sure I'm all stocked up."

He didn't give her a chance to answer. One hand went between her legs to play in her folds and the other went to one of her nipples as he bent to kiss her stupid.

Two hours later, Blade lay on the bed with Wendy, feeling like he'd been wrung out to dry...in a good way. He and Wendy were a perfect match, sexually. She was almost insatiable, and he'd had a fuck of a good time getting creative, making sure she was as satisfied as she could be.

He'd been true to his word. He'd made slow, sweet love to her until she was begging him to move faster, harder, anything. The teasing had been fun, bringing her to the brink of orgasm, then backing off, but it had been more fun to turn her over and fuck her hard and fast from behind as she writhed and moaned under him.

Then he'd run a bath for her as promised. Of course, he'd climbed in with her, and they were using the last condom he had within ten minutes of being soapy and slippery together.

She was perfect for him in every way. From her lush tits and her hard, tight nipples, which seemed to beg for his mouth every time he looked at them, to her wide hips and thick thighs he could grab and manhandle into position.

She wasn't stick thin, but neither was she fat. She was just right. Her brown eyes twinkled with excitement and happiness as they bantered back and forth, and they deepened with lust when he was inside her.

He lightly ran his fingers through her mussed hair as

they lay with their limbs intertwined in his bed. He had no idea where the pillows, other than the one under his head, had gone. The comforter had been shoved down to the end of the mattress at some point, and the fitted sheet had long ago been pulled up from the corners and was bunched under them.

The bed looked like a major battle had been fought there, and both Blade and Wendy were the winners.

He smiled, loving the feeling of intimacy that surrounded them. He felt closer to her at this moment than ever. After what they'd just shared, he wanted to open up to her, to share who he was.

He felt certain if he let her in, this time, she'd reciprocate.

"You know I'm in the Army, but what you don't know is what I do."

She was using her finger to slowly and sensually circle his nipple, but looked up at him at that. "I figured it was something out of the ordinary. If you don't have to move every couple years and you get to work with the same group of men all the time. I don't know a lot about the military, but from living in the area, I've learned that much at least."

He kissed her forehead. "You're right. My unit is Special Forces. We're Delta Force."

"Whoa," she said in an exhalation of breath.

"I guess you've heard of them?"

"Duh," she whispered. "Who hasn't?"

"You'd be surprised. Anyway, me and the guys have been together for a few years. The Army sends us in when there's a need for secrecy. I won't be able to tell you where I'm going, or even when I'll be back. But I want you to know that we're always careful. We have too much to lose to be careless about our safety. But you can't tell anyone. Who we are and what we do is a need-to-know kind of thing, and no one else needs to know."

"Why are you telling me this? I mean, if it's a secret and all, why tell me?"

"Seriously? After the last few hours, you have to ask?"

She blushed, but nodded anyway.

"This was not just sex, sweetheart. It was amazing, life-changing sex, and more. It was the start of *us*. I've never wanted to be with anyone the way I want to be with you. We clicked that night you first called me, and I've felt our connection grow every day since then. I want to wake up with you by my side and I want to fall asleep with my dick deep inside your body every night. I want to watch Jackson walk across the stage in a couple years and accept his diploma, and I want to watch him grow into the amazing man I know he'll be because of the role model his sister was for him. I want to come home from a mission knowing that you'll be here waiting for me. The thought of someone caring if I live or die while I'm in some shithole of a country makes me want to be all the more careful."

"Oh," she murmured.

"Yeah, oh," he agreed with a small smile. "Am I alone in this?" he ventured to ask.

"No," she said softly.

Blade relaxed. He hadn't realized how tense he'd gotten during the conversation. Other than his family, he'd never told anyone what he truly did before. He'd been nervous, but he should've known Wendy wouldn't ask him any questions he couldn't answer. They were finally on the same page. He relaxed.

After several minutes of dozing, he sleepily murmured, "Happy Birthday, sweetheart."

It was late afternoon and he knew they needed to get up, shower, and think about getting Wendy back to her apartment, but Blade was so sated and comfortable, he didn't want to move.

"Thanks."

"What are you, thirty-one, thirty-two?" Blade asked while tracing circles on her back with his fingers.

It was an innocent question—but she stiffened next to him as if he'd asked her something extremely personal and out of line.

"Something like that."

Blade went from relaxed and lazy to highly alert and suspicious in an instant.

The harmless question had simply popped out. He hadn't thought in a million years that she'd refuse to answer. It was such a simple, easy question—at least, it should've been if she trusted him.

And the thought that she didn't *killed* him. Even after everything they'd just done, she was still holding back.

"Which is it?" he asked tensely.

She propped herself up on an elbow and looked at him. "Does it matter?"

"Why won't you tell me how old you are, Wendy?" Blade asked point-blank.

She fell back down, resting her head on his shoulder, but it seemed more like an avoidance technique than a loving one. "Women don't like to be asked their age, Aspen. Drop it."

But he couldn't. Not now. "I'm thirty-one. Does it bother you that you're older than me? I don't give a shit, and neither do my friends. Why would you care?"

"I just do."

Suddenly feeling sick to his stomach, Blade sat up, dislodging Wendy from his chest. "Are you seriously not going to tell me how old you are after what we just shared?"

Eyes wide, she shook her head.

Blade ran his hand through his hair in frustration. He didn't understand what the big deal was. "I just told you something I've never told anyone before. Something that could get me a big fat reprimand by my commander if he knew, and you won't even tell me your *age?* You've *got* to be kidding me. Are you older than that? Thirty-five?" He was trying hard to understand what was going on behind her stubborn expression.

Wendy slid out of the bed and grabbed the fitted sheet that was hanging off the side of the mattress, holding it up to cover her body. "There's a reason I'm being evasive."

"Evasive, hell—you're just flat-out refusing to tell me. How about where you grew up? Or where you were before you moved here? Where you graduated from and what your major was? I don't know *anything* personal about your life other than the fact your parents died and you took over raising your brother. *Talk* to me, Wendy. I feel like I don't even know you."

"You know me," she protested.

"Every time I ask you anything, even something inconsequential, you blow me off—and I'm getting really tired of it."

"Maybe that's because what you're asking isn't inconsequential!" she fired back.

"Knowing how old you are isn't that big of a deal," Blade said.

"It is to me."

"Why?"

She pressed her lips together and stared at him.

"How long have you lived here?"

She stared at him.

"Where were you before you moved to Texas?"

She blinked, but again didn't give him anything.

"Why don't you like cops?"

Once more, she refused to answer. Simply stood there, wrapped in his sheet, looking like she wished she was anywhere other than with him. And that hurt. Majorly.

"How many other men have you done this to?"

That got him a flinch. But he pressed on. "How many other men have you been with and refused to tell them anything other than the basics? How many others have you pushed away because you wouldn't tell them something as simple as your fucking age?"

"Fuck you, Aspen," she said finally. "You don't know anything about it."

"I know I don't!" he yelled. "Because you won't *tell* me. For all I know, you move from place to place, dragging your brother along, reeling men in with your beauty and vulnerability, then when they get sick of you hiding whatever it is you're hiding from them, you move on."

She didn't make a sound, but the hurt in her eyes was clear to see.

Blade was frustrated and sad. How they'd gone from making love one second, to fighting the next, he had no idea.

Most of all, he hated that he didn't even know what they were fighting *about*.

Taking out his frustrations on Wendy, he growled,

"Tell me something, *anything*, that'll make me feel less like you're just using me for sex right about now."

"Just because we fucked doesn't mean I have to tell you every little thing about my life!" Wendy shouted, trying to sound hard and tough.

But to Blade, she simply sounded desperate.

And her words made him mad. No—*furious*. He was standing there begging her to let him get closer, and she was absolutely refusing. Not only by evading the stupid fucking question about her age, which wasn't even the point anymore, but by throwing the amazing sex they'd had in his face as if it meant nothing.

He spoke without thinking.

"Right. And that right there makes you no better than the whore who tried to pick me up in the bar. I might as well've gone home with *her*; at least she was honest about just wanting me for sex. I bet she would've told me how old she was without all the fucking games *you've* played."

He regretted the words as soon as he said them.

Wendy paled and clutched the sheet closer to her body.

Blade needed some air. He'd had the best afternoon of his life and thought he'd been starting something permanent with Wendy. Hell, he'd thought for the last few *months* that was what they were doing. But she'd apparently just wanted sex.

Disgusted with himself *and* with her, Blade got off

the bed. He stalked over to his dresser and grabbed some clothes. "I'll get dressed in the guest bathroom. I'll take you home as soon as you're ready."

He didn't look back as he left his room. If he did, he might change his mind and go to Wendy and take her in his arms and tell her everything would be all right, and that he didn't mean any of the awful words he'd flung at her.

But he didn't. And therefore, he didn't see the absolute devastation on her face. The regret and self-recrimination, or the tears that streamed down her cheeks as if a faucet had been turned on full blast.

CHAPTER THIRTEEN

The ride back to her apartment was completed in silence. Aspen didn't say a word, and neither did Wendy. She'd managed to stop crying long enough to find her clothes. They'd been kicked under the bed during their afternoon sex fest.

When she'd gone downstairs, Aspen was waiting by the door. He opened it without a word, gesturing for her to precede him. He didn't help her into his Jeep and barely waited for her to buckle up before tearing out of the parking lot as if he couldn't wait to get her home and out of his life.

And she supposed that was exactly how he felt.

Wendy couldn't tell him how old she was. If she did, it endangered Jackson. In ten months, she could tell whoever she wanted that she was really only twenty-seven, but by then, it would be too late for her and Aspen.

She wanted to tell him. Had almost done so more than once. Had almost broken down and told him everything, but she'd held back...and now it was too late. He'd washed his hands of her.

Feeling more depressed than she had in a long time, Wendy stared down at her fingers as Aspen drove her across town. He stopped in the parking lot of her crappy apartment complex and she found the courage to say, "I'd tell you if I could."

"Yeah, okay. I gave you plenty of chances to talk to me, Wendy. More than enough. See you around."

His words were clipped and emotionless.

That was it. She'd found and lost the man she wanted to spend the rest of her life with. She wanted to be pissed at him for not giving her a chance to explain, but she couldn't. This was on her—because she *couldn't* explain. He was reacting exactly how she'd figured he would once he heard her story, which was part of the reason why she hadn't wanted to tell him.

Without another word, she slipped out of the Jeep and headed for the rickety stairs that led to the second floor and her apartment.

When Aspen left before she was halfway up the stairs, she knew that was it. He *never* left before making sure she was inside safe and sound. Ever.

Until now.

The decisions she'd made when she was a young, hormonal teenager had never weighed so heavily on her shoulders. Wendy had no idea how she was going to tell Jackson that she'd screwed things up with Aspen. She hoped that he might still agree to teach her brother self-defense. It wasn't as if Lars and his gang of assholes were going to stop harassing Jackson anytime soon.

Just because Aspen wasn't in their life anymore, didn't mean everything else stopped as well.

With her fingers shaking, Wendy unlocked her door and slipped inside. Everything seemed duller now. The bright pillows on the couch seemed to mock her. The dingy gray walls seemed even more pathetic.

Sinking into a depression she hadn't felt for years, Wendy dropped her purse on the dining room table and headed for the shower. She could still smell Aspen on her. As much as it hurt, she needed to get his scent off. She didn't need the reminder of how amazing he was. Of how badly she'd screwed up.

Why hadn't she just lied and said she was thirty-two? She'd still be in his bed if she had.

But she didn't want to flat out lie to him. Not even about her age. That's why she'd simply been avoiding answering his questions.

Yes, some people would claim that not telling him was kind of the same thing as lying, but not to her. Protecting Jackson had become second nature. She'd learned how to evade answers and change the subject like a pro. But of course, Aspen saw right through her. He was probably trained in the art of interrogation.

Not only that, but if the law caught up with her, it could hurt *him* too. Anything that brought attention to a Special Forces soldier had to be a bad thing. And if she was arrested, that could really be bad for him.

No, she'd done the right thing. Protecting the men in her life was the most important thing...even if doing so made Aspen hate her.

His last words replayed themselves in her head.

I might as well've gone home with her; at least she was honest about just wanting to be with me for sex. I bet she would've told me how told she was without all the fucking games you've played.

She didn't blame him for being upset with her, but that was beyond upset. He was furious...and hurt.

She wanted to call and tell him it had never been about the sex for her. That she loved spending time with him. Talking to him. But it was too late now. Way too late.

Shedding her clothes, Wendy climbed into the luke-warm shower and lifted her face up to the spray, letting it wash away the tears she continued to shed. She had to get herself under control before Jackson got home. He'd take one look at her and know something was wrong.

Even as she tried to shake herself out of the funk she'd fallen into, Wendy slid down the tile to the shower floor. She curled her arms around her updrawn knees and bawled.

Cried for all she'd lost before it was even hers.

Cried for all she'd given up in her life.

Cried for the unfairness of everything.

Jackson lay in his bed later that night, fuming.

Something had happened, and Wendy wouldn't tell him what.

Her eyes were puffy as if she'd been crying, but she'd pretended everything was normal, asking how his afternoon at Jenny's had gone.

When he'd tried to pry, she'd snapped at him to leave her alone, that she was fine.

But she wasn't.

Her phone hadn't rung. She and Aspen had talked every night for the last few months. He'd thought it was a bit ridiculous, but now he'd give anything to hear the low tones of Wendy's voice coming from her room as she spoke to him.

Clenching his hands into fists, Jackson stewed.

He'd thought Aspen was a good man.

He'd introduced them to his friends. Had gone out of his way to help with self-defense. Had even seemed upset over the condition of their apartment building and the dangerous people who also lived there.

Why would he do all those things if he was just going to break up with Wendy? It didn't make sense.

Jackson wasn't an idiot; he knew what Wendy had done a decade ago was illegal. They'd talked about it often enough over the years. But he also didn't care. She'd done the right thing. If he'd had to stay in that last foster home another night—hell, another hour—he wouldn't be the same today, and he knew it. She'd saved his life, and she'd only been sixteen. He didn't know if he'd be able to do what she did if he was in the same situation.

Picking up his phone, Jackson contemplated calling Aspen right then and there and chewing him out. His finger actually hovered over the button before he took a deep breath and put the phone down.

No. He needed to do it man-to-man. Wanted to make sure Aspen knew what he was giving up in his sister. Jackson realized whatever had happened between them probably wasn't all Aspen's fault. He knew his sister, knew she was stubborn and pretty closed off sometimes, but he'd also hoped Aspen wasn't the kind of man to run at the slightest hint of drama. Because Lord knew, he and his sister had their fair share.

But he was certain that Aspen would never find a more loyal, protective, and loving woman than Wendy.

His mind made up to talk to Aspen in person, Jackson immediately began to figure out how and when he'd make that happen. Monday and Wednesday, he had robotics club. Tuesday and Thursday, lacrosse practice. Jenny had rehearsals all week as well, and he needed to be there when she was done, just in case Lars and his buddies decided to come back.

But Friday he could skip lacrosse and head to Aspen's condo. Well, he could have Rob take him there. Jenny's family was going out of town for the weekend and they were picking her up right after school.

He'd have a couple hours where Wendy would think he was at practice to have his talk with Aspen and get Rob to drop him off at home later. Maybe he'd suggest to Wendy that they should have one of their famous taco nights on Friday. She always liked those because they were easy to make, relatively inexpensive, and there was always lots of leftovers.

Then they could watch a movie. He'd even let her pick. He hated the sad look in her eyes. Wanted to help her move past Aspen and whatever he'd done to make her so unhappy.

His plan set in his mind, Jackson began to formulate what he wanted to say to Aspen.

It was late by the time he finally fell asleep, but he had a plan. It would be uncomfortable, and embarrassing, but his sister was worth it.

By the time he was finished, Aspen would regret whatever it was he'd said or done.

By the time Friday rolled around, Blade was miserable and completely regretted the way he'd acted toward Wendy. He was an asshole. Why did he care how old she was? He didn't. But ultimately, that wasn't the issue. He wanted her to trust him, and it was obvious she was hiding something big from him. And that killed.

The bottom line was that he'd overreacted and treated her as if she was the enemy. On her birthday, no less. He could've backed off, let her have some space, then tried talking to her later when she wasn't so upset. But no, he had to get in her face and push the issue.

In his defense, the frustration over the fact she was avoiding his questions and keeping some big secret from him had gotten to a point where he couldn't hold back anymore. But that was no excuse for saying some of the things he had. He especially regretted comparing her to the woman at the bar. *That* had been a dick move.

He'd tried calling more than once, but she was either ignoring his calls or she'd blocked him.

He missed her. Was worried about her and Jackson. And he couldn't do a damn thing if she wouldn't talk to him. Let him apologize.

He missed their talks every night.

Missed hearing stories about "her" residents at the retirement home.

Worried about the situation with Lars and the other bullies.

He'd been slowly introducing her to the guys on his team, but hadn't had time to get through them all yet. Emily and Casey loved her, wanted to see her again, and he knew the others would too.

But unless he could fix what he'd broken, they wouldn't get that chance.

Work had been tense; the team had been on standby to be sent to Guantanamo Bay in Cuba. There weren't a lot of detainees left there, but the ones who remained were some of the worst of the worst. There had been an uprising in the detention center, and because of the limited number of staff stationed there, the brass had thought they'd need to send reinforcements, but in the end, they'd sent two SEAL teams from California instead of the Deltas.

Blade was glad, because as much as he loved serving his country, it didn't feel right to head off on a mission without making things right between him and Wendy first.

He'd been home for about twenty minutes and had practically worn a hole in the floor with his pacing, trying to decide whether or not to head over to Wendy's apartment and demand she talk to him, when his doorbell rang.

Thinking it might be Wendy, he raced to it and opened it without bothering to look through the peephole.

"I need to talk to you."

It was Jackson. And he didn't look happy.

"Is Wendy all right?" Blade asked. That was his first thought, that Jackson was there because something had happened to his sister.

"Not like you care, but yes."

Blade was thrown by the hostility in the boy's response, but asked, "And Jenny? Lars hasn't pulled any more of his shit?"

The anger in Jackson's face eased a bit and morphed into confusion. "She's cool, and I haven't seen much of Lars lately. We need to talk," he repeated.

Blade looked past him to the parking lot but didn't see Wendy's car like he'd been hoping. If she'd been there, he would've gone out and begged her to come in and talk to him. "How'd you get here?"

"My friend, Rob, brought me. He's waiting in the parking lot. This won't take long."

Blade opened the door fully and gestured for Jackson to come inside.

He did and turned to face Blade when he got far enough inside the condo.

"What's up?"

"What did you say or do to my sister?"

Blade studied the young man in front of him and decided to be honest. "I asked her how old she was. When she wouldn't tell me...I wasn't very nice."

When Jackson flinched and looked away from him for the first time, Blade was even more sure there was a lot more to the innocent question than he knew. "I fucked up. I know it. I've been trying to call her all week, but she won't pick up. I miss her. I love her, Jackson. I love your sister with everything I have, and it's killing me that I don't even know what our stupid fight was about. Talk to me. *Please*. Tell me what I'm missing so I can appropriately apologize, and it'll never happen again."

Without a word, Jackson wandered into the living room and sat on the couch. Blade followed, sat on the other end of the couch, and waited. He hated that the first person who heard that he loved her wasn't Wendy, but it couldn't be helped. He instinctively knew he needed to win her brother over before he could get anywhere with Wendy. If Jackson didn't want him with his sister, that would be that. Yeah, he was only a teenager, but Blade knew how close the two of them were.

Besides, he liked Jackson. Wanted him to respect him, not look at him as if he was no better than the dirt on his shoe. Because that's how Jackson had looked when he'd opened the door, and it sucked.

"She just turned twenty-seven," Jackson said in a low, even tone. "And I'm not sixteen. I'll be eighteen in ten months."

Blade quickly did the math in his head. "So, you were what...six when your folks died?"

"Yeah. And Wendy had just turned sixteen."

"And she got custody of you at that age?"

Jackson looked Blade in the eye as he said, "No."

Everything clicked into place as if Jackson had just spent the last thirty minutes telling him the details. "She's protecting you," Blade surmised.

Jackson nodded. "Yeah. Until I'm eighteen. Then we can both relax a bit. Me more than her, though."

"Will you tell me what happened?"

"Do you really love her, or are you just saying that to try to get me to tell you shit?"

"I love her," Blade returned immediately. "I don't give a damn what you tell me, my love for her won't change. I'm not going to do anything that will put either of you in danger."

Jackson nodded. "After Mom and Dad died, Child Protective Services took us both in, but they wouldn't put us in the same foster home. Something about how they didn't have any families in their database who wanted both a teenager and a little kid. Wendy didn't take that well. She was good at sneaking out, did it all the time when our parents were alive. She snuck out of her foster home every night and came to mine. But eventually, she got caught."

"Didn't you have any relatives who would take you in?" Blade asked, already not liking this story.

Jackson shook his head. "Not really. I think Dad had a sister, but they didn't get along and when she was contacted, she didn't want anything to do with us."

"Bitch," Blade murmured.

Jackson didn't react. "The state didn't have any choice but to keep us apart, but Wendy did everything she could to see me every day. I was scared. I missed Mom and Dad and didn't really understand what was going on. I was switched to three different homes, but somehow Wendy always found me. Her foster parents got fed up with her sneaking out all the time and stealing money for rides, so they told the authorities they didn't want her anymore."

"Jesus, she was just a kid. She wasn't a shirt someone could return as if it didn't fit," Blade bitched.

"Anyway, so she was sent to live in some sort of group home for unruly teens or something. But she snuck out of there too. She told me that they wanted to put her under house arrest, but because she wasn't actually breaking any laws when she left the house, they couldn't. And yeah, the last home I was in...wasn't good."

Blade's teeth clenched at the way Jackson said that. He hated that the young man next to him had been through something obviously horrible.

"The last night I was there was the worst. If Wendy hadn't shown up, I don't know what kind of person I'd be today...or if I'd even be around at all."

"Tell me about it?" Blade asked quietly.

"My foster parents had a bipolar sixteen-year-old biological son. When his parents weren't around, he'd pick on us foster kids. There were three others in that home with me. Once, he killed the family cat and hid it in the basement, and when his parents weren't watching, he forced us down there and showed us how he'd killed it. It was awful and scary."

"What happened your last night there?"

"The parents went out on a date and left their son in charge of all of us. I was six, the others in the house were four, five, and eight. Two girls and two boys. Ronald, the son, herded us all into the basement. There were dog crates down there from previous pets that had also mysteriously disappeared. I think the parents knew their son was sick, but they didn't know what to do about it. Anyway, he made us get into the crates, then he started to fuck with us."

"Fuck with you how?" Blade bit out.

"He'd poke us with sticks. Tell us he was going to leave us there all night and not tell his parents where we were. He didn't let us eat anything and didn't let us out even when we had to pee. We all ended up going in our pants, and he laughed at us when we cried. Then he took John, the eight-year-old, and tied him to one of the support beams with rope. He smeared the cat's blood he'd saved all over poor John...and told him he was going to gut him like he did the cat."

Jackson paused and took a deep breath. Blade wanted to go to him, put his hand on his shoulder and let him know that it was okay, but he wasn't sure what the boy's reception would be. So, he did nothing, just sat on the edge of the seat cushion and felt helpless.

After a moment, Jackson continued. "John was crying so hard he had snot running down his face, and the girls were hysterical. I was trying to figure out a way to run and get help, assuming at some point Ronald would let me out of the cage to do something to me too. But then Wendy was there. She'd snuck out of the group home again and had come to visit me. She used to throw little rocks at the window of the room I was staying in, and I'd crawl out onto the roof and slide down a tree and we'd sit in the backyard and talk.

"But when I didn't answer after she threw the rocks that night, she said she looked in every window and everything was dark in the house. She was going to go back to the group home, figuring the foster parents had taken us all somewhere as a treat, when she saw the light on in a basement window. She looked in and saw what Ronald was doing. She broke into the house and ran down those basement stairs as if she were possessed. She had a baseball bat in her hand. I guess Ronald was so surprised to see her that he just froze. She walloped him across the stomach and he dropped like a stone. She hit him a few more times, and I heard something break when she hit him in the legs."

"Jesus," Blade breathed.

Jackson ignored him and went on. "She untied John and got the rest of us out of the cages. She took us upstairs and locked Ronald in the basement. He was screaming and crying, but she told us to ignore him. She sent John and the girls up to their rooms, telling them to call 9-1-1, then she took my hand and we walked right out the front door."

Jackson lifted his head and looked Blade in the eyes. "She kidnapped me, Aspen. Took me right out of that house and we didn't look back. We had nothing. No extra clothes. No food. Nothing to drink. She brought me back to our house. The one we had when our parents were alive. I guess the authorities were still trying to settle all the legal shit with it because all our stuff was still there. I wanted to stay, but she said we couldn't. I remember sitting in my old room and crying because I didn't understand why we couldn't live there.

"Wendy helped me pack a bag with things that I wanted to take with me. Didn't even complain that the toy cars and stuffed animals I filled it with weren't practical. She put clothes for both of us into her own backpack, used the hidden key to unlock the safe under Mom and Dad's bed and got our birth certificates and some money that was there. Why the lawyers or police hadn't already found the safe and taken it, I'll never know, but thank God they hadn't. Then we left. Wendy bought bus tickets and we rode for three days and nights on that stinky bus until we got to Florida.

"We lived on the streets for a month before Wendy finally found a job. It was only bussing tables, but she lied about her age and they agreed to pay her in cash. We lived in a shitty motel for two years. She finally decided it was time to move on and we went to Louisiana. She didn't have any proof of what grade I was in, or anything to show that I had ever *been* in school. But she went to the elementary school near where we were staying and said she'd been homeschooling me. She had some forged papers about my supposed progress, and in order to prevent anyone asking questions about my age, made me a year younger than I really was.

"They tested me, and I was placed into the second grade, even though technically, according to my age, I should've been in third. Wendy did her best to teach me while we were on the run, but she worked a lot and we were so scared someone would figure out she was underage and take me away. Looking back, it seems silly to worry so much about someone questioning why I tested into the second grade when according to my age I should've already have mastered that information, but Wendy was really worried that any little thing that seemed off would make the authorities question her, so she told them I was younger than I was.

"We've moved around a lot since then, but when she got the job here at the retirement home, I could tell she really liked it. So, we stayed. I'll be eighteen in less than a year, and then no one can take me away from her and put me back into foster care. But the thing is...she's probably in a lot of trouble for what she did. If it was just her, a runaway teenager, no one would care. But she broke into that house, hurt Ronald, and kidnapped me. I might be free when I turn eighteen, but she'll always have to look over her shoulder.

"So, that's the long and ugly story about why she wouldn't tell you how old she was. Twenty-seven. She took over looking after me when I was six and she was sixteen. She never finished high school, never got her GED, and she's been more of a mother to me than my own was. I don't remember much about my mom, but I'd do anything for Wendy. Even come over here and tell you that you fucked up. Big time. You'll never find anyone else as loyal and protective as her. Sometimes people have a good reason for not wanting to talk about themselves."

Blade got up and moved closer to Jackson. The boy stiffened, but Blade ignored that. He kneeled on the floor at his feet and looked up at him. "I know I fucked up. I've been trying to get ahold of her to beg for her forgiveness ever since."

"Is your car broken?"

"What?"

"Your Jeep. Is it broken down?"

"No."

"Then you could've come to her. You know where she works. You know where she lives. It's not like she's been hiding from you. I know for a fact that even though she blocked your number, she still hoped you'd show up. Every day that's gone by and you haven't, the light in her eyes has died a little more. I'm pissed at you, Aspen. You made my sister so happy, then you killed the happiness faster than that." Jackson snapped his fingers to make his point.

"Things have been...tense...at work," Blade said, knowing that didn't make the fact he hadn't gone looking for Wendy any better. He should've.

"Whatever. What could've been so harsh on an Army base?"

In that moment, Blade realized that Wendy hadn't told her brother what he did, who he was. She'd kept his secret even though he'd hurt her in the worst possible way.

"Me and my friends are Delta Force," he told Jackson evenly. He had no qualms in telling the teenager who and what he was. The boy was going to be his brother-in-law. There was no way he was going to let Wendy get away now that he'd heard her deep dark secrets. Besides, Jackson obviously knew how to keep a secret as well. Had been keeping them his entire life.

"No shit?"

"No shit."

"Damn! Are you going to have to go off somewhere right now?"

Blade shook his head. "Luckily, no. It was touch and go for a while, but we were called off this afternoon."

Jackson stood, and Blade did as well. "Okay. Well, I'm going to go. I just wanted to set the record straight."

"I'm glad you did."

Jackson nodded and turned to go.

"I'm sorry about your parents, and I'm sorry about what you went through. But you should know, I'm also proud of you."

At that, Jackson turned back to face him, one brow arched.

"Wendy needs a champion, and you might be younger than her, and still in high school, but you're one hell of a champion. And you're right. I was an asshole. I fucked up. But I'm going to make it right. For both of you."

Jackson eyed him for so long, Blade was sure he was going to tell him not to bother, then eventually, he said, "I like you, Aspen. But you not only hurt my sister, but me too."

"I'm sorry. I can't say that enough. I've worried about you all week. About that situation with Lars and his asshole friends. I finally heard back from my commander and it looks like their parents *were* stationed here at Fort Hood, but most of them have moved. Chuck's parents are the only ones still working on post. Lars was enrolled at the local community college but dropped out earlier this year. His parents probably think he's still taking classes. He lives in an apartment near the college with two of those assholes who hang around with him."

"Losers," Jackson murmured.

"Exactly. The commander is going to touch base with Chuck's parents, but because the others don't have anyone living on the Army post, there's not much the authorities there can do."

Jackson nodded. "They haven't been around much this week. I only saw them once, and they didn't even approach me. I'm thinking you scared them away."

Blade wasn't sure he agreed, but kept his mouth shut about it for now. "You're going to continue to let me help you with those self-defense classes, aren't you?"

"Are you going to make things right with my sister?"

"Absolutely."

"And if she tells you to fuck off?"

Blade chuckled. "I actually expect her to. I was a dick. But I'll just keep trying. I won't give up on her. I love her."

"And if she's arrested for kidnapping?"

"I have a feeling that's not going to happen, but we'll deal with it if it does," Blade said.

Jackson shook his head. "That's what she thinks is going to happen. That once I'm eighteen and get my license and generally put my info out there into cyber-space more, someone from California will track her down and she'll be put into custody."

"But she has a driver's license. And I'm assuming

she's not working for cash at the retirement home. Isn't *her* info already out there? Does she pay taxes?"

Jackson furrowed his brow. "Yes, but I guess so far, she's just been lucky. We've both been lucky."

Blade shook his head. "I think it's more than that. Jackson, she was a minor when that happened. That doesn't mean she'll get away scot-free, but I think there were enough extenuating circumstances that if anything, she'll just get a slap on the wrist. Besides, if someone does find out where she is, I have friends who can help her."

Jackson looked unsure. "Really? You're not just saying you think she'll be off the hook to try to get on my good side?"

"I wouldn't do that to you, or her," Blade said.

Nodding, as if he'd come to a decision, Jackson said, "She's working at the call center tonight, but tomorrow I have a robotics competition. It's at the school gym. It starts at eleven. She'll be there."

"Do you mind if I bring a couple friends?"

"You haven't introduced her to all of them yet, have you?" Jackson asked with uncanny insight.

Blade chuckled. "Nope. And I might need reinforcements to help tell your sister that I might fuck up sometimes, but I'm not a bad guy."

"Good luck. You're going to need it."

Blade held out his hand. "I appreciate you coming over, Jackson. And looking out for your sister."

Jackson shook his hand and said, "You don't have to thank me for that. I'll always look out for her. We only have each other."

"You only *had* each other. Now you have me, my team, and their wives and girlfriends. You guys aren't alone anymore."

Jackson looked surprised for a moment, then nodded and dropped his hand. "Thanks."

"You're welcome. I'll see you tomorrow."

"Make sure to wear your groveling shoes," Jackson quipped as he opened the front door and grinned at him.

"Will do," Blade said and watched over the teenager until he reached a four-door Honda Civic. He kept watch until the car disappeared around a corner after leaving the parking lot. Only then did he close the door and lean his head against it.

The story Jackson told him broke his heart. He could just imagine Wendy as a teenager, sneaking out of her foster home so she could be with her brother. And to know they'd been homeless? And that she'd sacrificed so much for her brother? It only made him love her more. And made him more upset with himself for treating her as badly as he had.

All the comments Jackson had made in the past about his sister protecting him and doing what she needed to do made a lot more sense. Blade didn't know why the authorities hadn't knocked on her door before now. She was using her social security number to pay taxes, and she'd obviously given it to human resources at her job. And she had a driver's license. She wasn't exactly hiding.

But the more he thought about it, the more he realized *Wendy* thought she was hiding. She was acting as if she was some big bad criminal. No friends, flying under the radar, keeping mum on basic details about her and her brother.

What she didn't seem to realize was that she hadn't been caught because it was likely that no one was looking. Thousands of kids are missing around the country. Too many for any specific state to focus on looking for just one without just a good reason. Their entire fight was based on a false assumption on her part—that if someone knew where she was, they'd come and arrest her and take Jackson away.

Blade didn't know how, but he was going to do everything he could to fix this for her.

But first, he'd apologize. Then apologize again. He'd keep doing it as long as he needed to until she accepted that he was sincerely sorry for what he'd said and done. There was no other option than for her to forgive him because he couldn't live without her. Didn't want to. He loved her. Totally and all-encompassing.

CHAPTER FOURTEEN

W endy wearily climbed into the bleachers at the high school gym. She was exhausted. Her schedule wasn't any different than it usually was, but working two jobs this week totally kicked her butt.

She knew it was because she didn't have Aspen to talk to. She'd gotten so used to decompressing every night by talking to him on the phone, that *not* having that was affecting her more than she was comfortable with.

She missed him.

He'd been a dick to her, but then again, she'd been less than honest with him.

She understood why he was so upset. He'd taken a risk and told her about his job as a Delta Force soldier, and she wouldn't even tell him how old she was. But she'd been hiding it for so long now, it was second nature. Besides, the last thing she wanted to do was drag him into her mess. If the authorities found out he knew her secrets, they'd punish him too.

She was more sad about the entire situation than anything else. She wanted to go to his condo and apologize, but he'd been *so* mad. Wendy wasn't sure he'd even open the door once he found out she was standing on the other side.

She didn't do conflict well, something Jackson was always telling her she needed to work on. When Aspen started to get mad at her, she'd just frozen up. She'd wanted to tell him that she was protecting her brother, and him, but she couldn't get the words out. Then he'd turned cold and had left the room.

Settling on the highest bench in the gym, Wendy put her elbows on her legs and rested her chin on her hands, staring down at the setup for the robotics demonstration. Today was more for fun than an actual competition. Four different teams were there, and their robots had a series of about ten tasks to perform. They started out easy and progressively got more and more difficult. Jackson was convinced the robot his team had made would easily be able to do whatever was assigned. They were still working on the robotic arm they'd been constructing, but the competition for that wasn't for another few months.

Thinking about the prosthetic arm made her sad all over again, because she realized that Aspen's friend,

Fish, was supposed to be in town soon. She couldn't remember exactly when it was Aspen said he'd be there. But he wouldn't be coming to the school to speak to the robotics club anymore. Not when she and Aspen weren't even talking. That sucked. Jackson had been so excited too.

Wendy wasn't paying attention to her surroundings and was startled when someone sat down in front of her. At first, she was irritated; there were plenty of empty seats—but then she looked at who was sitting there.

It was a man. A very *big* man.

She jerked in surprise when another man sat next to her.

For a moment, she panicked slightly, but when neither of the men did anything aggressive or otherwise threatened her, she took another look at them.

The one in front of her had turned so he was straddling the bench. He was extremely tall. She figured he was probably about a foot taller than she was. He had short dark hair and his skin was also dark, as if he had some sort of exotic background in his lineage. He gave her a slight chin lift in greeting—and suddenly she realized that he had to be one of Aspen's friends. He carried himself in the same way. He seemed very alert, and she had no doubt he knew exactly who was sitting where in the large gym.

The man sitting next to her wasn't as tall, but he

exuded the same sort of competence as the other one. When she glanced at him, he had his eyes on her, as if she was the only person in the room. It was a little unnerving, but she'd seen Aspen do the exact same thing. He was also muscular and had brown hair and dark eyes.

Both men were good-looking, but she definitely wasn't in the market for a man, and therefore didn't care much what they looked like.

"Um...hi?" she said tentatively.

The man next to her held out his hand. "Hi, Wendy. I'm Ghost. And that's Coach. We're friends with Blade."

"Yeah, I figured," Wendy said as she shook his hand.

When he didn't say anything else, she asked, "What are you doing here?"

"We're here to watch Jackson's thing," Coach said.

Wendy's brows drew down. "But you don't know him."

"Sure we do," Ghost said. "We helped Blade out when he was teaching him how to defend himself and his girlfriend."

"Oh." Wendy wasn't sure what to say to that. She'd heard Jackson talking about Aspen's friends who had shown up to train with them, but hadn't paid much attention.

A thought struck her—these guys must be Special Forces soldiers too. Suddenly she felt nervous. She wasn't sure what to say or do. She didn't want to blab anything she wasn't supposed to, but she didn't want to be rude either.

"Relax, Wendy," Coach said as he turned and leaned his elbows back on the bench beside her, looking down at the course set up on the gym floor. "We aren't here to cause any problems."

She wanted to ask why they were *really* there, but wasn't brave enough. Maybe they didn't know she and Aspen had broken up? Crap.

After an awkward silence, Ghost leaned forward, rested his elbows on his knees and said, "Blade fucked up. He knows it, we know it, and you know it. The question is, are you going to continue to make both of you suffer for it, or are you going to talk to him about what happened?"

Wendy flinched. That answered the question of whether they knew they'd had a fight. It was bad enough that *she* knew she'd overreacted, but it was even worse that Aspen had talked to his friends about what had happened.

"He didn't tell us anything," Ghost said, as if he could read her mind. "That's not the kind of man he is. He admitted that he'd said some shit he didn't mean and wished he could take back, and you were pissed at him. Rightly so. That's it. But believe me, when I tell you, he's devastated about it."

Wendy looked at him in shock.

Ghost went on. "I'm his friend, but I'm also his team leader. His head hasn't been in his work this week. He's lagged behind on our runs, he doesn't banter back and forth with us like usual, and when we were on standby to head out for a mission, he was distracted and not 'present' when we discussed possible scenarios as to what might happen."

"You were on standby for a mission?" Wendy asked quietly.

"Yeah. Just got the word yesterday that we weren't going…this time. But then again, we could get a call ten minutes from now that the situation has changed and we'd be wheels up within the hour."

Wendy thought about that and cringed. She obviously hadn't really understood what being a Delta Force soldier meant. Of *course* they could be called up at a moment's notice. If someone was kidnapped, if there was an uprising, or a terrorist needed to be taken out… she assumed that was the kind of thing Aspen and his friends did.

She'd been naïve, thinking only about the fact he was in the Army, not the specifics of what that meant. Aspen and the men in front of her put their lives on the line every single time they were sent on a mission.

It made her refusal to tell him how old she was seem silly now.

"Here's the thing," Coach said quietly. "Blade likes you. A hell of a lot. He wants to apologize. To talk to you. That's all you need to do. Talk. If you guys can't work out whatever happened, okay. But as his friend—one who has seen how much he's suffered this week—I'm asking if you'll please give him a chance to tell you how sorry he is."

Wendy swallowed, then said, "He was really upset with me, and I can't blame him. But I don't do well with conflict. He got mad and it was as if I literally couldn't talk. If he starts yelling at me, I'm going to react the same way."

Ghost reached out and put his hand on her knee. It didn't feel sexual in the least. He was treating her as a friend.

"He's not going to get mad. He'd like to talk to you right now. Here. If you want, we can sit nearby. Not near enough to hear what you're talking about, but we'll be able to read your body language. We can intervene if we think it's not going well."

Wendy wasn't sure she was ready to talk to Aspen, but really, here and now was a good solution. Besides, they both needed to move on. Good or bad. She needed to know if they could salvage things between them or if they might as well call it quits for good. "Okay. Should I call him?"

"No need," Ghost said and gestured to the door of the gym.

Wendy looked up and saw Aspen standing just inside the door. He was staring at where she was sitting with his friends. His hands were in his pockets, and he looked as unsure as she'd ever seen him.

"Ready?" Coach asked softly.

Wendy looked down at the gym. Jackson's team wasn't up yet. They were going to go last. She had time to talk to Aspen before it was his turn. She nodded nervously.

Ghost lifted a hand and gave Aspen some sort of signal and he immediately pushed off from the wall and headed up the bleachers toward them.

Ghost and Coach stood and moved to the side.

Within moments, Aspen was there.

"We'll be over here," Ghost said, gesturing to the right.

Wendy took a deep breath and nodded.

Aspen sat next to her, leaving at least two feet of space between them. She appreciated him not crowding her, but hated the distance at the same time. God, she was a mess.

"Hi, Wen," he said softly.

"Hey." She had absolutely no idea where to start or what to say.

She needn't have worried.

"I'm sorry," he said immediately. "I was a dick and shouldn't have pushed you so hard. We'd had the most amazing afternoon ever, then I went and ruined it."

"It wasn't you. I should've just answered your question."

He shrugged. "If it means anything, it wasn't so much that you wouldn't tell me how old you were, it was more that I knew you were hiding something from me, and I hated that. Every time I asked you something and you deflected the question, I got more and more frustrated. Then we made love and I thought I'd broken down those barriers. When I realized that I hadn't, it hurt, and I took it out on you when I shouldn't have. You should know, I feel closer to you than anyone in my entire life, including my sister. What we did, what we shared, had broken down all *my* barriers. It's why I told you about being a Delta. Then, when you wouldn't even share how old you were, it hurt. Bad. I lashed out and said things I'll never forgive myself for saying."

"I'm twenty-seven," Wendy said softly.

"I know."

Her head whipped around and she stared at him. All sorts of scenarios about how he found out her age ran through her mind. Her breathing sped up and she began to have a panic attack. If he'd searched for her online, or if he'd contacted someone in law enforcement and they knew where she was and what she'd done, she might lose Jackson again! She couldn't do it. She—

"Easy, sweetheart," Aspen said, putting his hand behind her neck and gently urging her to lean over. He'd scooted over while she was panicking and was now right at her side. "Slow down your breathing. You're okay.

Jackson came to talk to me yesterday. That's how I know. He told me everything."

Wendy sat up at that, noting that Aspen still had his hand on her nape. The heavy weight felt good there. "What?"

"Apparently, he was pissed at me and came over to my condo to tell me off. He told me how old you were, how old *he* was, and what happened after your folks died. I'm so sorry, Wendy. So sorry that happened to you, and you were put in that situation. It's not fair, and the system definitely let you and your brother down."

Wendy didn't care about him knowing what she'd done. It wasn't important at the moment. "He told you about that night?"

Aspen stared at her for a beat, as if trying to read her mind. "Yeah. He told me about the bipolar kid, and what he did to him and the others, and how you came in like a Valkyrie and kicked his ass and saved them all."

Wendy was shocked. She couldn't be more shocked if Aspen had told her he was married with twelve kids and couldn't be with her after all. "He's only talked to me about that night once," she said softly. "And even then, I knew he was leaving stuff out. I didn't want to push. He had nightmares for weeks. Months. He wet his bed for at least a year after we left. You're *serious*? He told you what happened in that basement?"

She saw Aspen's jaw tighten and his nostrils flare as

he understood what she was saying. "Did he ever talk to a counselor?"

Wendy huffed out a breath. "No. I was afraid someone would find out that I wasn't eighteen, I'd stolen him, and he'd be taken away again. There was no way he was going to survive being put in another foster home, even if it was loving and wonderful. He clung to me and wouldn't let me out of his sight for weeks. We went everywhere together for the longest time. I can't believe he told you," she said with a slight shake of her head.

Aspen's fingers grazed along her jaw as he removed his hand from her nape. He scooted a little closer and took her hand in both of his and held it tightly on his thigh. "He told me because he was defending you. He wanted to make sure I understood how badly I'd fucked up. He wanted me to know how loyal and protective you are. And I have to say, he did a hell of a job. I'd already come to the conclusion that I said all the wrong things that day. Hurtful things that if I could take back, I would. But I can't. All I can do is apologize and tell you it won't happen again."

Wendy shrugged.

"Look at me," Aspen begged.

She didn't want to, but she turned her head toward him and lifted her gaze to his.

"I swear to God it won't happen again. I don't care how old you are. I don't care how old Jackson is. I don't care what you did when you were sixteen, except to say that I'm proud as I could be of you. All I care about is that you forgive me and that we can move on from this.

"I love you, Wendy Tucker. Twenty-seven, thirty-one, seventy-eight. If your past comes back to haunt you, I'll move heaven and earth to make sure Jackson is safe and you have the best representation possible. You aren't alone anymore. You've got me and my friends at your back."

"Aspen..." Wendy choked out, not sure what she wanted to say. But he didn't give her a chance, simply continued blowing her mind.

"There'll be times I can't physically be here for you, but that doesn't mean you're alone. You've met my sister and Emily. You haven't met the other women yet, but when we get sent on a mission, they band together until we're home. I know it's asking a lot, but I'm begging for your forgiveness. I was an asshole. A grade-A dick and I said things I didn't mean. I'm sorry. I'm *so* sorry. Do you think you can at least give me a chance to show you it'll never happen again? That I'll never fly off the handle like that in the future? Will you ever be able to trust me?"

His words were sweet, and Wendy knew she'd replay them over and over in her head for years to come. But she was still fixated on those three words he'd thrown out there so easily as if he'd said them to her hundreds of times before. "You love me? How is that possible?"

"How is it *not* possible?" he countered. "From the moment I picked up that telephone all those months ago and heard your voice, I was hooked. Then I met you, and you blew all my expectations out of the water. You're gracious and more forgiving than an asshole like me deserves. You've forgiven me not once, but twice now. There won't be a need for a third. Oh, I'll do stupid shit like forget to pick up something at the grocery store or leave beer cans lying around after a night in with the guys, but I swear to you that I'll never hurt you like I've done thus far in our relationship.

"I don't expect you to say it back, I haven't earned that right yet, but I wanted you to know where I stood. That this isn't about my ego or simply wanting to get back in your good graces so I can get you in my bed again. I love you, Wendy. This past week has been unbearable. I've missed you something awful. Those late-night talks of ours somehow became more important to me than anything else, and not having them made my nights depressing as hell. Do you think you can possibly forgive me? Give me another chance?"

How could she not? Wendy nodded. "I've missed you too."

"Thank fuck," Aspen said with a whoosh of air and leaned into her, putting his arms around her and hugging her tightly.

How long they clung to each other, Wendy didn't

know, but after a while, she heard Ghost say from nearby, "Jackson's group is up."

Wendy pulled back and saw that Ghost and Coach had scooted closer and were watching the action on the gym floor.

Aspen picked up Wendy's hand and kissed the back of it reverently before putting it on his thigh again, covering it with his own.

"Is cheering allowed at this sort of thing?" he asked with a twinkle in his eye.

Wendy smiled at him. "Yup."

Without warning, Aspen turned his head and yelled, "Go get 'em, Jack!"

Jackson looked into the stands where they were sitting and beamed up at them. He gave them a thumb's up, then turned his attention back to the controller in front of him.

Wendy took a deep breath through her nose and let it out in relief. She thought she'd lost Aspen forever. But not only was he there, he'd said he loved her. And Jackson had told him what he'd gone through at the hands of that sick teenager all those years ago. She still didn't know what was going to happen to her, or if the authorities would catch up to her, but for the first time in a really long while, she didn't feel alone.

And that felt amazing.

CHAPTER FIFTEEN

"Not like that," Wendy said with a laugh, pulling the spoon out of Blade's hand. "You have to mix it like this." And she proceeded to show him the "right" way to mix cake batter.

Blade didn't give a shit how to stir. What he *did* give a shit about was the fact that Wendy was standing in his kitchen in his condo, making a mess. It had been so long since he'd done more than pop in a microwave meal or grill a steak that he was happy to see flour on the counter and floor, egg shells in the sink, and about a thousand dishes that needed to be washed.

Wendy laughed as he moved behind her and pulled her into him. His hands rested on her belly as she stirred the cake batter. He put his chin on her shoulder and simply held her as she worked.

The last three weeks had been a learning experience

for them both. He learned when to back off on his questions and she was learning how to open up. They were both relearning trust. Blade tried not to take it personally when she changed the subject or evaded answering his questions about her life over the last ten years, and Wendy was slowly realizing that Blade wasn't asking so he could mock her or get information to use against her. He was genuinely trying to get to know her.

One night, she and Jackson were over at his condo visiting. They were watching television and Blade asked the teenager what he wanted to do with his life. A lively discussion ensued about the benefit of doing his first two years at the local community college versus going to a four-year university right away. Wendy had excused herself, and when she hadn't returned several minutes later, Blade went looking for her.

He found her in his bedroom, sitting on his bed with tears streaming down her face. Alarmed, he'd immediately asked what was wrong, but she simply shook her head. Instead of getting upset with her, he took her into his arms and rocked her. Eventually, her tears slowed, then dried up, and she told him that she felt like a failure for not even having her high school diploma. That she was scared to even register to take the GED for fear of someone finding out what she'd done and arresting her.

Blade had explained that her information was already out there. That if the authorities really wanted to find her, it wouldn't be hard. Especially since she'd been filing taxes for years. *That* had triggered another bout of panic. She'd stared up at him with scared eyes, but he held her in his arms and told her he'd always be there for her. Eventually, she'd calmed down, apologized for not telling him she was upset, and they'd rejoined Jackson.

Her brother knew something was going on, but to his credit, he didn't bring it up, trusting Blade to do the right thing when it came to his sister.

They hadn't made love since getting back together, and Blade was okay with that. The time never seemed right. Their fight had seemed to bring them back to square one and he was moving slowly, making sure Wendy knew he was on her side and always would be. They'd worked through what had happened that awful afternoon and Blade didn't think Wendy was holding on to any residual feelings of resentment or anger toward him, but he could tell sex wasn't exactly at the forefront of her mind.

And that was okay.

They'd fallen back on their routine from before that afternoon. Talking on the phone and texting. They'd had dates with and without Jackson. They were getting to know each other without any secrets between them. Blade told her what he could about being a Special Forces solider and Wendy opened up more and more about what she and Jackson had experienced over the last decade.

She was amazing.

Tough as nails and ferocious as a lion defending her cub.

Blade's love for her was as strong as ever, but he hadn't said the words since that day in the gym.

"How was work today?" he asked as Wendy stirred the batter.

"Pretty good. I talked to my boss like you suggested and she was super supportive about me applying for the supervisor position. I'd be in charge of ten aides. Scheduling and performance evaluations and stuff like that. It would mean less time with the residents for me, but I'd still be able to work with them part-time."

"And the pay?"

She smiled up at him. "Is enough that I could quit the call-center job."

Blade beamed at her. "So, we'd have more time to spend together."

She rolled her eyes.

"Right?" he insisted, moving his hands to her sides and tickling her.

She shrieked and tried to wiggle away from him. She was holding the wooden spoon so she couldn't grab his hands and try to pry them away from her sides.

"Say it!" he teased.

"Okay, okay, I'd have more time to spend with you!"

Holding her to him, Blade buried his nose in the side of her neck and nuzzled her. "Damn straight you would."

She sighed and leaned against him affectionately.

"I'm proud of you," Blade told her softly.

"Thanks. Me too. I've come a long way from the thug of a teenager I was to now," she joked.

"You weren't a thug," Blade said. "You were sowing your wild oats."

Wendy chuckled. "I doubt my parents would have agreed. They were at their wits end with me."

"Do you miss them?"

"Every damn day. I'm sad they never got to see what a great man Jackson has become. I wish they could see me too. I hope they'd be proud of me."

"They would be," Blade said without hesitation. "How could they not?"

As usual, when things got intense, Wendy changed the subject. "Have you heard from Fish?"

Blade nodded. The trip he'd planned to their area hadn't happened because his new prosthetic arm wasn't quite ready. Jackson and his friends had been disappointed, but Fish had Skyped with them one afternoon, and that seemed to be just as good for the teenagers. Blade had been amazed at the depth of their questions for Fish and how advanced the robotic arm they were making had been.

"He's not sure when he'll be coming out, but when

he does, he said he definitely wants to meet with your brother and his friends. He was highly impressed with what they were doing."

"Cool," she said with a proud smile.

"When do you have to leave?" Blade asked. He wanted her to stay the night, but hadn't pushed.

"The party Jackson is at is supposed to go until around midnight. I told him he could stay the entire time as long as he came home right after."

"Is Jenny there?"

Wendy chuckled. "*Everyone* is there."

"I'm assuming this isn't a school-sanctioned event," Blade said dryly.

"Nope. But I'm not worried about Jackson. He knows how to stay out of trouble. I told you before that I started letting him taste beer and wine and stuff. He's seen some of his friends get shit-faced drunk and how stupid they acted. It turned him off. He might have a beer or two, but he won't get drunk."

"And that's just one more way that you've done an amazing job of raising your brother," Blade told her.

Wendy put down the spoon and turned in his embrace. She lifted her arms and put them around his neck. "Most of the time I have no idea what I'm doing."

"Something else to be proud of," he told her with a smile.

"Anyway, can you take me home around eleven-thirty? That way I can be home when he gets there."

"Of course." He glanced at his watch and saw it was nine-thirty. "We've got time to watch a movie if you wanted."

Wendy looked up at him for the longest time. He tried to read her mood, but was having trouble doing so.

"I want to make love...but I'm scared."

"Of what?" Blade kept his tone even and soothing, even though his dick immediately got hard at the thought of being inside her once again.

"Of saying the wrong thing. Of screwing up like I did last time."

"Oh, sweetheart. We've been over this. That wasn't your fault. It was mine."

She shook her head.

"We'll get there," Blade said. "When it seems right for both of us. How about we put this cake in the oven, pop in a movie, then make out until the cake burns and it's time for me to take you home?"

She chuckled. "Sounds perfect."

Blade kissed the tip of her nose and hugged her for a second. "I'll go choose the movie, you finish up in here. And don't do the dishes. I'll take care of them tomorrow."

"But they'll be all crusty and gross tomorrow," she protested.

"Leave them, woman," Blade said with a scowl, although he ruined it by laughing at the frown on her face.

"Fine, whatever," she grumped.

Smiling, Blade went to the other room to pick out something extremely boring so they could make out and not be distracted.

"And don't pick a military movie!" Wendy called when he was out of sight.

Grinning, Blade decided on *Patton*. He'd seen it a million times and knew Wendy wouldn't be interested in the slightest. It'd be the perfect background as they made out like teenagers.

———

Jackson stood in the middle of his friends with an arm around Jenny. They'd been at the party for a while now. David and Patrick were there with the girls they were dating, and Rob was around somewhere. He and Jenny had hung out with the guys on the lacrosse team for a while, but they'd migrated to standing with the others from his robotics club in the last half hour.

Jenny had seen a few of her friends here and there, but for the most part, the kids at the party were juniors and seniors. Jackson was somewhat impressed that people weren't getting shit-faced drunk, but were simply hanging out, feeling mellow and having a good time.

There were a few people smoking pot, but they were mostly kids he didn't know and didn't hang out with.

"Any word on when Fish will be in town?" Dan

asked. He was the captain of the robotics club, and he'd been integral in coming up with improvements to their robotic arm after talking with the Army veteran via Skype.

"Unfortunately, no," Jackson said. "But he told my sister's boyfriend that he was willing to answer any further questions we had for him."

The others were excited about the prospect and began a conversation about what else they wanted to ask the veteran and whether their latest plans for the robotic arm would actually work.

Jackson felt Jenny shiver and leaned down. "Cold?"

"A little," she told him, looking up at him with her big green eyes. He'd been half in love with her the second he'd seen her. Her red hair fell past her shoulders in waves and her pale skin had freckles all over it. He didn't know he was a sucker for freckles until he'd met her.

She was a lot younger than he was, more than she or her parents knew, but Jackson was moving slowly with her. She was inexperienced and a little naïve, but he loved that about her. He hadn't pushed her to do anything she was uncomfortable with, but earlier that night, they'd made out behind one of the cars in the lot, and it had been amazing. He'd kissed girls before, had even had sex not too long after Wendy had given him the condom talk, but nothing had affected him as deeply as simply kissing Jenny. She was special, and the fact that she was with him made Jackson feel both scared to death he would let her down somehow and proud as fuck at the same time.

When they were kissing, she'd taken his hand in hers and put it over her breast. Jackson had gotten hard the second he'd felt her small nipple pushing against his palm. He hadn't done more than squeeze her tit over her shirt, but even that had made him feel ten feet tall. She'd trusted him not to hurt her and not go any further than she wanted.

"You wanna go home?" he asked, rubbing his nose against hers affectionately.

She smiled up at him. "Do you think we can just go somewhere quiet and talk for a while?"

Jackson shifted until he was holding her hand. He squeezed it and said, "That sounds great." He hoped she might want to kiss a bit more before he took her home as well.

He bid farewell to his friends and looked for Rob. He was their ride home. He saw him with a group of other boys. He led Jenny that way and told Rob they'd be hanging out near the entrance to the parking area. It was really just a large field that had been cordoned off, but it served its purpose...namely, to keep the cars away from the fires and the people.

Rob nodded and said he'd be ready to go in about thirty minutes. Looking at his watch and seeing it was eleven, that worked for Jackson.

He led Jenny over to the parking area and gestured to a large log on its side. It had obviously been placed there as a barrier, but it was a perfect seat. He straddled it and encouraged Jenny to do the same. As soon as she'd sat facing him, Jackson scooted as close to her as he could, pulling her legs over his own. The position was intimate and cozy. He locked his hands together at the small of her back, giving her stability as she perched on the log.

They'd been sitting there, talking and kissing, for about fifteen minutes when Jackson heard something behind them. He turned to see what it was, expecting to see Rob, but was knocked off the log when something hit him in the side.

Because Jenny was mostly sitting on his lap, she went flying as well. Jackson ended up halfway on top of her on the hard grass and dirt. He moaned in pain but immediately shifted so he wasn't crushing her.

The second he moved, someone hauled him upright with a hand gripping the back of his shirt.

Jackson's first thought was of Jenny. To protect her.

Instinctively, he bent his leg and kicked back at the person holding him. Whoever it was fell to the ground with a groan, but instantly more hands were there, grabbing at him.

Jackson knew he was in over his head immediately. He tried to do what Aspen and his friends had taught him, but there were just too many hands hitting him. Too many feet kicking him.

But the tipping point was the baseball bat that someone kept using to hit him in the side.

He fell to the ground and tried to get up, but it was no use. He curled into a ball to protect his kidneys and head, but it didn't stop the beating. The guys kicking his ass were relentless in their assault.

Jenny screeched then, but the sound was immediately cut off.

Looking up, Jackson saw Lars holding her against his chest. He had his hand over her mouth and was smirking down at him.

"Back off, boys," he ordered, and immediately the guys beating on him stopped. They didn't move away, as if they were afraid he was going to leap up and try to get to Jenny and Lars. Jackson couldn't catch his breath, and he knew moving was going to be extremely painful. But he couldn't just lie on the ground and let Lars hurt Jenny.

"Lookie what I found," Lars taunted. "A cute little freshman to have fun with."

"Leave her alone, asshole," Jackson growled, forcing himself up to his knees.

"What are you going to do about it?" Lars asked. "You can't even stand up. Some protector *you* are." He looked over at one of his friends and nodded.

Before Jackson could think to protect himself, the

boy with the bat—he thought it was Chuck—hit him again.

Doubling over in pain, Jackson fell once more, panting, trying to catch his breath. It felt as if he wanted to cry, but it hurt too badly for any tears to form.

Lars leaned over Jackson, still holding Jenny. "Me and the boys are going to have us our own private party since we weren't invited to this one. We're gonna show your girlfriend a *real* good time."

Jackson saw Jenny's beautiful green eyes, wide with terror, fill with tears as she struggled against Lars's hold. But at five feet three, she was no match for the man's superior height and strength.

Jackson felt helpless. He needed to get up. To help Jenny. To make sure Lars and his cronies didn't hurt her.

Lars stood upright and picked Jenny up off her feet. She tried to kick him, but he merely laughed. "Come on, boys. I think it's time we showed Jenny what a real man is like." And without another glance at Jackson, Lars spun on his heels, still holding the frantically struggling Jenny. He headed toward a beat-up old pickup truck on the edge of the lot, not far from where Jackson had been kissing Jenny.

The four guys each kicked and punched Jackson another couple times for good measure, then ran laughing after Lars.

Jackson lay on the ground in despair, panting for a moment. His vision blurred from the blood dripping into his eye from a cut over it. He couldn't quite catch his breath, but he forced his aches and pains back. He watched as one of the guys got into Lars's truck and the others ran toward another pickup a few cars over.

He could see Lars in the cab of his truck, trying to kiss Jenny, and laughing as she continued to fight him.

A wave of hatred swept over Jackson, and he was moving before he'd even thought about it. He managed to get to his feet, even though he could only stand all hunched over, and with a hand over his kidney, he limped as fast as he could toward Lars's truck. Jenny was putting up the struggle of a lifetime against the two men, and as much as Jackson wanted to rip open the door and rescue her, he knew he was outnumbered, and he'd only get himself and Jenny hurt even more.

Seeing there was no tailgate on the truck, and a large tarp covering something in the back, he made a split-second decision. Jackson tried to be as quiet as he could —not that Lars would hear him over Jenny's shrieks of terror and his own evil laughter—and eased his aching body onto the truck bed, covering himself with the foul-smelling tarp.

He would've laughed at the irony that Lars, the piece of shit, was hauling a load of crap around in the back of his truck, but he was too scared, worried about Jenny, pissed off, and hurting to even crack a smile.

He'd gotten settled not a moment too soon because the truck engine started and Lars peeled out of the parking area seconds later. Jackson moved slightly so he could lift the back of the tarp and see where they were going, then reached into his front pocket for his phone. For once in his life, he was thankful that Wendy hadn't been able to afford the huge, expensive smartphone he'd wanted. It wouldn't've fit in his pocket and would probably be lying on the ground back where he'd been beaten up.

Making sure to keep the phone under the tarp so the light on the screen wouldn't alert Lars or his buddy if they happened to look behind them, Jackson clicked on his sister's name.

He needed help. Immediately. And there was only one person, or group of people, that could help him and Jenny right now.

———

Blade ignored his raging hard-on and concentrated on making sure Wendy was pleasured. She was sitting astride his lap and they'd been making out for the last twenty minutes or so. At first, they'd only been kissing, but as time went on, and she got more and more aroused, they'd progressed to her shirt coming off and Blade's lips on her tits.

She was rubbing herself against his erection and moaning in satisfaction, and Blade had never felt as relieved as he did right then. He'd been afraid she'd never be able to let go enough to trust him to make her feel good again. But at the moment, she obviously wasn't thinking about anything but her pleasure.

Her hands were in his hair, gripping tight. Grabbing at him when she wanted him to suck harder and pulling on his hair when he nipped her a bit roughly. He grinned. She loved his mouth on her. He'd skipped this the last and only time they were together, concentrating more on her juicy pussy and the delicious taste of her there. Mentally rebuking himself for his shortsightedness, Blade closed his eyes and did his best to see if he could make her orgasm with only his mouth on her tits and her dry humping his lap.

Just when he thought she was going to go over the edge, her phone rang, killing the mood.

Wendy jerked in his arms and opened her eyes. She didn't seem to be all there, and Blade smiled. "Easy, sweetheart. It's just the phone."

Keeping hold of her, Blade reached over and grabbed her cell off the table next to the couch they were both sitting on. Looking at it, he held it up and said, "It's Jackson."

"Will you answer it?" she asked, sounding almost sleepy, but he knew it was still her arousal coursing through her system.

"You got it. Hey, Jackson, the party over?"

"Need...help."

Blade immediately tensed. He sat up straight and urged Wendy to stand.

The passion wiped off her face in an instant.

"What's wrong?" Blade asked Jackson.

"Lars. Beat me. Up. They. Have Jenny."

His words were staccato and he sounded as if he had marbles in his mouth. Blade could also hear a lot of wind noise.

"Where are you?" He stood even as he asked and was reaching for his own cell phone to text the guys for help.

"What's happening?" Wendy asked from next to him.

"In the back of...his truck. Hiding. Don't know where," Jackson said. "Ask Wendy. She'll track me."

Blade immediately looked at Wendy and said, "Your brother's in trouble. I need to find him. He said you could track him? What does that mean?"

He had to give Wendy credit, she didn't freak out. Didn't start yelling at him to give her the phone. The blood drained from her face, but she immediately said, "Find-a-phone. It's an app. We can both see where the other is as long as the phone is on."

Blade nodded and sighed in relief. Putting the phone back up to his mouth, he told Jackson, "Don't turn your phone off, whatever you do. I'm getting ahold of the others. We're on our way."

"Five guys...two trucks. Hurry, Aspen. They've got Jenny. Want to hurt her."

"I'm coming, bud," Blade said, hoping the kid could hear the conviction in his tone. "Stay hidden. Don't get yourself more hurt than you already are."

"Don't care about me. It's Jenny...I'm worried about," Jackson said.

Blade understood that. He didn't like it, but he understood. "I'm going to hang up, but I'm always here. If something changes, call me. I'm coming for you both, hear me?"

"Yeah. Tell Wendy I love her."

Blade clenched his teeth. "Will do. Hang in there, Jackson." And with that, Blade clicked off the phone and held it out to the scared woman in front of him. "Pull up the app," he said.

Wendy had thrown her shirt back on and immediately began clicking on her phone. Blade pushed send on the text he'd typed to Ghost and clicked on Truck's number.

Wendy held out the phone and Blade nodded his thanks.

"Hey, Blade, what's up? It's late."

"I need your help. Wendy's brother has been beaten up and they've kidnapped his girlfriend."

"On my way. Where are we going?" Truck said without hesitation.

Blade looked down at Wendy's phone and eyed the

app. "Looks like those assholes are taking her out to the northeast side of post."

"In the restricted training area?" Truck asked.

"Looks like it. Jack crawled into the bed of the truck and I've got his position pulled up on Wendy's phone. She has an app."

"Find-a-phone?" Truck asked.

"Yeah, that's it."

"I've got that myself," Truck mused. "Where are we meeting? You've contacted the others?"

"Sent Ghost a text."

"I'll call the commander and give him a heads-up and get ahold of the others on my way. We'll go through the back gate, assuming that's how these guys went too. Meet there and consolidate to go in together?"

"Yeah. Jackson said there were five guys with Jenny."

Truck growled, "Assholes."

"Yeah," Blade agreed.

"I'm on my way," Truck said again, then hung up.

Blade turned his attention to Wendy. He didn't have a lot of time, but he needed to reassure her before he left. "We've got this," he told her, taking her shoulders in his hands. He could feel her trembling under him. "I'm going to find your brother and bring him home to you safe and sound."

Wendy nodded and brought her hands up to his face. "Is it Lars?"

Blade nodded grimly.

"Dammit. I knew him disappearing wasn't a good sign. I told Jackson he wasn't going to just let things go. And he has Jenny?"

Blade nodded again. "I gotta go, but will you do me a favor?"

"What?"

"I'm going to call my sister and ask her to come over here. I don't want you to be alone."

"I'm okay."

"Please, sweetheart. Let me do this."

"But it's late."

"She's up. Truck is calling Beatle and the others now. I have to take your phone with me, so I won't have a way of letting you know everything is fine once we get to Jackson. But if Casey's here, I can call *her*."

"Oh...that makes sense. Okay."

Blade leaned down and kissed her hard and fast. "Jackson said he loves you—but you should know, I've got this."

A tear fell from her eye and trickled down her cheek, but she didn't move to wipe it away. "I know."

Blade hated that tear. Hated that at the moment, he couldn't take her in his arms and comfort her. He kissed her cheek, tasting the salt left behind, and stepped back. He nodded at her, then spun and headed for the parking lot and his Jeep. He was glad he had the vehicle; they'd need it to navigate the back forty of Fort Hood. There weren't a lot of roads back there and they'd need the four-wheel drive.

The other thought that went through his head was that if Lars was taking Jenny back there, he didn't have plans to return with her. No one wandered into that area on a whim.

There were thousands and thousands of acres of land on the Army post. It'd be easy to rape and kill the teenager and hide her body where it would never be found.

Thank God Jackson had the wherewithal to get in the back of the truck. If they were lucky, the app would lead the Deltas straight to them and give Lars and his gang the surprise of a lifetime. He didn't know it, but he was heading straight into an area the Delta Force team knew like the back of their hand. They'd done their share of training there.

Tonight, Lars's reign of terror would end once and for all.

"Hang in there, buddy," Blade murmured, thinking about Jackson as he headed out of the condo complex and raced toward one of the many back entrances to the post, his eyes alternating between the road in front of him and the app on Jenny's phone. The blinking red dot his only comfort at the moment.

CHAPTER SIXTEEN

Wendy paced nervously. Time seemed to be moving extremely slow. Not knowing what was going on was killing her. If anything happened to Jackson, she didn't know what she would do. He might be her brother, but right now it truly felt as if he were her child.

A knock on the door startled her out of her musings and she went to answer it. Standing on Aspen's doorstep was his sister. But she wasn't alone. There were five other women with her. Wendy recognized a couple, but not all of them.

Numbly, she opened the door.

Casey immediately pulled her into her arms. The hug was just what Wendy needed. She grabbed hold of Aspen's sister and held on as if she'd never let her go.

She felt them being shuffled backward, but didn't release her.

"It'll be okay," Casey said soothingly. "The guys got this."

Taking a deep breath and getting herself under control, Wendy eventually pulled back.

"Here," someone said from next to her.

Wendy turned and saw a brunette about her height holding out a tissue.

"Thanks," Wendy said and wiped her tears and blew her nose.

"Come on," Casey said, hooking her arm with Wendy's. "Let's go sit and I'll introduce you to everyone."

Having no doubt the other women were the wives and girlfriends of Aspen's teammates, Wendy docilely followed Casey into the living room. She sat in the middle of the couch and Casey plunked down next to her while Emily sat on the other side. Casey latched onto Wendy's hand and Emily rested a hand on her thigh.

Wendy felt surrounded...and loved. She'd felt alone ever since her parents had died. As if she had the weight of the world on her shoulders. But these six women, most of whom she didn't know, had managed to make the oppressive load of doom that hung around the room lift a bit with just their presence.

"You know Emily," Casey started, nodding at the pregnant woman next to her.

"Hi again," Wendy said.

"Hi," Emily returned. "Annie is spending the night at a friend's house tonight, otherwise she'd be here too."

Wendy nodded, and Casey went on. "So, from left to right. That's Rayne. She belongs to Ghost. They've been together the longest and she's kind of our matriarch."

There were subdued chuckles all around before Casey went on. "Harley is the tall drink of water in front of you. She's the oldest and smartest of us all. She designs video games and if you give her a computer, she'll be lost for hours."

"Blade told me about you," Wendy said softly. "Jackson would love to pick your brain."

And just like that, the tears were back. Simply saying her brother's name was enough to make her remember what was happening and why the women were there in the first place.

"Easy," Emily said in a soft tone.

Wendy tried to control herself and nodded.

"Kassie is the other prego chick. She's with Hollywood, and once you meet him, you'll understand his name. He's gorgeous and could definitely give ol' what's-his-name a run for his money for *People Magazine's* Sexiest Man Alive."

"How he took a second glance at me, I'll never know," Kassie said with a smile. "But now that he's mine, I'll cut a bitch if she even tries to take him from me."

Wendy wouldn't have believed she could smile, but that did it.

"And last, but certainly not least, is Mary. She's the short chick."

"Hey, I'm not that short," Mary protested.

Wendy had to disagree. She was pretty petite, at least compared to everyone around her. She had short hair with a streak of pink in it, and even though she wasn't as tall as her friends, there was something about Mary's countenance that made her the most intimidating of the bunch.

"Hi," Wendy told her and the others. "Thank you for coming over, although I'm not sure why you're all here."

"We're here to support you," Rayne said. "To hold your hand when you cry, to wait with you until we have more information. It's what we Army wives and girlfriends do."

Wendy was overwhelmed. "But you don't know me."

"But we know Blade," Kassie said.

"And in case you had any doubt, you are definitely a part of our group now," Casey said. "I've never seen my brother so enamored with a woman. He's dated, but he's never been serious about anyone before."

"Fletch said he was a major pain in the ass when you guys weren't talking."

"Oh, yeah, Coach wanted to wring his neck," Harley added.

"Truck told him to get his ass to your place and apologize before they had to knock some sense into him," Mary added.

Wendy smiled weakly at everyone—but all of a sudden, they weren't looking at her anymore. Everyone was staring at Mary.

"What?" the woman asked defensively.

"You've been hanging out with Truck?" Rayne asked, her brows arching in surprise.

Mary shrugged. "It's not like that. I just happened to see him the other day in passing."

Wendy realized that it wasn't just Rayne who seemed surprised to hear Mary had spent some time with Truck. She didn't know the dynamics of the group well enough to figure out why though.

"Can you tell us what happened?" Kassie asked Wendy, breaking the tension in the room.

Wendy nodded. Then took a deep breath and told the other women the whole story about Lars and his bullying.

The seven Delta Force operatives were traveling in two vehicles toward the small red dot on the map. Blade knew without the app, they never would've found

Jackson and the others in a timely manner. They were well into the restricted training grounds on the post. Lars and his friends had chosen well. It was pitch dark and no one would accidentally stumble upon them as they did whatever they had planned for poor Jenny.

Blade pushed down a little harder on the accelerator. The dot had stopped moving a couple minutes ago, and every minute that went by was another minute closer to Jenny being hurt—and possibly Jackson again.

"Everyone knows the plan, right?" Ghost asked, his voice low and deadly in the silence of the Jeep.

Ghost, Truck, and Beatle were in the Jeep with Blade, while Fletch, Hollywood, and Coach were following in Fletch's Highlander. They were all wearing their night-vision goggles so they could more effectively sneak up on Lars and the others. They were careening down the dirt road with their headlights off at a highly dangerous rate of speed.

Ghost had his phone on speaker and was communicating with Hollywood. They'd been discussing the best way to sneak up on, and take out, Lars and his gang.

"Affirmative," the soldiers in the other car said practically in tandem.

"The main unknown in this scenario is Jackson. He said there were five men and two vehicles. Blade, we've got the five covered, you're responsible for Jackson. Understand?"

Blade pressed his lips together and nodded. He

wanted Lars, but Ghost was smart enough to know better than to let him get anywhere near the punk. He'd kill the bastard and feel no remorse for it. His job was to get to Jackson and make sure he was safe and out of the way so the team could take down the kidnappers.

Truck's job was Jenny. He was the biggest and strongest of the group, and if he needed to manhandle someone in order to secure the girl, he would. He'd do whatever was necessary to get her out of the line of fire to safety.

"We're coming up to the coordinates. About half a mile dead ahead," Blade said as he took his foot off the accelerator. They needed to get as close as they could to the location without giving themselves away.

When they were within a quarter mile, he stopped his Jeep in the middle of the road. He noticed Fletch angled his car behind him, also blocking the road. Nodding, knowing if Lars or one of his friends tried to run, they'd have to slow down to go around their cars, giving them a shot to catch up, he climbed out.

Adrenaline was coursing through his veins and all Blade wanted to do was get to Jackson. To make sure he was safe. Wendy couldn't handle it if anything happened to her brother. He was going to make sure Jackson got back to her safe and sound. She was relying on him, and he wouldn't let her down.

Without a word, the team headed toward their targets. They moved swiftly through the scrub brush that this part of Texas was notorious for. They made no sound as they moved in on the five assholes who would dare kidnap and assault two teenagers minding their own business.

Blade again had the thought that this probably wasn't the first time this group of men had done this sort of thing. One didn't start a life of crime by kidnapping and gang-raping a girl.

No, they'd most certainly done this before. Perhaps taking their last helpless victim to this same exact spot.

Making a mental note to have their commander get in touch with the local cops about missing teenagers or women, Blade adjusted his night-vision goggles and moved faster to where the app said Jackson waited.

It was go time.

"What's taking so long?" Wendy grumbled. She'd gotten past the weepy stage; now she was anxious and angry that she hadn't heard anything. She hated not knowing what was going on. Hated not knowing if Jackson or Jenny was all right. Hated not knowing if Blade was hurt or not.

It was silly, all her concern should be for her brother, but she couldn't help worrying about Blade as well.

Yes, he was a badass Delta Force soldier, but bullets didn't care about that. He could still be shot, or beat up, or cut with a knife. She couldn't stop thinking about everything that could happen to him, and she couldn't stop those scenarios from playing over and over again in her mind.

"Stop worrying," Rayne ordered. Harley had pulled a laptop out of her bag and was at the dining room table clicking away at the keys. Kassie and Emily were sitting on one side of the couch, talking about babies and weird pregnancy cravings. Casey was baking something in the kitchen.

That left Mary and Rayne with her. Wendy paced, Mary was standing near the wall, and Rayne was sitting at the other end of the couch.

"I can't help it," Wendy said. "I keep imagining all the horrible things that could be happening."

"Yeah, I was like that the first few times Ghost and the others went on a mission. I knew better than most what actually happens on some of their missions."

"What do you mean?" Wendy asked.

Rayne went on to explain how she'd been caught in the middle of an Egyptian coup, and Ghost and the rest of the team had appeared as if out of nowhere to rescue her. "There I was, in Truck's arms, bleeding as we ran out of that government building, knowing someone was probably going to shoot us at any second. It was awful."

Wendy had stopped pacing and stared at Rayne with wide eyes. "Seriously?"

"Yup. Then the very next mission he went on, Ghost was hurt and didn't bother to tell me. I was pissed."

Mary chuckled. "That's an understatement, Raynie."

The two women smiled at each other. "I missed you," Rayne told her friend. "How come you've been avoiding me?"

"I haven't."

"Bullshit," Rayne said. "When you were sick, we were together every day. I held you as you puked into the toilet and even got in the shower with you to make sure you didn't keel over. And lately, I think I've seen you like twice in the last six months." Her voice lowered. "It's like I don't even know you anymore. I don't know how work is going, or how you're feeling. I *miss* you, Mare. We live in the same damn town and I miss you."

"I'm sorry," Mary said, her eyes downcast. "It's been a weird time for me."

"Just tell me you're done holding me at arm's length," Rayne insisted. "I want my best friend back."

"I'm done holding you at arm's length," Mary repeated. "The last thing I ever want to do is hold you back from the wonderful life you were meant to have."

Mary's confession seemed to upset Rayne, for some reason. "What does that mean?" Rayne asked.

"It means that you're practically married now," Mary said. "You have a life outside of me. After I got sick, I told you time and time again that you shouldn't wait for me to get married. That was something we agreed on one night when we were drunk and depressed. It's ridiculous now. You have Ghost and all the other women here. It's not just the two of us anymore."

Rayne sighed. "I know what you told me, but I really thought you and Truck were going to make it work. He loves you, Mare. I wasn't actually going to insist on us getting married together, but...after I saw you and Truck together? I really thought if I waited long enough, you guys would get together officially, and we really *could* have that double wedding ceremony."

"Raynie," Mary said softly, then pressed her lips together as if she was trying not to cry.

"I love you, Mare," Rayne said. "We've been friends forever, and I guess I'm finally realizing the harder I pushed you, the more you pulled away. That was my mistake. I'm sorry."

Wendy felt like an interloper. She didn't know what the history was between the two women, but felt a pang of jealousy that they had a friendship as close as they did. She'd always wanted that for herself, but had never been in a position to have it. She'd moved too much and had too many secrets. Not to mention being busy raising her kid brother. None of that was conducive to making lasting, close friendships.

"I love you too," Mary said in a low voice. "I promise I'm done keeping my distance."

The two women smiled at each other until Kassie said, "I think we should call the commander."

"I'm not sure," Rayne replied. "Ghost said we were only to call him in an emergency."

"I think this constitutes an emergency," Kassie argued. "Our men have been gone long enough to have found and taken care of those assholes by now. And even if they haven't, maybe he can give us an update."

"Does he even know what's going on?" Harley asked from the table.

"I don't know this commander guy, but Blade said Truck was going to call him," Wendy said.

"There. It's decided. I'll do it," Kassie said, pulling out her phone. "I'm pregnant and shouldn't have this stress." She smirked. "Besides, I think the commander is scared of me and Emily. He doesn't want us to go into premature labor or anything."

Everyone chuckled.

Several minutes later, Kassie hung up her phone with a sigh. "He doesn't know anything yet," she announced. "He said he'd make sure he told the guys to call as soon as they could."

Wendy sighed and plopped down on the floor, curling her arms around her drawn-up knees. "Do you guys think this place needs some color? Blade said he wouldn't mind if I spruced it up a bit. I could use your help to figure out what to buy. It'll keep my mind off of things."

"Hallelujah!" Casey cried as she entered the living room, throwing her arms up in the air in triumph. "I've been after him ever since he bought this place to jazz it up. He refused to let me help. He's obviously in love with you, Wendy. There's no way he'd invite you to decorate his precious condo if he wasn't."

Wendy blushed. He'd said that he loved her, but a part of her hadn't really believed it. Having his sister's confirmation went a long way toward chipping at the insecure part of her that taunted she wasn't good enough for Blade.

"So, you'll help?"

"Of course. Harley, we need to use your computer!" Casey told the other woman.

Harley rolled her eyes. "Whatever. Let me finish up this one line of code where the soldiers kick the asses of the scumbag terrorists who kidnapped a helpless teenager, then you can use it."

"She's a little bloodthirsty," Emily mock-whispered to Wendy.

Wendy couldn't help but smile. God, she wouldn't have made it through the waiting if these women hadn't come over. She liked them—all of them. Liked the dynamic between them all and how close they seemed. She only hoped she'd have the chance to continue to get to know them better and be a part of this close-knit group.

Blade crouched behind one of the pickups in the clearing and scowled. There were four men gathered around an injured and bleeding Jackson. The fifth man held Jenny in his arms, one hand over her mouth. She was struggling and crying, but she was no match for the man's strength.

Lars and his cronies were taunting and kicking Jackson, telling him how much they were going to enjoy Jenny and there was nothing he could do about it.

"We're going to take turns with her right in front of you, pretty boy. You'll be helpless to do a damn thing. Now...aren't you glad you stowed away in my truck? It's really too bad, we were looking forward to telling you all about what we did to her later...you ruined our fun. But then again, now you get to watch it firsthand."

"You won't...get away...with this," Jackson said, his words broken and painful to hear. He was holding his side and blood dripped from cuts on his face.

Lars laughed. "We already are."

And with that, he began to kick the weak and helpless Jackson.

Blade saw Jackson attempt to use some of the self-defense moves he and the others had taught him, but nothing he did was very effective against the four men ganging up on him.

Blade was moving before he thought about making

sure the others were ready. He couldn't sit back and watch Jackson get beaten to death. Not when he could do something about it. His mission was Wendy's brother, and that meant making sure he was safe from the others. He could certainly get some licks in as he made his way to his target.

Blade arrived at the circle of men around Jackson before the rest of his team. He took out one man with a powerful kick to the back of his knee. He fell to the ground with a thud. He was on another before they even realized he was there. He punched the man in the back, right in his kidney, then grabbed him by the shoulders and kneed him in the face hard as he fell.

Before he could move on to another, his team was there. They swarmed around the rest of the men like avenging angels.

"Blade—Jack," Ghost ordered, even as Blade turned to take down another one of the bullies surrounding Wendy's brother. He wanted to kick all the men's asses, but he was too well trained to disobey Ghost. He headed for Jackson and threw himself on his knees in front of the battered teenager. He put a hand under his chin and pulled his face up so he had no choice but to look at him.

"We're here, Jackson. You did it. We're here."

"Jenny," Jackson said, his eyes darting to the right, trying to find the girl.

Blade looked up to see a standoff—Lars had a gun

pointed at Jenny, the guy who was holding her, and Truck and Ghost.

"Put down the gun," Ghost ordered. "It's over, Lars."

"I'll fucking shoot her," Lars bit out. "Back off and let me go to my truck."

"Dude, you can't shoot her. I'm standing right here!" the man holding Jenny said.

"Fuck off, you pussy," Lars told his so-called friend. "You were the one who wanted a first go at her, Chuck. You were the one who begged to hold her so you could feel up her tits while we dealt with her boyfriend."

"Yeah, but I didn't know you had a gun or were gonna go all crazy and shit!"

"Listen to your friend," Ghost interrupted. "Put the gun down and let's talk about this."

"I'm not stupid," Lars said. "The second I do, you're gonna be all over my ass and my face'll be in the dirt."

"True, but you won't be dead," Ghost countered calmly. "You aren't getting out of this."

"Fuck this," Chuck said, and he let go of Jenny, holding his hands up and backing away from her.

Fletch was on him immediately, wrenching his arms behind his back so forcefully he cried out in pain.

Blade watched helplessly from nearby as events unfolded as if in slow motion. Truck moved to go to Jenny, to protect her now that she wasn't being held captive. Lars pulled the trigger on the pistol. And Ghost leaped at Lars in a flying tackle.

The crack of the gun was loud in the quiet Texas night, but Jenny's scream was louder.

Jackson yelled, "No!!!" and struggled to stand, to get to his girlfriend even as both she and Truck fell to the ground in a tangle of limbs. Truck managed to not fall on top of the diminutive teenager and Blade heard him groan as he hit the dirt.

Lars swore viciously and cried out as Ghost and Hollywood subdued him. And "subduing" him included beating the shit out of him and shoving his face in the dirt, just as he'd feared. Blade wished he could get a punch in for Jackson, but his teammates had the bully under control easily and didn't need any assistance.

"Sit-rep," Ghost yelled, even as he continued to hold Lars's face to the ground.

"Clear," Coach said. He had control of two of the thugs who'd been beating Jackson.

"Clear," Fletch said as he finished tying Chuck's hands behind his back.

"Clear," Beatle said from next to the unconscious third man who'd been punching Wendy's brother.

"Clear," Blade said as he helped Jackson sit up carefully.

"Clear," Hollywood grunted as he kicked Lars hard once more then backed away slowly.

"Negative," Truck said in a voice no one recognized. Instead of the gruff, no-nonsense tone they were used to, it was weak and pained.

"Uh...I think h-he's hurt," Jenny stuttered. She was kneeling next to Truck, who lay on his back.

"Fuck," Hollywood exclaimed as he ran for their fallen comrade. "Call the commander!" he yelled as he got to Truck. "We need a chopper. He's been shot."

Blade watched in disbelief as a puddle of blood began to form under Truck's body. "That's not good," Blade said in a low voice.

The team did their best to stabilize Truck before the chopper arrived. Blade worried about Jackson, but the teen waved off his attempts to look him over, saying he was okay and to help with Truck.

Jenny took over holding Jackson upright, so Blade helped Fletch and Coach deal with Lars and his friends. Within fifteen minutes, they heard the sound of a helicopter coming in hard and fast. Ghost stepped off to the side to mark the landing zone.

Blade was surprised to see the commander running toward them, along with the medic.

"Sit-rep!" he barked.

Ghost updated the commander as to what had happened and what Truck's situation was. Within minutes, the medic and Hollywood had Truck on the gurney and ready to be transported to the chopper.

"My wife," Truck said urgently, reaching for the commander's arm.

Blade's head whipped around at his friend's words.

He saw the rest of the team staring at Truck as well. Was he delirious?

"Yeah?" their commander asked, leaning over Truck to hear him better.

"Tell my wife I'm okay. Not to worry. She'll worry," Truck said.

The commander patted Truck's shoulder. "I'll take care of Mary. I'll get her to the hospital, don't worry."

Truck nodded, and his eyes closed.

The commander then turned to the rest of the team. "Get this trash back to post. I'll meet you there, along with the MPs. We'll figure out as many charges as we can to make sure this shit doesn't happen again. I'll also have this entire area searched with a fine-toothed comb. If these assholes have done this before, we'll find evidence of it and get them locked up behind bars and throw away the key."

The medic and the commander picked up the gurney with Truck on it and rushed him toward the helicopter. The team watched without a word as he was placed inside the chopper and the big machine lifted off the ground and raced back toward post.

"Holy shit," Coach said. "Did he say what I think he said?"

"Truck and Mary are married," Hollywood confirmed.

"That sneaky son of a bitch," Fletch muttered.

"That fucking asshole," Ghost bit out, clearly beyond pissed.

Blade turned to look at him in surprise. They all knew Truck loved Mary, so he didn't understand Ghost's anger.

"Rayne is going to be devastated," Ghost said—and clarity hit Blade.

Yeah...she so was. They all knew Rayne had put off her marriage to Ghost until Mary was ready to get married as well.

Suddenly the fact that she and Truck had gone behind all their backs to do the deed didn't sit so well with Blade anymore.

"Fuck!" Ghost swore again. "I do *not* want to have to tell Rayne that she's been waiting for nothing. I wonder how long it's been."

No one said anything, as no one knew the answer to that question.

"Come on," Beatle said evenly, but they could all hear the frustration behind his words. "We need to get these assholes back to post and let the MPs deal with them."

"I need to get Jackson checked out and Jenny home," Blade informed everyone.

"They'll need to talk to the MPs," Ghost said. It was obvious he was trying to control his temper.

"It's late. Wendy'll be worried sick, not to mention

Jenny's family. Can I bring them in tomorrow?" Blade asked.

Ghost ran a hand through his hair. "Yeah. I think that should be okay. Oh-nine hundred and no later though. Otherwise, I'll have the commander on my ass."

"Yes, Sir," Blade said, helping Jackson stand. He had to put an arm around the boy's waist to help him stay upright.

"Hollywood, you and Coach drive the assholes' trucks back. I'll go with Fletch, taking Lars and Chuck. Beatle, throw the others in the back of that pickup with the load of shit in it and watch over them until you get to the MP station. Okay?" Ghost asked.

"Sure thing, Sir."

Everyone moved to do as Ghost ordered. No one said another word. The night had been intense, what with the threat to Jenny and Jackson, Truck being shot, then finding out he was married but hadn't told any of them.

It was hard to understand. They shared everything with each other. The trust levels between them were high and unbreakable. He didn't know why Truck would want to break that, but they wouldn't know until they spoke to the man himself about it.

With a heavy heart, he helped Jackson into the backseat of his Jeep and waited until both he and Jenny were buckled in before heading toward Temple at a

SUSAN STOKER

slightly slower pace than when he'd left. Jenny refused to be dropped off at her house, saying she was going wherever Jackson went. And since he was bringing the boy to the emergency room, that's where Jenny went too.

Blade picked up the phone to call Wendy. He knew the entire girl posse was at her house waiting for information. Someone would drive her to the hospital, making sure she didn't wreck on the way there.

He thought about Truck and Mary. He wasn't sure what he'd say to Mary when he saw her next. There was no question that he'd tell Wendy about the pair being married; he vowed never to keep stuff from her if he could help it.

But he knew, without a doubt, feelings were going to be hurt. And he hated that.

Damn Truck. What was he thinking?

CHAPTER SEVENTEEN

W endy lay in bed, snuggled in Aspen's arms. She and Jackson had spent every night for the last week in his condo and had moved a lot of their stuff there as well. After her brother had been assaulted and Jenny kidnapped, Wendy felt safer with Aspen.

But it was more than that.

She could tell that Aspen needed her there as well.

"How's Truck doing?" she asked softly.

"Good. He went home today."

"And Mary is there looking after him?"

"Um hum," Aspen murmured, his body tensing.

Wendy knew that talking about Truck and Mary was a sore point with her man. She didn't really understand all the nuances, but what she did know was that the circle of friendship had definitely taken a blow.

When Aspen had called from the hospital, saying

Jackson and Jenny were safe, Wendy had been over-joyed, but he'd sounded tense. He should've been happy that he'd found her brother and that Jenny was all right, but it was obvious something else was bothering him.

She was still on the phone with Aspen when Mary's phone had rung. When she'd heard Truck had been hurt, Mary's face had lost all its color and she'd swayed on her feet, almost passing out. Rayne had taken the phone from her before Mary could protest, and she'd heard the tail end of what the commander was saying as a result.

"You're *married?*" she'd asked incredulously, backing away from her best friend.

"It's not what you think!" Mary responded quickly.

"Yes or no," Rayne had demanded.

Mary sighed. "Yes."

Rayne's lips had pressed together, and she'd had a look of such betrayal on her face, it made Wendy flinch. But Rayne took a deep breath and turned to the others. "Truck's been shot. The commander says it looks worse than it is. He's in surgery right now, but the doctors said the bullet was a through and through and he'll be okay."

The others all breathed out a sigh of relief.

"Oh—and Mary and Truck are husband and wife. Apparently, they got married at some point and didn't tell us. You probably want to get to your husband, Mary. I'm sure Casey will take you to see him."

And with that, she'd gathered up her stuff and

walked out of the condo without a backward glance at her best friend or any of the other women standing around speechless.

Wendy had been a bit jealous of the closeness of the women and men of Aspen's Delta team, but that closeness had been severely tested. Now everything was tense and awkward between some of them. Aspen had admitted that Ghost hadn't even been up to see Truck since he'd been hurt.

She hated that for the team.

"You want to talk about it?" she asked Aspen gently.

"No." He rolled over until Wendy was on her back looking up at him. "Move in with me," he demanded, didn't ask.

"What?"

"Move in with me. I want you and Jackson here with *me*. You've been here for the past week and I've never been happier. I love coming home to you and I love waking up with you. I love how it takes you forever to get out of the bed in the mornings and I love seeing your shit strewn across the vanity in my bathroom."

"But...what about my place?"

"What about it?" Aspen asked. "The building's a piece of shit. And not safe. I want you both where I know you won't be mugged going to and from your car. I love you, Wendy. So damn much. Your brother too. Seeing him hurt, and those assholes beating on him, made me crazy. I not only love you, but I need you. You make my life less lonely. I like having someone to talk to when I get home. I like having *you* to talk to. You make my life complete. If you're worried about living in sin, don't. I'm going to ask you to marry me sometime soon. We can be engaged for as long as you want once we set a date. And we aren't going to run off and have some bullshit secret ceremony either. All our friends will be there to celebrate with us."

"But...what I did could get you in trouble," Wendy said quietly. "I wouldn't be able to live with myself if you got in trouble because I kidnapped my brother."

"We'll deal with that. I'll have a guy I know make inquiries. I said this before, but you were a minor when that happened. I'm not saying that you won't have to answer for it, but I think having Jackson vouch for you and testify as to what he was going through in that last foster home will go a long way toward leniency. That, and the fact he's well-adjusted, smart, and amazing."

"I won't make him testify," Wendy said urgently. "I won't make him do anything he's not comfortable with."

"Easy, sweetheart. I have a feeling he'll gladly do it if it'll help you."

Wendy sighed. "It's hard for me to not pay my way."

"You aren't paying rent when you move in here," Aspen said. "No fucking way. Keep your money for you and Jackson. Although you know anything he needs, I've got plenty of money to help out. You can quit that call-center job, and you're going to get that promotion at the retirement home. You can keep your own checking account...I'll never do anything that will make you feel insecure."

"I don't feel insecure when I'm with you, Aspen, it's not that."

"Then what is it?"

"I just...it would kill me if we moved in and our relationship didn't work out."

Aspen laughed. Laughed so hard, he started to snort.

Wendy glared up at him. "What's so funny? It's a legitimate concern."

"No, sweetheart, it isn't. I'm not letting you go. Ever."

"You can't promise that."

"Yeah, I can. I know full well that you can do so much better than me. I'm going to do everything in my power to make sure you never regret calling me that first time and continuing to talk to me. You'll never be unsatisfied in our bed. You'll never go hungry. You never have to worry about me cheating on you. You don't have to worry I'll ever be resentful of your relationship with Jackson. You're it for me, Wen. I think I knew it the first time we talked. Give us a chance."

Wendy's eyes filled with tears. She'd been on her own for so long, it felt amazing to know she wasn't anymore. That she'd have a partner in Aspen.

Not wanting to cry, and wanting to cheer him up after the shitty week he'd had, she teased, "I'll never be unsatisfied in your bed? Seems like it's been a while since you've done any satisfying here, buddy."

His lips quirked up in an evil smile. "That so?"

"Yup."

"Say you'll move in permanently and I can tell your landlord to fuck off, and I'll satisfy you."

"And if I don't?"

"Then we'll snuggle down and go to sleep."

"You're blackmailing me with sex?" Wendy asked in disbelief.

"Yup."

Knowing her decision was already made, Wendy decided to give a little back. "Hmmmm, guess we're going to snuggle then." And she turned onto her side and pushed her ass out, rubbing against his erection.

"You little wench," Aspen complained. "You're gonna be the death of me."

Wendy waited until he'd thrown an arm around her waist and pulled her back against his front to say, "Yes."

He froze behind her. "Yes to what?"

"To all of it." Wendy sat up and pushed Aspen onto his back and straddled his thighs. "Yes, we'll move in. Yes, I'll quit that stupid call-center job. And yes, I'll marry you."

Without a word, and with only a sparkle in his eye as warning, Aspen grabbed her hips and turned, throwing her over until she was on her back once again. His hand went to the boy shorts she'd worn to bed and pushed down the front of them. His talented fingers immediately began playing with her clit, even as he leaned down and kissed her as if this was the last kiss they'd ever share.

Wendy shoved her hands into his boxers and gripped his rock-hard ass, squeezing him and trying to pull him down on top of her.

He didn't move closer though, simply continued his assault on her clit and her mouth until she was squirming desperately under him.

"Aspen," Wendy gasped. "Fuck me."

He groaned in response and lifted up high enough to frantically shove her shorts down her legs. As if his desperation was contagious, Wendy did her best to help him remove them. One long finger slipped inside her body and Wendy's knees fell open wider, giving him access. He pumped in and out of her several times, as if testing her readiness, then he brought his finger up to his mouth and licked it clean.

His eyes met hers and almost burned with their intensity. Without a word, he reached down and pushed his boxers just far enough that his rock-hard cock popped out. Fisting the base, he rubbed the head over her clit several times, then down between her folds. Once he'd lubricated himself in her excitement, he pressed the head just inside her body. Then he stilled.

"What?" Wendy asked. "Why are you stopping?"

"I'm not wearing a condom," Aspen said in a croak.

"I don't care."

He groaned again. "Wendy..."

"Fuck me, Aspen. I need you!"

"You *will* marry me, Wendy," he said as he ever so slowly pushed inside her body. "I'm not letting you renege."

"I don't want to. If you're crazy enough to want me, then I'd be an idiot to turn you down. Besides, I need to save you from all the whores who try to pick you up in bars."

He chuckled then, and Wendy felt the movement deep inside her.

"God, you feel amazing like this," Aspen said, holding absolutely still inside her.

"You too. But...I need you to move," Wendy begged. "Please."

He lazily pulled out and pressed back inside. "Like this?"

"No. Harder."

"But doesn't this feel good?" he teased.

"If you mean it feels good like I'm reading a boring book on a lazy Sunday afternoon, yeah."

"Oh, you'll pay for that," Aspen warned as he reached down with one hand and grabbed her ass cheek, pulling her harder into him.

"I love that you can be slow and sweet. But I want out of control. Give it to me hard and fast."

"You sure? I can be romantic," he said.

"Fuck romantic right now! Fuck me, Aspen. Seriously. I love it like that, as you should remember."

And with that, Aspen commenced taking her hard. He fucked her on her back, on her knees, and while she straddled him. He made her come three times before finally giving in to his own desire. Wendy could feel her wetness coating her thighs and the sounds they were making were porn-movie impressive.

Jackson was sleeping on the first floor in the office, since stairs were still too painful for him, allowing her the freedom to be with Aspen without reservations.

He had her on her back once more and was fucking her wet channel. Her ass was propped up by two pillows, and every time he thrust inside, he hit her G-spot. Wendy moaned and gripped his thighs as he reached his peak.

"Once more, sweetheart. I want to feel that hot pussy grip my dick once more before I fill you with my come." He used his thumb to rub her clit in a relentless motion as he spoke.

"Oh, God," Wendy moaned as she felt another orgasm approaching. Her legs shook as she went over the edge, and she watched as Aspen's eyes closed and he threw his head back. The tendons in his neck bulged, and it was the sexiest thing she'd ever seen in her life.

She felt his come begin to leak out around them, but didn't move. It was fucking hot, and she almost couldn't believe this amazing man was hers. Almost.

He fell on top of her, nearly crushing her, but Wendy didn't care. She didn't deserve Aspen, but she wasn't letting him go. Wrapping her arms around him, she ignored the way her thighs protested being spread around his hips. She ignored the wet spot growing under her ass. She ignored the way it was hard to take a full breath. She simply soaked in the moment of contentment.

CHAPTER EIGHTEEN

A month later, Wendy was as happy as she'd ever been, all things considered. Lars had been charged with trespassing, attempted murder, assault, and kidnapping. His friends had all been charged with trespassing, assault, and kidnapping. Chuck's parents were also in trouble, seeing as he still lived with them on the Army post. The authorities said that Chuck had apologized, cried, and desperately begged that his parents not be reprimanded and allowed to stay on post, but it had done no good.

Two teenagers from a neighboring high school had come forward, after seeing the publicity about what had been done to Jenny and Jackson, and had admitted they'd also been bullied, then assaulted by the group. More charges were pending, but Wendy was confident the thugs wouldn't be a problem for them anymore and they were getting what was coming to them.

Jackson and Jenny were as close as ever. He'd recovered from the beatings and Jenny had been by his side the entire time. Wendy wasn't worried about their relationship at all. She had a feeling, even with the difference in their ages, that they'd make things work. They had a special connection that went deeper than just the bond they had because of what Lars had done.

The most amazing thing that had happened was when Aspen asked permission to talk about her situation with a friend of his named Tex. He explained that Tex would be able to use the computer to search for information about her discreetly.

Trusting Aspen, Wendy had agreed.

That had led to her, Jackson, and Aspen flying out to California to meet with the authorities in her hometown. Wendy had been terrified to turn herself in, but Tex had given them the name of an incredible lawyer, who'd reassured her that all would be well.

And she'd been right.

The authorities hadn't been pleased with her actions, but because Jackson was still with her, safe and sound, in school, and had told the detectives everything that had happened to him in the foster home—and what his sister had done for him while on the run—they'd ultimately let her off the hook.

They'd reprimanded her, of course; told her that she

should've come to them when she'd found out what was going on in the home Jackson was in. That if they'd known, they could've gotten him the help he'd needed. She didn't handle the situation properly, which was something she knew, but luckily, they hadn't seemed inclined to lock her up for the choices she'd made as a scared teenager.

She had to pay restitution for the time and money spent ten years ago looking for Jackson, but in the end, it seemed all her moving around and trying to fly under the radar had been for naught.

She'd thought they'd been lucky. But in reality, their case just wasn't important enough for the State of California to spend even more money hauling her back across the country.

"You can get your degree now," Jackson told her once the detectives had said no charges were going to be brought against her. "We're truly free!"

And they were.

Back home in Texas, Truck had been released from the hospital and had no lasting issues from being shot, other than having another scar. Wendy had met the man once and had been taken aback more by his size than the gnarly scar on his face.

There had been no more get-togethers with Aspen's friends or their women. The betrayal of Truck secretly marrying Mary had fractured the once-close friendships. The women were upset at Mary, and the men were upset at Truck. Aspen said work was strained and the tension was affecting their previously seamless group. He even admitted the commander had noticed and had suggested splitting them up if they couldn't work together anymore.

Their friend, Fish, had finally arrived in town, and he met with Jackson's robotics club. He'd been impressed with everything they'd done and had offered more invaluable suggestions for their design. There hadn't been a barbeque though. Wendy had been looking forward to it, but since none of the men were really talking outside of work, that was inevitable.

After speaking with Casey one night, Wendy learned that Fletch had decided to sell his house. The construction had been completed, but he'd decided there was just too much shit that had happened there, and both he and Emily wanted to start fresh. Wendy could tell Aspen was upset about it, but he refused to say anything to Fletch.

Wendy felt helpless, not knowing how to help Aspen. She wanted to do something, but when she'd asked, Aspen had told her that being with him, being there in his condo when he got home, was enough. Their sex life was as amazing as ever and she reveled in the way he took her hard and fast every time. Slow and romantic sex did nothing for her. It was pleasant enough, but didn't make her come over and over, like when Aspen slammed into her and forced her orgasms.

Evenings were much more pleasant now that she didn't have to go to the call center a few times a week. She didn't get cussed at or hung up on and it was amazingly nice.

They were eating dinner one evening when Aspen said, "There's an Organizational Day on the post this weekend. Want to go?"

"What's that?" Jackson asked. "And can Jenny come?"

Aspen smiled. "Of course you can bring her. And it's basically a fair. There will be food trucks, games, music, and face painting and balloons for the smaller kids."

"Cool," Jackson said.

"It sounds fun," Wendy said. "Are the others going?"

Aspen sighed. "Probably."

"But you don't know?"

He shook his head. "We haven't talked about it."

Wendy put her hand on Aspen's arm. "You need to talk to them about this. You need to get past it. I'd hate to see you lose such amazing friends over this."

"You don't understand," Aspen said, putting down his fork. "Everything we do and say while on a mission affects everyone else. We have to absolutely trust each other to not do anything stupid and get us all killed. What Truck did broke that trust in a big way. Hell, Hollywood told us when Kassie was pregnant, even when he wasn't supposed to. We've always known everything everyone does even before we do it. Somehow,

Truck keeping this huge secret made us all question our blind loyalty to each other. We're now wondering what else is being kept from us."

"Have you asked him about it?"

Aspen sighed and shook his head.

"Don't you think you should? I mean, I don't know Truck all that well, but he had to have a *reason* for keeping his marriage from you guys."

"I know you're right. I miss my friends, and I hate how it's hurt the friendships between the women as well."

"Yeah. The only one I've talked to is Casey, and she's said that everyone is taking sides."

"That's what I've heard too," Aspen agreed.

"Rayne is devastated and hasn't talked to Mary since she found out. Emily is on her side. Harley and Kassie think Rayne should talk to Mary and find out why she married Truck, and what's up. Casey is Switzerland, so to speak. She says it's sad, because Kassie and Emily used to talk about their pregnancy all the time and they were looking forward to their kids being raised together, but now they aren't even speaking to each other."

"I don't know how to fix this," Aspen said. "It's a fucking mess."

"Talk to him," Wendy ordered.

"I will."

"Good."

They finished their meal, and that night, when they were in bed and Aspen was sending her over the edge for the second time, Wendy had the thought that no matter what, things could only go up from this point on.

The next day after PT, Blade had had enough. The guys were all grumpy and things were beyond awkward between them.

"Enough is enough," he said, glaring at his friends. "We're acting like a bunch of junior high school girls." He turned to Truck. "Why didn't you tell us you got married? We're a team. We tell each other shit. We knew when Kassie was pregnant way before Hollywood told anyone else. We knew about Emily's baby before anyone too."

"Coach and Harley went and got married without telling us," Truck said defensively. "Why didn't anyone yell at *him*?"

"That was different," Fletch said.

"How?" Truck asked.

"It just was. He didn't keep it a damn secret for *months*," Beatle said.

Truck sighed. "I can't tell you all the details because it's not my story to tell, it's Mary's."

"That's a cop-out," Ghost seethed. "I'm pissed at you,

man. You know how badly I want to put my ring on Rayne's finger. She's been holding out because she was sure Mary and you would fall in love. You could've at least told *me*."

"You're the last person I could tell," Truck said. Then pressed his lips together and shook his head. "Leave it, man. It's done."

And with that, Truck walked away.

The other men stared after him in disbelief, disappointment, and confusion.

Blade sighed. He'd wanted to end their feud by offering Truck a chance to explain why he hadn't told them about his marriage, but instead, it made things worse.

Saturday was a beautiful day. The sun was out and it wasn't too hot for once. There were families everywhere, enjoying the activities of Organizational Day. A local country band was playing on a stage at the far end of the field and there were several food trucks set up serving free food for the Army families.

Jackson had wandered off with Jenny as soon as they'd arrived, and Blade was enjoying walking around with Wendy. They were holding hands and talking about nothing in particular. Everything was fine—until he'd seen Truck and Mary. They were easy to spot, the difference in their heights almost comical. There was nearly a foot between them, but somehow, it worked. Mary had her fingers intertwined with Truck's and they were laughing at something.

A pang of sorrow hit Blade as he watched them. It was the first time he'd seen Mary look like she openly enjoyed being with Truck. Everyone knew they belonged together, and they should all be thrilled that it seemed as if they'd worked through their issues. But because of Truck's secrecy, their union had broken the team instead of bringing them closer together.

Blade also saw the others walking around. Sadly, everyone was keeping away from each other. It was depressing, and nothing he'd imagined would ever happen in a million years. They'd been through so much together. From Rayne's rescue, to laughing with little Annie, to Coach nearly dying on his first jump with Harley, to the latest with Fletch's house being blown up by a psychotic pedophile.

That didn't even begin to cover what the team had been through on missions. From Africa to South America and the Middle East. They'd had each other's backs for years. Saved each other's lives time and time again. It almost felt as if they were going through a painful divorce right now. Thinking about the good times between them was like a knife being thrust into his chest.

Blade wrapped his arm around Wendy's waist and pulled her into his side as they walked.

"Are you okay?" she asked.

"No," he told her bluntly. "This sucks. I miss my friends."

"What can I do to help?" she asked.

"Unfortunately, nothing, I—"

Blade's words were cut off by a loud popping sound.

Knowing immediately what it was, Blade threw Wendy onto the ground a little rougher than he meant to and covered her body with his own, even as he was looking around for the source.

The gunfire sounded again, and Blade turned his head to look in the direction it came from.

Standing on the stage was Chuck, one of Lars's friends. The members of the band were rushing away behind him as Chuck yelled and continued to randomly shoot into the panicking crowd.

Blade's eyes swept the grounds and caught Ghost's. His team leader was on the ground hovering over Rayne, much as he was doing to Wendy. Ghost used his head to gesture to the right. Looking in that direction, Blade saw Truck and Hollywood. Before long, he'd made eye contact with all six of his teammates, and they'd silently and quickly made a plan using hand signals.

"See that set of bleachers over there?" Blade asked Wendy urgently, pointing to their left.

"Y-Yeah."

He could tell she was freaked out, but she was listening to him. "I need you to go over there as fast as you can. Stay down low and make sure you don't run in a straight line. Can you do that?"

"Yeah, but what are *you* going to do?"

Ignoring her question, he went on. "Rayne and the others will meet you there. Once you're all there, hunker down and *do not* move, no matter what. Hear me?"

"Okay, but, Aspen, what are you going to do?" she repeated.

"Me and my team are going to stop this motherfucker," Blade said. Then he kissed her hard. When there was a lull in the gunfire, he pulled her to her feet and pushed her toward the bleachers. "Go. Now!"

Blade watched as Wendy took off running toward the relative safety of the bleachers. Nothing was foolproof, but the women would be much safer there than lying in plain sight on the grassy field.

Then, as if the last month hadn't happened, Blade and his team did what they did best...worked together to bring down the shooter.

Ten minutes later, Blade stood with his teammates as they waited for the MPs to clear the area. They'd surrounded Chuck and disarmed him within five minutes of his rampage starting. They didn't have weapons, but hadn't needed any. Basically, they'd bum-rushed him when he'd paused to reload his rifle.

The boy was now sobbing and begging them to let him up, to let the MPs shoot him. Crying that he'd ruined his parents' lives and they'd be better off without him.

With Truck and Ghost holding him down, the rest of the team had secured his weapons and ammo and made sure Chuck wasn't going to be a risk to anyone else. By the time the MPs had gotten there, the younger man was limp and non-combative.

Truck told the Military Police what Chuck had been babbling. Basically, he'd been shooting the ground to avoid hurting people, but in the hopes the police would still kill him and end his misery.

He was hauled off quickly and, after making eye contact with their women to ensure they were safe, the Delta team stood together at the bottom of the stage, waiting to be dismissed.

"I fucked up in not telling you guys about me and Mary. But if I had to do it again, I wouldn't change anything about what I did," Truck said, breaking the silence.

"We've talked about this shit already. Rayne is devastated," Ghost bit out.

"I know. And I regret that—but Mary was dying. She couldn't afford treatment when her cancer returned, and I married her so she could be under my insurance."

Everyone was immediately silent upon hearing that. Truck had said it was Mary's story to tell, but none of them had expected that bombshell.

"The ceremony was when we all went out to Idaho to help Fish, wasn't it?" Hollywood finally asked.

Truck nodded. "Yeah. She was at a low point and agreed. But I knew if I put it off, she'd find her second wind and refuse."

"She been living at your place?" Ghost asked.

"Mostly. Yeah."

"I figured. The few times Rayne convinced her to meet up, it's been somewhere other than her apartment."

"She hasn't been back there much. At first, she was too sick. Now that she's better, it's become a habit to stay with me, I guess," Truck said with a shrug.

"You should've told us," Coach said.

Truck nodded. "I know. I'm telling you now because this stupid feud between us is affecting our work. I don't want the team to be split up. But the other reason why I didn't say anything before is because I'm convinced it's only a matter of time before Mary tries to divorce me. She married me for my insurance...well, I *made* her marry me so she could use my insurance. And now that she doesn't need it anymore, I have a feeling she's gonna want to go her separate way."

"She's okay now though?" Blade asked.

Truck sighed and nodded. "Yeah. She saw a doctor last week and he gave her the all clear. She'll be on drugs for at least the next seven or eight years, and she's considering breast reconstruction, but the cancer seems to be gone for now."

"Here's the thing," Beatle said. "We were pissed at you, Truck. And your betrayal of our trust hurt the team. But...today proved that deep down, we still trust each other implicitly. Right?"

Everyone agreed.

"So, we need to stop this petty shit and fix this rift between us."

"I agree," Fletch said. "I miss you guys. Annie misses you guys. She's also been asking when she'll get to see Wendy again. And the rest of the women. I need to break in my new house with a barbeque."

The men smiled at each other, and Blade felt the tension drain from his body. They were back. The team was together again—and it felt fucking amazing.

"I'm not sure it'll be as easy for our women to fix their relationships," Ghost said. "What you did really hurt Rayne."

Everyone looked over at the women where they were standing behind the bleachers. Mary and Rayne were at opposite ends of the little group, and both had their arms crossed over their chests. Wendy and Casey were talking quietly, and Emily was standing next to

Rayne with her arm around her waist. Kassie and Harley were standing closer to Mary and talking to each other.

"I'm going to fix this," Truck told his friends. "I don't know how, but I will. Mary is the most stubborn woman I've ever met, but she's also one of the most compassionate and loving as well. I know you guys think she's a bitch, but you don't know her like I do. She's torn up inside that Rayne is mad at her, and she hates that the group has been broken because of what we did. Will you guys help me?"

"Abso-fucking-lutely," Ghost said.

"You got it," Hollywood agreed.

One by one, the men vowed to do whatever was necessary to bring their group back to where it had been.

"Are you gonna let her have a divorce?" Fletch asked.

"No," Truck answered. "I love her. She's prickly as all fuck, but she's learned to be that way because of her past. I've seen her caring, loving side, and I know you will too. Eventually."

"Anyone got any more secrets they've been keeping from us?" Ghost asked dryly. "Figure we might as well get everything out now."

Everyone chuckled.

"I'm going to ask Wendy to marry me soon," Blade piped up. "Her and Jackson have moved in, and I want to give them both the stability they didn't have in the last decade."

Beatle put his hand on Blade's shoulder. "Congrats."

"Thanks."

"What about you?" Hollywood asked Beatle. "If Blade and Wendy get engaged, you and Casey are going to be the only ones not married or engaged."

"What, I don't count?" Ghost asked grumpily.

Hollywood rolled his eyes. "We all know you're going to marry Rayne the second she says the word. It's only a matter of time. So? Beatle?"

He smiled at the group. "I don't have a ring yet, but she agreed to marry me the other week."

Everyone slapped Beatle on the back in congratulations.

"Anyone else got anything to say?" Ghost asked the group.

"Mary and I got married at the courthouse, but I want the white dress and the walk down the aisle and a big-ass party," Truck told Ghost, looking him straight in the eye. "She might protest and say she doesn't want a fuss, but fuck that. She beat cancer, twice. I want to throw her the biggest party this town has ever seen."

Ghost looked at Truck, then turned and met both Blade and Beatle's eyes before saying slowly, "What if we had four weddings in one, then had the town's biggest fucking party afterward? You think your women would go for that? Or do they want their wedding days all to themselves?"

"Wendy would love that," Blade said immediately.

"She's never had close friends, and without family other than Jackson, I know she'd feel awkward if all the guests were mine. So, hell yes for me."

"Beatle?" Ghost asked with a cock of an eyebrow.

"I can't speak for Casey until I talk with her about it, but I'm pretty sure she wouldn't object. She's been really shaken up and depressed over the last month everyone's been fighting. I think if they could all make up and work together to make this happen, it would be epic."

The men all nodded their heads at each other.

"If I can make a suggestion?" Fletch asked.

"Sure," Ghost said.

"Maybe we can wait until after Em and Kassie have their babies. I know they'd love to stand up with their friends, but I have a feeling Em would hate to be nine months pregnant in all the pictures," Fletch said.

"Not a problem for us," Hollywood agreed. "Kassie's about to pop any day now."

The others chuckled.

"No worries. We aren't going to have everything planned in the next three months anyway," Ghost said.

"Hell, it might take that long to get the girls talking to each other again," Truck mumbled.

"We're all on the same page, right?" Ghost asked.

Everyone nodded in agreement.

"Okay. After the debrief with the MPs, we'll head home with our women and make sure they're good. But starting tomorrow, Operation Fix This Shit will commence. Yeah?" Ghost ordered.

Everyone agreed and headed across the field toward the women waiting anxiously.

Ghost put his hand on Truck's shoulder before he could leave. "I was pissed at you, Truck, but I get it now."

"Do you?"

"Yeah. I'd pick Rayne over all you assholes every day of the week and twice on Sunday."

Truck gave his friend and team leader a lopsided smile. "'Preciate that."

Ghost punched Truck in the arm. "I can't believe you convinced Mary to marry your ugly mug."

Truck chuckled. "Don't get too excited yet. It's not like we have a normal relationship."

"Seriously?"

"Seriously. We sleep together every night, but we haven't slept together, if you know what I mean. At first, it was because she was nauseous and sick, but she's still being stubborn now that she's all better."

"Well, if anyone can break down her barriers, it's you," Ghost said with one hundred percent conviction. "I can't wait to watch this."

"A little compassion would be nice," Truck mumbled. "I've got the worst case of blue balls in the history of man."

Ghost barked out a laugh. "Serves you right." Then

he got serious. "I need to fix Rayne's relationship with Mary, Truck."

"I know. We'll fix it."

"Swear?"

"Swear. One way or another, those two are going to be thick as thieves again, and they'll get their double— no, quadruple—wedding."

Ghost smiled. "That, I'll take. You're a good man, Truck."

"Not all the time. I've found that I'm selfish as fuck."

"We all are in our own ways. Come on, our women look like they're going to burst. We'll talk tomorrow and put together a plan to get those two back on track... and to mend the rest of the women's relationships too. Glad you were here today, Truck. As usual, your size made taking that guy down easier."

"My pleasure," Truck said.

Blade watched from the side as Ghost and Truck shook hands then went to collect their women.

"What's going on with you guys?" Wendy asked Blade when they were headed toward the parking lot. "You were all mad at each other, and now you're not?"

"Sometimes all it takes is a little danger to put things in perspective," Blade told her. "Now come on, I want to get you and your brother home. I think we all need a little 'us' time. I was scared as shit that you'd get hit by a stray bullet."

"I love you," Wendy told Blade as she stood on tiptoe to kiss him.

His eyes lit up. "That's the first time you've said it."

"Uh uh. I've said it before," Wendy protested. "That night you asked me to marry you, in fact."

"No, sweetheart, you haven't. Believe me, I should know. You oohed and ahhed and screwed my brains out, but you never came right out and said the words. I've been waiting for this moment for weeks. And you can't take it back now."

"I don't want to take it back," she reassured him. "Now take me, Jackson, and Jenny home. I'll feed you, then when Jackson takes Jenny home, I'll show you how much I love you."

"Oooh, baby, I love it when you talk dirty."

Blade put his arm around Wendy and led her to his Jeep. Things weren't perfect with the team, but they were well on their way to getting there. The next few weeks and months would be interesting, but he'd put his money on Truck every time.

Truck opened his apartment door and waited for Mary to enter before following then shutting and locking the door behind them. She'd been quiet on the way home, and he wanted to ask what she was thinking, but wanted to do so when they were in his apartment and she couldn't run from him.

He made her a cup of tea, with a liberal splash of bourbon, and got her settled on the couch. He sat next to her and pulled her into his arms and they sat in silence.

After a while, he asked, "You okay?"

"Of course."

Truck resisted the urge to roll his eyes. Of course she'd say that.

"Did Rayne say anything to you today?"

"No."

"Did you say anything to her?"

"No. There's nothing to say. I hurt her."

"If you talked to her and told her why, she'd understand."

Mary shook her head. "No, she wouldn't. She was there throughout every step of my first bout of chemo and radiation. She wouldn't understand why I didn't want her there a second time."

Truck didn't exactly understand it himself, so he let it go. When she reached forward to put the empty mug on the coffee table, he asked, "Ready for bed?"

"Yeah. Truck?"

"Yeah, baby?"

"Are things okay between you and your team now?"

"You saw that, huh?"

"Yeah."

"They're not perfect, but we're getting there."

"Good. I didn't mean to get you in trouble with your friends."

Truck kissed the side of her head and left his lips there as he said, "You didn't get me in anything. Whatever consequences my actions have are on me. Not you. Understand?"

She stared at him for a long moment, and again Truck tried to figure out what she was thinking, without luck. "I know you mean that, but I also know it's not true." She looked away. "I need to get ready for bed."

"Need help?"

Mary stilled and glanced over at him. "What?"

"Need any help?" Truck repeated. Throughout their marriage, he hadn't ever crossed the line between being a friend and being more. But the longer he spent around her when she wasn't sick and hurting, the more he *wanted* to cross that line. It was time he started pushing a bit more.

"No."

"Are you sure? I'd be happy to help get you out of those clothes."

"Truck!" Mary exclaimed and smacked him on the arm. "No!" Her cheeks were flushed and she didn't meet his eyes. If he was a betting man, he'd say she was open to the idea, but needed a bit more convincing.

"Just thought I'd make sure. I'll be up to join you in *our* bed in a bit," he said, emphasizing the "our" a bit more than usual. Then he put his palm on Mary's cheek and turned her to face him. He leaned down and covered her lips with his own.

Using his tongue, he traced the seam of her lips until she gasped, and he took the opportunity to taste her for the first time.

Every other time they'd kissed, it had been a closed-mouth, chaste thing, but Truck was done with that. Mary was his. In every sense of the word. She was skittish, but he could work with that.

When she didn't pull away from him in shock or slap him in the face, Truck continued his lazy exploration. Her tongue shyly twined with his, and he nearly groaned. His cock was hard as steel and he could feel himself leaking precome.

Jesus, he was ready to blow with just the feel of her little tongue playing with his own. He reluctantly pulled back, satisfied for now with how things had gone, and kissed her forehead. "Go on, baby. I'll be right there."

Without a word, and with a stunned look on her face, Mary stood and headed down the hall to the master bedroom.

Truck knew her complacency wouldn't last. It was one of the things he loved most about her. That she gave as good as she got, and that she'd never sit back and let him dictate everything in their relationship. She was a challenge, and a man like him needed that. He needed *her*.

She might not realize it, but the day she'd said "I do" had changed her life forever.

She was his, just as he was hers.

They'd fight and make up and fight again. And Truck looked forward to every single second of their give and take. Eventually, she'd give him everything he wanted, and he'd take on the responsibility for making her happy for the rest of their lives.

He couldn't wait.

Make sure to pick up *Rescuing Mary*, the final installment of the Delta Force Heroes series. Truck and Mary have been through a lot, but their trials and tribulations aren't over. Find out what happens in their story!

JOIN my Newsletter and find out about sales, free books, contests and new releases before anyone else!!
Click HERE

Want to know when my books go on sale? Follow me on Bookbub HERE!

Would you like Susan's Book Protecting Caroline for FREE?
Click HERE

Also by Susan Stoker

Delta Force Heroes Series

Rescuing Rayne

Assisting Aimee - Loosely related to DF

Rescuing Emily

Rescuing Harley

Marrying Emily

Rescuing Kassie

Rescuing Bryn

Rescuing Casey

Rescuing Sadie

Rescuing Wendy

Rescuing Mary (Oct 2018)

Badge of Honor: Texas Heroes Series

Justice for Mackenzie

Justice for Mickie

Justice for Corrie

Justice for Laine (novella)

Shelter for Elizabeth

Justice for Boone

Shelter for Adeline

Shelter for Sophie

Justice for Erin

Justice for Milena

Shelter for Blythe (June 2018)

Justice for Hope (Sept 2018)
Shelter for Quinn (TBA)
Shelter for Koren (TBA)
Shelter for Penelope (TBA)

Ace Security Series
Claiming Grace
Claiming Alexis
Claiming Bailey
Claiming Felicity

Mountain Mercenaries Series
Defending Allye (Aug 2018)
Defending Chloe (Dec 2018)
more to come!

SEAL of Protection Series
Protecting Caroline
Protecting Alabama
Protecting Fiona
Marrying Caroline (novella)
Protecting Summer
Protecting Cheyenne
Protecting Jessyka
Protecting Julie (novella)
Protecting Melody
Protecting the Future
Protecting Alabama's Kids (novella)

Protecting Kiera (novella)
Protecting Dakota

Stand Alone

The Guardian Mist
Nature's Rift
A Princess for Cale
A Moment in Time- A Collection of Short Stories
Lambert's Lady

Special Operations Fan Fiction

http://www.stokeraces.com/kindle-worlds.html

Beyond Reality Series

Outback Hearts
Flaming Hearts
Frozen Hearts

Writing as Annie George:

Stepbrother Virgin (erotic novella)

ABOUT THE AUTHOR

New York Times, *USA Today* and *Wall Street Journal* Best-selling Author Susan Stoker has a heart as big as the state of Tennessee where she lives, but this all American girl has also spent the last fourteen years living in Missouri, California, Colorado, Indiana, and Texas. She's married to a retired Army man who now gets to follow *her* around the country.

She debuted her first series in 2014 and quickly followed that up with the SEAL of Protection Series, which solidified her love of writing and creating stories readers can get lost in.

If you enjoyed this book, or any book, please consider leaving a review. It's appreciated by authors more than you'll know.

www.stokeraces.com
susan@stokeraces.com

facebook.com/authorsusanstoker

twitter.com/Susan_Stoker

instagram.com/authorsusanstoker

goodreads.com/SusanStoker

bookbub.com/authors/susan-stoker

amazon.com/author/susanstoker